Snowdown at the Old Schoolhouse

Margaret Amatt

LEANNAN
PRESS
INDEPENDENT PUBLISHER

LEANNAN PRESS

First Published by Leannan Press 2023

Book Cover designed by Margaret Amatt

eBook ISBN: 978-1-914575-61-7

Paperback ISBN: 978-1-914575-58-7

Chapter One

Marcus

February last year

Tie: straight. Microphone: straight. Cuffs: straight. Watch: dead centre.

'Twenty seconds,' the producer muttered in Marcus's ear.

His hand strayed to his tie, and he straightened it again, then the microphone, his cuffs and his watch. Seriously, this was ridiculous. OCD? Maybe. Or his tried and tested system to dispel those last-minute nerves. Even after all the years on camera, he still got them.

The light turned green and anchorman David spoke, 'And now for the weather. Here's our very own studio pinup boy, the heartthrob that is Marcus Bowman, with the Valentine's Day forecast.'

Studio what? Heat rose in Marcus's cheeks and he bit back all the replies he wanted to throw at that smug face. David thought himself such a smart arse and always had some wisecrack. *But to call me that on air?*

'Thank you, David.' Marcus fixed his trademark grin in place. What else could he do? And David knew it. 'Sadly, for all the lovers out there hoping for a bright and sunny Valentine's Day, I'm going to have to disappoint you. The day starts grey and overcast for most and continues like that throughout. The east may get a few brighter spells later on but these will be short-lived before the next band of rain comes across the country.' He motioned his hand over the green screen behind him, flicking the remote to change the charts, keeping half an eye on the monitor in front. When he started out, he used to examine it closely, making sure his movements were accurate, but these days it was instinctive.

'Oh dear,' David said as Marcus handed back to him. 'He may be called Bowman but his arrow has shot wide today. That's not what we'd hoped for. But maybe Cupid will deliver a brighter message for you today.'

As soon as the light went red, Marcus pulled off the microphone and shook his head.

'Don't worry about him,' Jonathan, one of the cameramen, muttered. 'It's jealousy.' He gave Marcus a stoic pat on the shoulder.

That may be but it was also insulting.

Pah. David was just being a dick. Only he didn't get how even the slightest whiff of bullying triggered Marcus. Being labelled a 'pinup' wasn't that bad but coming from David it felt demeaning.

Marcus could avoid social media if he wanted to. And there was stuff on there he'd never read. It'd wrecked his marriage and made him a reclusive hermit for the safety of his family.

Forget it. Just forget it.

Leaving the studio, he strode into the main newsroom of e-Broadcast Scotland. The weather desk was in a separate section jutting off the main open-plan room. It was still open down one side, so it felt part of the main room but afforded a bit more privacy and was slightly detached from the noisy clamour, though maybe that was psychological.

He pushed through the bustle of people chattering into phones, clicking at keyboards, or carrying papers, towards the long, angled weather desk covered in monitors, seeking the familiar. But wait. Something was wrong. The leather chair he usually sat at was completely askew and atop his beautifully tidy desk was a bright red shiny envelope. Valentine card? Someone's idea of a joke? Every year, he received them from adoring members of the public but the card glowing like a beacon on his desk had clearly been placed by hand in full view not in his in-tray. Perhaps David? Or some other joker?

Please no.

Still frowning at his desk, he ploughed forward past workstations and ran the gauntlet of cables and papers.

A chair rolled back and collided with his leg.

'Ow!' He jumped but not before the casters ran over his left foot. 'Jesus Christ. What the hell are you doing?'

'Sorry, sorry, so sorry.' A pair of doe eyes, framed by long lashes, goggled at him. Marcus's jaw stiffened. Willow. It had to be her, didn't it? She was staring hard, like she was trying not to blink. Her pale skin verged on unnatural most of the time. Now her cheeks glowed pink but her knuckles were white on the chair arms. 'Are you ok? My mistake.'

'Just watch what you're doing, ok?' he muttered, keeping his focus on the shoe she'd just run over and flexing his toes. He made a point of not looking at her. He never looked at her if he could help it. 'There are more subtle ways to take a man out.'

'Um, ok.' Her rosy lips twitched like she was trying to smile, but it wasn't happening for her. Why was he looking? *Must not do that.* 'I'll try to be more subtle next time.'

He pulled a fake smirk. 'Make sure there isn't a next time.'

'Right. I will. Sorry.'

'Yeah, whatever.'

'Sorry' She blinked and her face fell. Well, he was acting like a jerk. It wasn't her fault that David had pissed him off good and proper.

'What were you jumping out for anyway?' He folded his arms. *And why am I prolonging this conversation?*

'I just needed the stapler. It's behind you.' She pointed, and her eyelashes fluttered like teasing butterfly wings.

He turned around, lifted it from the shelf, and handed it to her. 'There you go.'

'Thanks.' She took it from him, and he registered the coolness of her skin. A fleeting thought of taking her small, pale hands in his and warming them passed through his mind. *Jesus, no.* Looking was bad enough. Touching, absolutely not. Jonathan, the cameraman, was her uncle, or cousin, or something. And who'd want 'the studio heartthrob', or whatever David had called him, anywhere near his young relative? Especially a man with a reputation like Marcus Bowman. If Jonathan found out how often Marcus thought about Willow he'd probably swap the camera for a shotgun.

'Now, can I get past?'

'Sure.' She whirled it around.

He stalked off, suppressing a twitch under his left eye. Did he have to be so gruff? He didn't engage in office banter, small talk or anything not strictly professional and sometimes he just couldn't help his grumpy moods. Lack of sleep and a demanding family situation didn't help. David definitely made it worse and that bright red envelope shining on his desk was today's last straw.

He placed his hands on his hips, narrowed his eyes and glared at it. Who would have the nerve? His gaze hopped back to Willow. Her hair streamed over her shoulders in messy trails, crossing and winding over her bright red top. *Stop bloody looking!* She fingered an oversized heart necklace, obviously trying hard not to look back. Marcus watched a fraction longer than necessary. *Where's my damned self-control?* He tossed the envelope behind the monitor and took his seat. He sensed her eyes on him, heard the click of a stapler. Why was she staring? Did she put the card there? Surely not? Why would she do that? Unless to irritate him. Maybe David had put her up to it. It seemed much more his style than hers. No doubt it would have something lewd, insulting or suggestive on it. Possibly all three.

He glanced at the envelope behind the monitor. If he didn't open it, it would sit there taunting him for the rest of his shift. He grabbed it and ripped open the offending red paper, praying it didn't start playing music or other sounds... Ones that wouldn't be appreciated in the newsroom. The picture on the front was plain, bordering on dull after what he'd expected: a shiny red heart balloon with a cartoon couple holding it. He flipped it open and read a handwritten message.

Weather you like it or not, you warm my cold front a lot.

And strike my soul like a bolt of lightning.

It's snow joke! In fact, it's frightening!

When you're near, I'm on cloud nine; it's dreich when we're apart.

I love you, Mr Bowman, the raining archer of my heart!

He stared at the words. *What the...?* His lip curled up. Who on earth had written that? Not David. He wouldn't have wasted his time and that poem had clearly taken time. Someone had put thought into that. Silly as it was. Kind of sweet. *I'm losing my grip.*

His eyes flicked back to Willow. *Internal facepalm – yes, he was doing it again.* Those sweet, sassy words matched her to a T. Her gaze was resolutely stuck to the computer screen, her smile wider than strictly necessary for staring at a monitor. For a fraction of a second, he toyed with the idea of marching over and asking her if she left it. But surely not. She was a colleague. A too young and off-limits colleague.

He shouldn't be looking at her and she shouldn't be looking at him. For different reasons. He didn't have an uncle waiting in the wings to warn off unsuitable colleagues. He *was* the unsuitable colleague. He never dated workmates and he wasn't on the market. End of. *Now, concentrate and no more looking.*

He straightened his tie and turned his attention to the weather charts. His hand strayed to a miniature sudoku book he kept on his desk. Doing the puzzles when he was stressed helped him to focus. He picked it up and flipped through it.

A hand landed on his shoulder and he dropped the book back in place.

'Could you not have brought us sunshine?' David's grinning face hovered above him.

'I just make the forecast, not the actual weather.'

David laughed. 'Just as well all your lovies don't know what a prat you are in real life.'

'Bugger off.'

'I will, gladly.' David strolled over to Willow's desk. 'Hello, Willow. You got my printouts?'

'Yes. I certainly do.'

'Lovely. You got a Valentine's date later?' he said. 'A young thing like you? Got the men lining the street outside, waiting for you?'

Patronising, much? Marcus rolled his eyes on her behalf, his ears alert for the answer. A twinge of curiosity leapt into his chest. Willow may not be right for him, but he didn't like the idea of her with anyone else, which was something he had to stop. *Get over yourself and stop being a creep.* He let out a grunt.

'Ah, that would be telling,' Willow said.

David laughed. 'Very secretive. But I hope you do. And I hope he spoils you. You deserve it. Your smiles brighten our day. Makes a change from Mr Grumpy Guts.'

'Thank you.'

Marcus flipped him the bird behind his back as he ambled off. He caught Willow's eye and she shook her head. *What?* But that was exactly why she didn't need him in her life. Little Miss Smiles could keep bringing sunshine to everyone and anyone while he kept things real.

CHAPTER TWO

Willow

Today will be grey for
Valentine's Day.

Marcus had read the card. Yikes. What did he think? Willow wouldn't like to hazard a guess even if they were face to face, but from the back, it was impossible. Usually he was cool and impassive, though David wound him up – everyone knew that, including David himself, who often goaded Marcus so obviously on purpose. When grumpy Marcus came out, it wasn't a pleasant sight. Very occasionally he completely lost it and that wasn't something Willow wanted to witness. Would the card make him mad rather than happy?

Oh no. This was a bad idea. Could she curl up and hide under the desk? Why the hell did she ever think sending that card was a good idea? She'd meant it as a joke. Kind of....

She loosened the neck of her top and focused on her screen. Whatever happened, she had to remain calm. A difficult task when six foot five inches of sexy male was sitting less than two metres from her, so close his trademark woodsy fragrance drifted into her consciousness, forcing her to look up. Was it her imagination or had he looked over more than usual this morning? He definitely had. Normally, he didn't look at her at all. Well, she had almost knocked him over. Trust her to pick that exact moment to push her chair back in her clumsy fashion. She fiddled with a trailing lock of her over-long blonde hair and checked him out for the hundredth time today. After he'd gone to all that effort to look hot AF this early in the morning, it would be rude not to. And hot was an understatement; she meant scorching hot. In a past life, he must have been a Roman gladiator: dark hair, tanned skin, smouldering eyes and a rich deep voice. And that was before you looked below his chin.

He was usually togged in a suit and tie in the studio, occasionally minus the jacket in the summer months. But Willow and the rest of the country had goggled at his broad slick chest and six-pack when he'd gone topless for his new show *Destination Forecast*. He was ripped like a model and most people didn't even remember the places he'd visited; they'd been too busy drowning in a pool of drool to notice.

Yup, she fancied the pants off him. At least the fantasy version of him. The one she imagined had a kind and caring personality to go with his good looks. Clearly she'd been struck by a blunt object that morning if she thought that card would make him happy. He probably suspected a David prank and it would do nothing but infuriate him.

He tapped on his keyboard, interrupting her virtual undressing, then drummed his finger on the desk as his screen loaded. She'd happily chuck work out the window and ogle those broad shoulders for the rest of the morning.

Would you check how his hair is trimmed to utter perfection at the nape of his neck? His barber must have precision clippers and a slide rule. Why was she looking again? He flicked his head round and eyeballed her. *Holy hell.* Heat attacked her neck and her cheeks. She must look guiltier than a kid caught with her hand in the biscuit tin. He shook his head before turning back to his screen. Maybe guilty vibes were streaming from her like neon lights. Had she made herself obvious? Before today, they'd only occasionally talked... or she'd talked and he'd grunted noncommittal responses. He was generally more interested in organising his pen collection in a neat row or swearing at people.

She should get on with her work but the view was too interesting, and not just Marcus. From here she could sneak a look at the row of monitors in front of him displaying various weather charts and satellite images from the meteorological super computers. What she wouldn't give to be in that seat. Weather had always fascinated her. Grey days were just as interesting as bright ones. In fact, more so. Watching signs and analysing conditions had become something of a hobby, especially when Marcus's counterpart was working. Polly Morgan liked to be the face of the forecast but not to make her own predictions. Willow helped with that but wouldn't dare do it with Marcus. He liked to do everything himself and hated being wrong – an almost impossible task for a forecaster. It sometimes made his forecasts a little generic, though she'd never have the nerve to tell him. She stifled a yawn. The early shift always killed her. *Who invented four a.m. starts?* Or more to the point, who kept scheduling her on them?

'Willow!' A voice rang across the room and a head of long, glossy chestnut hair came into view, heading her way. Ginny Lord, the producer. Her elegant hand waved, and gold sparkled on her fingers and wrists.

The way she shouted Willow's name confirmed her dragon-like status; it was audible over the crowded newsroom. Willow tightened her smile and sat up. *Ouch*. A pain travelled up her back. Nothing unusual, just the one she always got when she tried to look taller by forcing her noncompliant spine into a straight line.

Marcus threw Ginny a look meant to kill; he hated interruptions. Willow screwed up her face. When volcano Marcus blew, everyone ducked for cover. This could be one of those moments. He was the only person who ever back-chatted Ginny. She was almost fifty, tall, slim and more glamorous than anyone else in the room – except Marcus, of course.

Ginny sailed past him, ignoring his evil eye, and marched straight to Willow's desk. Willow shoved her long straggly hair behind her ears, but it still trailed over her shoulders and down her back, almost to her bottom. It hadn't been cut for years and it was probably the part of her body she loved the most.

'Yes...' *Your majesty?* The words stayed silently lodged in her head. Sometimes she felt like she should curtsey in Ginny's presence, but being cowed in her seat was enough.

'I need to talk to you about the vacancy.'

Heat rushed into Willow's cheeks again and she tugged on her necklace. Was Ginny going to offer it to her? A hundred thoughts danced through her head. Could she do it? Why would Ginny give it to her? Perhaps for the same reasons she got her current job? To please a relative? To fill a quota? Before she could manufacture any answers, Ginny went on.

'I've just had a call from an old friend. His daughter is very keen to do it.'

'Oh... Right.' Willow blinked, catching sight of Marcus. Was he listening? Something about the way he'd stopped typing suggested he was. The vacancy wasn't to replace him but Polly, who was going on maternity leave and Willow wasn't looking forward to the change. If it was someone who didn't need help, she'd be stuck with all the boring admin jobs.

'She's in Glasgow today.' Ginny checked her watch. 'She wants to nip in for a visit. I can't show her around as I have a producers' meeting. A highly inconvenient clash, I might add.' With a quick glance at Marcus, she leaned over Willow's desk and added quietly. 'I want you to give her the tour. Remember, although she still has to do an interview, we want to sell the place to her. She's got a family of very successful journalists behind her, and she'd be a good name to have on board.'

'Ok.'

'I'm just going to have a quick word with Marcus. I want him on his best behaviour.'

Willow smirked as she stalked over. *Good luck with that.*

Sadie Greene was proper weathergirl material: at least five foot ten, fully made-up, immaculately dressed, with perfect poise and the voice of self-certainty. Willow shuffled before her, leading her through the jungle of desks, clattering keyboards, flashing monitors, and buzzing phones. Wouldn't it be just the thing if she tripped over something? She took her sticks just in case. Having them shouldn't be a cause for shame but no matter how much the world had progressed, she still felt people's focus on her, eyeing the sticks or watching the way she walked, and she didn't like it. She didn't need pity or whatever they intended with their well-meaning glances.

Sadie didn't look at her with pity or concern or anything really. In fact Willow might as well have been invisible. Sadie already seemed to know several people. Willow stood back, twirling a lock of hair around her index finger as Sadie greeted friends with hugs, pecks on the cheek, and exclamations of, 'Great to see you again, darling.'

When she reached Marcus, he stood to shake hands with her, and their eyes met. *Oh god.* Willow shrank back, feeling even smaller than usual. Did she have to witness this? Marcus and Sadie should walk down the aisle right now; they were made for each other. He was so tall next to Willow, but next to Sadie, he looked just right. Willow's stomach lurched, which was stupid. She lusted over Marcus all the time but knew nothing would ever happen. *I'm a dreamer, not delusional.* For starters, he had to be ten years older than her, and she suspected he was with someone, but he was famously tight lipped about his relationships. Oh no, the card? Her cheeks started to blaze with heat. What if he had kids and he was someone's dad? *I'm an idiot.* You didn't get to his age, being that hot and well-off without attracting loads of interest. A fact she'd conveniently let wash over her when writing that card.

Sadie flicked her elegant hair over her shoulders and smiled broadly, her lashes practically batting. Was she drooling as much as the commoners? Marcus smiled but it was the fake one he pulled out for the cameras. Willow could spot it a mile off. His eyes flicked to her and he blinked before looking back at Sadie.

Like a beaten dog thrown a scrap of affection, tingles of excitement zipped through her. *Seriously? I am actually a lovesick fool.* Time to get a grip! Would he ever in a million years be interested in her? She glanced down at the splints on her legs and swallowed.

Nope. Not a chance. If she could turn back time to this morning, she'd make sure that card never reached his desk.

It had vanished and she suspected he'd chucked it straight in the bin.

After Sadie's tour, she spotted him storming towards the recording studio. He straightened his tie and didn't look back before disappearing through the door.

No one else was on his side of the office and Willow snuck into his black leather chair; *mmm, nice and soft and still warm.* The heat penetrated her deep down, easing the ache in her thighs the walking around the office earlier had caused. The monitors were still on and she scrolled through them. Her elbow caught Marcus's lined-up pens, knocking them to the floor. *Oops.* She scrambled to pick them up – bending down was never the easiest move – and replaced them in what she hoped was the right order. Once they were sorted, she leaned forward and scanned the incoming data on the monitors. It was immediately obvious what he was working on. An area of low pressure in the Atlantic was moving in their direction and he was tracking it. It could cause stormy weather depending on the wind speed.

His desk bent around to accommodate all the screens with two seats so he could leap from one to the other, interpreting the data. Polly usually allowed her to sit in the spare seat and do the cross-referencing for her. Willow viewed the next monitor. Things got even more interesting. Another front on the east side was making its way towards the land. If those two fronts collided, what might happen? She made some mental notes, losing herself in the charts and making predictions. In her mind, she could hear herself forecasting to the nation; she was confident and no one questioned her abilities – either mental or physical.

Marcus's voice rang across the room. *Shit.* Willow got to her feet as fast as her joints would allow, which wasn't very fast at all. She hadn't meant to sit that long. He would reach his desk faster than she could get back to her seat. Now she was stuck.

A row of shelves around the weather room was laden with books, files, old electronics and stationery. Willow busied herself looking through a line of old box files, keeping her head low. Would he notice her? She couldn't get back to her desk without passing him.

Having a job in admin meant she could come and go as she pleased. She had an excuse to be everywhere and anywhere and she needed to use it right now. She couldn't stand here too long. Her legs were sore, but she was damned if she was going to let anyone know or demand special treatment. She took two tentative steps forward. Perhaps Marcus wouldn't even notice. A few steps further and he swivelled his seat around, his elegant Roman nose pointing her way. One neatly shaped eyebrow raised slightly.

'What are you doing?' he said. His jacket was off and his crisp charcoal shirt had the sleeves neatly turned back and precision-folded. What gorgeous forearms he had.

'Just, you know, tidying up.'

'Tidying up what?'

'The shelf.' She pointed with a smile.

'Oh-kay...' He turned back to his screens.

'There's always something to tidy on a shelf.'

'Sure,' he said. 'You'll go far with that attitude.'

'Thanks.'

'The further, the better.'

'Charming.' She made to move but her leg buckled, and she grabbed the back of his chair for support. It wobbled. 'That front is getting closer,' she said, trying to invent a reason for clinging to the back of his seat. 'I reckon it'll break tomorrow night.'

He glanced around, his eyebrows drawn together. 'Since when did you become an expert?'

'I didn't. I just like the weather.' She didn't let on that she helped Polly. Marcus got a bee in his bonnet about people not pulling their weight and technically she was just an admin assistant, nothing more.

'Yeah, so do thousands of people. But liking the weather and forecasting are two completely different things. You'd be more than somewhat out of your depth.' He looked at her again and a shiver coursed down her spine. He was actually talking to her, but he was so abrasive. Unfortunately, she couldn't stalk off with attitude. Could she even walk at all right now? Standing was taking all her energy and her sticks were unhelpfully back at her desk.

'That's not very nice,' she said.

His lip curled up very slightly at one corner. 'Ask David. He'll tell you I'm not very nice,' he said. 'Though several thousand viewers might disagree. I'll leave you to form your own conclusion.'

Was this banter? He never bantered. Everyone knew that. She was starting to overheat again but kept her cool. 'One day I'll show you just how good I am.'

He snorted and returned to staring at his screen but she still clung to his seat.

'Why are you still here?' He glanced up. 'Sit down.' He motioned her to the spare seat.

'I'm fine. I don't need a seat.' *Liar.* She winced. But seriously, she hated pity.

'Did I say you did?' He flicked her a pointed stare. 'I have a job for you.'

She cocked her head to the side and pursed her lips. Was he being nice in a roundabout way? Why? Did he think she needed sympathy? She sat on the spare seat, trying not to show how good – and vital – it was to rest her legs.

He casually leant back, resting his elbow on the armrest and rubbing his thumb and fingers together. His eyes travelled over her and she tingled like an outbreak of hives was on the verge of erupting.

Please don't ask me about that card. She'd die if he mentioned it. 'What is it you want me to do?' Her voice was weak.

'The storm, look.' He rotated to face the screen and pointed out its course.

She could see the trajectory herself but let him show her because she liked the sound of his voice. Something about it was calming and soothing. That was why people loved him on TV. That, and his looks.

'This ridge of low pressure is building,' he said. 'Trouble is, it's too far out in the Atlantic yet to say exactly when it'll hit.'

'Do you think it'll snow?'

'I'm a forecaster, not a frigging fortune teller, so I couldn't possibly comment. But between you and me, I'd say it's highly unlikely. However, if you open those other monitors, I can cross-reference the data from the other weather stations and see if I can get a handle on where it's going.'

'Sure.' She spun the seat around, fiddling with a puzzle book that was sitting on the desk as she waited for the data to load.

'Try one of them if you want,' he said, eyeing the book.

'Cool, sudoku. I love that.'

He frowned. 'You do?'

'Yes.'

'Have that book if you want it. Try the one on page six. It's a killer.' His rich brown irises glinted in the light from his monitors, and a smile as nebulous as a fine layer of Cirrostratus appeared on his chiselled face.

'Ok.'

'Just don't bother taking any more of my pens.'

'I haven't taken any of your pens.'

'Someone keeps nicking them. But anyway, keep the book.' His eyes met hers.

'Thanks.' She turned to the next monitor and brought up the right site. Had her face just gone bright red? Her cheeks were burning.

'If you get the one on page six, I'll buy you a bottle of champagne.'

'Why?' She flipped through the book.

'Because it's damn near impossible.'

'Challenge accepted.' She could buy her own book for a few quid, but the fact it had once belonged to Marcus Bowman made her want to keep it. Why was she so obsessed with him? This softening was making him even more appealing than usual.

'Where do you come from?' he asked. 'Your accent reminds me of someone.'

Willow shrugged. 'Perthshire originally.'

'That explains it. I come from there too.'

'Do you?' She spun back to look at him. 'Because if you do, you'll know people from Perth don't have an accent.'

His lips curled up into a proper smile and it was glorious, not like the fake TV one. 'Of course. How could I forget? So, do you still have family there?'

'My parents live here now.' They'd moved to Glasgow with her when she got this job. Willow let out a sigh. Wherever she went, they went too. 'I have an aunt and a couple of cousins in

Highland Perthshire. They live in a little town called Glenbriar, you might know it. It's very cute and touristy.'

'I know it very well. I... Someone I know used to live there.'

'Small world, isn't it?'

'Isn't it just?' Marcus rubbed his hands together. 'Now, haven't you got shelves all over the office waiting to be tidied?'

'I do, but don't you want me to note down any data for you?' She was so used to doing it for Polly.

'Do you know how to do that?'

'Sure, I do.'

'Go on then.' He turned back to his screen and Willow got to work, hardly daring to believe he was letting her help him. When she'd cross-referenced three of the main charts, she pulled the seat closer to him. Ok, maybe a bit too close. He smelled so good and the way his collar sat crisply at his neck was ridiculously seductive.

Suddenly aware of herself, she made to pull away, but he wheeled around and took the iPad from her hand. The touch of his skin on hers sent an energy current tingling through her nerve ends.

'Great.' He scrolled down with a semi-impressed expression. 'That's very helpful.'

'Do you want me for anything else?'

He locked his gaze on her, and for a split second, she froze. Was he thinking unspeakable things, or was her imagination in overdrive? 'Nope. I'm good.' He gave her a half smile.

She melted. He was actually smiling... *At me!* Could she move? She had to. With an effort, she shuffled forward.

'We should make this a date,' he said.

Heat attacked her neck and cheeks. She was so prone to blushing she got worse hot flushes than Ginny, who was in the grip of the perimenopause. 'I have a boyfriend.' *Why did she say that?* She didn't. Boyfriends weren't the easiest thing to come by.

Marcus looked away with a smirk. 'Maybe I do too.' He folded his arms and leaned back. 'But I meant a date as in a time of day when you come and help interpret the data with me.'

'Oh, er, right. Ok.'

He raised an eyebrow. 'Good.'

'Well, when you want me, you know where to find me.' She limped off in a highly unspectacular manner. He had a boyfriend? She'd imagined so many possibilities for his love life but not that one. Curse her. Why hadn't she thought of that?

CHAPTER THREE

Willow

*Scattered showers here
and there. Sunny spells
everywhere. Mostly dry,
yet a chill persists. Keep the
gloves out, that's the gist!*

March

Willow leaned in, checking the monitor and taking notes to cross-reference. Beside her, Polly sat back, yawning.

'I hate the early shifts,' she said. 'And it's a hundred times worse now I'm pregnant. I'm just so exhausted.'

Willow didn't want to say she knew the feeling. She didn't know how being pregnant felt, but fatigue was a regular visitor. No point in moaning though; she just did her best and dropped at the end of each day.

Marcus had been on the opposite shift from her for the past few days. Thank goodness. It lowered her chance of heart failure. When she saw him, she was worse than a kid at high school; it was a chemical reaction, pure and simple. Nothing she could do about it, except avoid him, which she didn't really want to do either. His presence was like her raison d'être. Without him, the office was dull and lifeless. And he'd been much more pleasant to her recently, letting her assist with data interpretation and cross-referencing charts. Even just getting to sit by him was a treat. Sometimes he chatted with her, which she was sure he didn't do with anyone else. Of course, it was about the weather and nothing personal, but it was something nonetheless. And better that way, as she had a totally boring life and nothing to tell him. His glamorous existence was unimaginable.

Only the forecasting kept her mind off him. She wasn't sure Polly actually knew what she was doing. On screen, she had presence and was very charming, but she left all the analysis to Willow. Ginny turned a blind eye to it – or so it seemed. Maybe she was counting the days until Polly left so she could replace her with someone more competent.

'Have you heard if there have been any more applicants for your post?' Willow asked her.

'Ginny is keeping schtum about it.' Polly glanced around, then leaned closer to Willow. 'Why don't you apply for it?'

'Me? But I don't have the right qualifications.' She didn't really have any, apart from a college diploma in business studies. 'And I don't have the nerve. I'm too shy to go on air.'

'I think you'd be fine. It's just like talking to David or whoever else is presenting. You forget about everything else after a while. And as for qualifications, you know more than I do, and you have experience working here, which is probably more than most of the other applicants.'

'I doubt it. One of them is Sadie Greene. I showed her around last week. You know she's Kenneth Greene's daughter and he's chummy with Ginny.'

'Yeah. I heard she was here, but I still think you should try. You'll never know if you don't, and...' She rested her hand on her large bump. 'There's a good chance it'll become a permanent post because I'm not sure I want to come back after I have the baby.'

'Seriously? Nooooooo.' *She can't leave me.* 'How will I survive without you?'

'You can transfer your help to Marcus.'

Willow's cheeks flamed at the thought. 'Er no. I don't think he'd want that.'

'Probably not. It would ruin his Mr Perfect image if he let someone help. I'm glad our shifts don't overlap too often. He intimidates me. But, here, I just remembered something.'

'What?'

'You know how he never talks about his private life?' She checked around, making sure no one was listening.

Willow knew only too well. She'd stalked him online and found out only what she already knew and what seemed to be the 'official' story. He'd been married to someone but was now divorced and his ex-wife didn't seem to be famous. Willow hadn't even found out her name. She'd found loads about him being a guest speaker all over the country, doing celebrity stints on cooking shows and mostly stuff about his new series *Destination Forecast,* a show about the best places to holiday if you were looking for certain weather conditions. He'd taken time away from the studio to do it, much to Ginny's chagrin, though she liked the ratings when he returned fresh from his travels all tanned and looking every inch 'Britain's sexiest weatherman'. He'd been afforded that title on many occasions. Once, he'd featured in Highland Home magazine, posing like a model in an unbuttoned shirt, in a warehouse-style apartment. But the article gave no personal details other than surface ones. Even with the titbit he'd thrown her about knowing people in Perthshire, she hadn't discovered anything else. She'd messaged her cousin, Hayley, who was a hairdresser in Glenbriar, and knew everything about everyone, asking her to find out what she could, but so far, she'd found nothing of note.

'Yeah, he never says anything about his private life, does he?' Willow fiddled with her cuff, not wanting to look too interested, but inside, dying to hear. Maybe he'd left his wife for a man and Polly had found out.

'Did you know he has three kids?'

'No.' Her heart hiccupped. Surely he'd been winding her up about having a boyfriend. Or did he have a boyfriend and three kids? *Oh god.* She'd been leching over someone's partner, someone's dad.

'I saw him with them outside one day. His wife, or partner, looked like a supermodel. Long dark hair, tanned. Kind of like the woman version of him really.'

'A woman?'

'Well, yes. Why?'

'He...' She stopped and shook her head. He'd been teasing her.

'He what?'

'Nothing.'

'You know what I think?'

'What?' Willow frowned. Where was this going?

'I don't think he's actually divorced. I think he and his wife made that story up. The oldest child looked about thirteen. I wonder if he had a kid before he was married. Then they stage a divorce, she disappears with the kid and they have two more in secret.'

'Why would he do that?'

'Privacy, I expect. And I don't blame him. I don't want this little one growing up in the public eye.' She patted her tummy again. 'Not that I'm anywhere near as famous as Marcus. We don't all have his looks. I don't know why he doesn't pack it in and focus on *Destination Forecast* or get a modelling job. He'd be snapped up.'

'He sure would.' Willow's heart was at her feet. He had a partner who looked like a supermodel. Well, there was never much chance he'd look twice at her. Now there was zero. In fact, make that minus twenty. She was a plain Jane and an average Jill with noncompliant joints, straggly hair and a funny wee button nose. Marcus was a gorgeous fantasy. She had as much chance of succeeding with him as she did of becoming a TV weather girl.

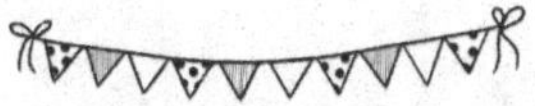

Willow flipped the page on her cute dog calendar to the fifteenth of March and smiled at the puppy staring back at her. One day she'd like a dog, though it wasn't really practical right now.

Her eyes travelled to the weather desk. She was back working shifts with Marcus. He hadn't looked at her or spoken to her since he arrived. And that suited her just fine. She had to wean herself off him for her own sake.

Like he'd read her mind, he spun around on his seat and caught her eye. Damn it. Why did she have to be looking?

'Come here.' He beckoned her.

She glanced from side to side, then pointed at her chest.

'Yes, you, Willow.'

She dragged herself to her feet and made her way to his desk. 'What is it? Do you want me to help with the charts?'

'Later. I'm fine just now. But look.' He craned his neck and scanned around, presumably checking for nosey people. 'I've got something for you.'

'For me?'

'Yes, you. I hear it's your birthday soon.'

'How did you know that?'

He tapped the side of his nose. 'I know everything.' With a smirk, he lifted a small parcel from the desk. 'With my compliments.' He handed it to her but didn't let go when she took it. 'And good luck.'

'Thanks... I think.'

'Got to dash.' He got to his feet and straightened his tie. Why did he have to be so ridiculously tall? She was like a child next to him. And that fragrance. She half closed her eyes, breathing it in. He marched towards the studio and she flopped into his seat. Tentatively, she peeled off the wrapping paper on the parcel. Inside was a small book, *The World's Most Difficult Sudoku Puzzles – only for geniuses,* and a very expensive looking handmade chocolate bar. Her lips curled up. Seriously? But a flicker of heat licked her insides. Marcus Bowman, the hottest weather presenter in TV history, had given her a birthday present. Was squealing for joy out of the question?

She needed to get some air and cool off. Bright spring sun split the sky but it was freezing. The half-predicted storms had come and gone with just rain and no snow, as Marcus forecast, leaving clear skies. The sun was shining, and the Clyde-side walk outside the studio looked so inviting. She grabbed a seat on a cold bench. It was Wednesday and she didn't have a shift the next day. Then it was her birthday on Friday. She pulled out her phone, opening the application form for the forecaster job – closing date today. She'd filled in all the boxes, as Polly suggested. All she had to do was hit send. Maybe she should ask Marcus's opinion. He seemed to be in a good mood, and he'd been kind to her recently, like a sort of mentor, but she wasn't sure she dared. If he didn't think she was up to the job, she couldn't stand his rejection. Maybe he was just humouring her by giving her presents. Would he?

Her finger hovered for a second. What to do? She had to decide for herself, but it wasn't easy.

Her parents cosseted her all the time. She'd been born with cerebral palsy and they'd felt they had to make the big decisions for her when she was growing up to keep her safe and healthy. She appreciated everything they did for her. Really, she did. They'd helped her land this job. Her uncle Jonathan was a cameraman and pulled some favours. But it wasn't quite right for her. Her heart wanted more. She loved forecasting more than anything else, but was she cut out for life on camera? She didn't want to be some token disabled girl they employed to fill a quota. She wanted to earn this on merit. What if she couldn't get over her nerves? She tried not to imagine the cameras rolling and her freezing, unable to form a sentence and just standing there. What would happen then? Or what if she did speak but it was utter nonsense that came out?

'Oh god.' She sighed into her hands. It wouldn't just be the talking. Some days, she could barely stand up straight. How would that look on TV? Would she be allowed crutches? A chair?

She'd never know unless she tried. This was her moment to be brave and step right out of that comfort zone she'd lived in for so long.

Her finger hit send. Gone. She'd done it. Shouldn't there be a thunderclap or something? She checked her emails immediately in case there was an instant reply from Ginny, asking if she'd lost her mind.

Huddling into her duffle coat, Willow messaged Hayley, her cousin. She had many friends and acquaintances, and Hayley was the most steadfast and reliable in her love and loyalty. If anyone would understand this move and champion it without question, it was her. She wouldn't care if Willow was underqualified or applying for a post several steps up the ladder. She'd simply cheer for her in the wings and be furious on her behalf if she didn't get it.

Willow shoved the phone into her pocket and headed inside.

All afternoon, she jumped at calls and couldn't focus, wondering if Ginny had got the application. Her cheeks were hot. Maybe she should go ask her. What would Ginny make of it? Had she made a complete tit of herself? Should she show face? What if she didn't get the position? How awkward would it be? Would Ginny tell everyone? How likely was it that she'd get it? Less than zero. *Oh god.* She should retract the application immediately. Nerves threatened to eat her alive and she hadn't got near a camera yet. This did not bode well.

And where was Marcus? He hadn't been at his desk since he gave her the birthday present. Her phone buzzed.

Hayley: Awesome! I can't wait to see you on TV. OMG, you will be excellent. Everyone will melt at your beautiful smile. Crossing everything for you. xxxxxxxxx

The words made her grin, but she couldn't bear the tension. She had to speak to Ginny. She headed for her door but stopped at raised voices.

'That is completely ridiculous,' Marcus said from inside Ginny's office. His tone was unmistakably smooth, even when angry. He wasn't shouting, but it sounded like he was in one of his explosive moods. 'She is so wrong for the post. You can't seriously be thinking of employing her. It undermines the profession completely if you start taking on people like her. I have a degree in mathematics. I did several years of training with the Met-Office. And for what? So you can employ some girl barely out of school with no qualifications at all?'

'Marcus, calm down.'

'I am perfectly calm.' His heated tone told a different story. 'This is nothing but lip-service and a paper exercise so you can tick a box and look good.'

'That's enough, Marcus. Put that ego of yours back in its box for a minute.'

Willow's soul froze from the inside out. She dragged her hands down her face, turned and walked away. Her heart slipped to the bottom of her stomach. If she'd doubted herself before, it was even worse now. Why had she kidded herself Marcus had softened towards her? And why did he bother trying to be smooth by giving her a book for 'geniuses'? Maybe she was allowed to be a genius admin assistant but he couldn't entertain her pushing her way into his patch.

The nerves in her stomach were so bad now she couldn't concentrate. With a shaky finger, she opened her computer and logged into the company system. She withdrew her application with a note to Ginny. No way was she cut out for that job. How could she do it knowing what Marcus thought of her abilities?

She didn't see him or Ginny again that day and maybe it was just as well. Her insides were burning and she couldn't concentrate.

The second her shift was done, she grabbed her coat from the staffroom and left. It wasn't a new job here she needed. It was a new job full stop. One far away from Marcus Bowman.

CHAPTER FOUR

Marcus

June the following year

'And that's the forecast.' Marcus held his smile, waiting for the light to go off. Then he could get the hell out for the day.

Toby's review meeting was coming up and Marcus needed to be prepared.

Family first, just not in the limelight.

He'd been woefully neglectful as he'd been filming another series of *Destination Forecast*. The trips to Iceland and Goa were complete but he was due to fly to Egypt and New Zealand later in the summer. This, coupled with his forecasting commitments, made it feel like he hadn't had a day off in forever. He was utterly exhausted – emotionally and mentally, if not physically.

'Now, Marcus, before we let you go,' David said, 'tell us what you make of this online sensation, Rocky Rainman the rhyming weather forecaster.'

Seriously? Surely that was an off-limits subject on air. Why would David think it a good idea to mention that character on live TV? Marcus had heard nothing but Rocky bloody Rainman for months. On his travels, he'd become aware of this overnight sensation when he was tagged in hundreds of posts and comments on every social media platform. He'd spent hours trawling, trying to figure out why his name kept getting dragged into things. Rocky Rainman was the bane of his life. He was sick of everything about him.

Now he had to keep his grin in place and answer like it was his favourite subject. Ginny would string him up by the balls if he insulted Rocky or made it obvious that he couldn't stand him.

'He seems like a very a keen amateur.' Marcus straightened his tie and flexed his neck.

'Indeed,' David said. 'For any viewers who haven't heard of Rocky Rainman, he's an internet forecaster, who not only brings his followers accurate weather readings but has a fun turn of phrase, often putting his forecasts into rhymes. So far, no one has uncovered his real identity, which adds to the intrigue. Marcus, do you think you'd be able to rival the Rainman with some sonnets of your own?'

Marcus ground his teeth behind his grin. *What a dick.* 'Poetry isn't exactly my strong point. I'll stick to making accurate forecasts.'

'Good to hear.' David raised his eyebrows at the camera, turning on the charm for the viewers. 'Because Rocky has amassed quite a following already. His predictions are, to quote a few popular comments, "unerringly accurate", "completely trustworthy", and "spot on". While he claims that some TV weather presenters "won't stick their necks out and make a bold forecast in case they get sacked, so we're stuck with insipid and vague forecasts that anyone could make". What do you have to say to that?'

For fuck's sake. *I don't know who's worse: David or Rocky?* Right now, it was hard to say. Marcus kept his face impassive. 'An interesting opinion, though I'm not sure what facts he's basing it on.' His experience of Rocky so far had led him to believe the guy was little more than an online bully who got a kick out of insulting him.

'Do you agree with his latest prediction that we're in for a heatwave this summer?'

If this smile wasn't so damn well practised, it would have slipped off Marcus's face and hit the floor, but it remained intact. Did the viewers know how fake it was? Probably not, or he wouldn't maintain the popularity he did. 'I haven't seen the exact forecast, but I'd say it's impossible to predict something like that with any accuracy. I mean, there's every likelihood that we'll have some hot days over the next couple of months. It's summer after all. But predicting a blanket heatwave in Scotland for the entire summer seems a little far-fetched.'

'Indeed. And I think the post in question was a lot more specific, however we'll leave it there for the day.' David smirked. 'Thank you, Marcus, for the forecast.'

Finally, the light went red. Marcus ripped off his microphone and stormed out of the studio.

'Jesus F Christ.' He threw himself into the chair at his desk and rubbed his face. All around the newsroom, monitors twinkled and flickered, taunting him with images of unknown faces. People who, for all he knew, could be Rocky Rainman. He focused on his desk and lifted a pen. Sitting atop the empty in-tray was his sudoku book. He grabbed it and flipped through it for a blank one. His mind floated back to February last year and that anonymous Valentine card. He'd never got to the bottom of that, though he'd suspected Willow. Pah. That was silly. The average age of his followers was mid-sixties and while he didn't knock it, he didn't want someone old enough to be his mother sending him a Valentine card.

He tapped the pad with his pen. Whatever happened to Willow? He often thought about her. More than was sensible. Just like he'd looked at her more than was good for him when she was here. She'd probably married that boyfriend of hers. But to leave without saying goodbye... That was harsh. She'd just walked out one day. The same day he'd given her a birthday present. Ginny got an email of resignation and that was that. Was his gift connected to her reasons for leaving? Had she seen it as something unwelcome or creepy? *Idiot – you brought it on yourself, always sneaking looks at her or faking reasons to have her sit by you.* Maybe he was just a sad old git whose head had been easily turned by a pretty young thing. *Christ, I really am a creep.*

He filled out a few numbers in the blank boxes and his breathing calmed. When he'd finished one square, he tapped out a quick update email to his counterpart, the princess who got the job in place of Polly because her daddy was a top producer and her mummy a well-known journalist. Sadie was only meant to do maternity cover for Polly but Polly hadn't come back after the baby was born. Marcus didn't blame her. He was done with early mornings, late nights and long shifts. Now *Destination Forecast* had taken off, he saw himself leaning more and more towards that. It wasn't the job he trained to do but neither was forecasting. People might think he got a lucky break into TV but he wasn't convinced it was such a great reward. Ginny was petrified he would jump ship to presenting and he'd be a liar to say it wasn't tempting.

He doodled on the pad. Nothing was to stop him from penning his resignation right now. Nothing except the entire world would think it was because he couldn't take the heat from Rocky Rainman. He was damned if he was going to give anyone that satisfaction. And quitting at the top would mean a mighty fall. No. He had one last mission before thinking seriously about a change of direction: expose Rocky and give him the payback he deserved. Ever since Rocky had appeared, the undertones of bullying had gnawed at Marcus. No one got away with that. Once he'd sorted out Rocky and the intrigue died down, so would the interest. He could move on without looking like a coward.

But none of that mattered today. He grabbed his jacket from the back of his chair and headed for his car. He had to sort things out for Toby.

It was an easy drive home over the Kingston Bridge to the south side where he lived in a beautifully kept street of Victorian houses. Sloped gardens surrounded by rails lined the avenue. A perfect leafy suburban home for him and his very eclectic and completely non-traditional family. He flicked the remote control, opening the iron gates and crunching up the gravel driveway to a space by the side door.

A couple of years ago, he'd done a photoshoot for Highland Home magazine in a warehouse apartment he'd rented for a week. It kept up the myth that he was living happily as a bachelor since his divorce, in a trendy upmarket city flat. Nothing like the truth.

His youngest brother, Toby, still lived at home with him. Four other siblings, Dario, Adella, Luca and Antony had flown the nest over the years and gone their separate ways. But his sister, Laurenia, as good as lived in his house, especially when her husband was away on the rigs. Marcus couldn't thank her enough. Without her being around, he couldn't have kept his job and looked after the others. Not with his hours and with Toby's issues. None of them had really wanted to leave Perthshire but the commute wasn't possible. Not with four a.m. starts and late finishes. But a heavy weight pressed on his chest when he thought about how much Laurenia had given up for their family. She'd sacrificed the chance of her daughters growing up in the countryside so he could have his career and Toby stay in a family home and not be taken into care.

He'd barely opened the door when a boy sprinted towards him, refuting his fragile appearance, and knocking Marcus off balance. Marcus staggered backwards before lifting his youngest brother off his feet in a bear hug. Toby didn't say a lot but, boy, was he affectionate.

'Hey, Toby.' Marcus clapped his back.

Toby made a growling sound as he dangled off Marcus's neck. He weighed next to nothing despite being almost eighteen but was more like a six-year-old in mind and emotion. Small for his age, while Marcus was six foot five and could lift him like a child. But Toby was moving on and would have to get used to not being able to do this. It was a wrench thinking about it. Nothing would be quite like home, but without school, Toby needed something more.

Two younger children ran into the hallway: Laurenia's daughters, Emily and Freya.

'Uncle Marcus,' Emily said. 'Mummy says I can go horse riding and I can get a hat and boots and everything.'

'Wow. Sounds great. I always wanted to horse ride.'

Maybe his uncle-duties could stretch to that. He wished he could do more; he'd missed so much – of everything. And for what? A career? Money? Money that paid for all his family to have better lives than they would have otherwise.

'What's going on out here?' Laurenia said, surveying the hall. 'You're all being so noisy.'

Marcus wrestled Toby off him. 'I'm hearing all about horse riding.'

'Oh, that. Listen guys, can we all get out of the hall? I'll put the TV on.' She ushered them into the lounge, aimed the remote at the TV and the kids dived onto the sofa like puppies in a basket. The opening music of an animated show started up. 'Marcus, come with me a sec.' She closed the door and he followed her into the kitchen.

'What's up?'

'I've been thinking. Once this review meeting is done and Toby's left school, it might be a good time for us to refocus. We can see what he needs but it also might be the chance to move back home.'

Marcus nodded, knowing exactly where she meant. This had never been her true home. She missed Perthshire, where they'd grown up, and she still had a lot of friends there. 'Of course. I understand, but what about Toby's care?' All the options they'd looked at were in Glasgow.

'Well, I've been investigating, and I found a place I think might work.'

Marcus scratched the back of his neck. 'Great.'

'Would you like to go and see it next week?'

'Of course I would.'

'Great. And are you sure it's ok?'

'Yes.' He rested his hand on her shoulder and nodded. How could it not be? After all she'd done for him? She'd bent to fit in with his life for five years. But his heart felt like a lead weight had landed. Perthshire wasn't the end of the world but it was way beyond a quick visit. And Laurenia wasn't just his sister, she was his friend... his only friend really. Everyone else who called themself his friend was more than likely a faceless acquaintance in a sea of people he'd met over the years.

'I guess there's no chance of you moving too?' she said.

He shook his head.

She sighed. 'Why not? Just pack it in. You'd get more jobs presenting and you wouldn't have to be in the studio all the time.'

'I'm not ready to give up yet.'

She cocked her head. 'Why? You look wasted. Just resign. You seem to have lost your passion for forecasting.'

Her words echoed his feelings from earlier but the timing was all wrong.

'Did you hear what David asked me on air?' he said, ignoring her question.

'I wasn't watching. What did he ask?'

'About that Rocky Rainman character. He's hacking me off so much.' Marcus gritted his teeth.

'I know,' she said. 'But isn't that just another reason to leave?'

'No. The opposite. If I go now, he'll think he's won. He's a bully and it feels like war.'

'Yeah.' She sighed and rubbed her forehead. 'I hate the way he brings you down. I try not to read it but things pop up on social media. His followers sign off with things like, *trust in Rocky, only weatherman you'll ever need.*'

'Don't I know it. And that's not the worst of it. Some of the stuff is just nasty. Cherie left me because she couldn't stand all the online speculation and that was long before Rocky. This is something that's impossible for me to ignore. Rocky's followers constantly tag me in the posts to make sure I know who they're talking about. Apparently, my forecasts are "insipid and vague". He doesn't get that it's not my job to be sensationalist. Even when I've deleted apps from my phone, I see things at work or David points it out. I can't avoid it. It's a newsroom. It's our job to know everything that's going on everywhere.'

'It's horrible and clearly someone who's out to get you.'

'I go between thinking it's someone who's got it in for me or just a random unknown with no idea the trouble they're causing.' He narrowed his eyes and leant on the work surface.

'I'm sure it's someone who knows exactly what they're doing.'

'I wish I could find out who it is. I'd give them more than a piece of my mind, that's for sure.'

'In his posts he calls himself *Scotland's number one weatherman* and puts *take that MB* and stuff like that at the end of posts. He's always trying to discredit you.'

'Yup. And it's working.'

'Maybe it's a forecaster from another channel.'

'I wonder. I don't think Shaun Wilson on Radio Scotland has ever liked me. I wouldn't put it past him to do something like that. Snotty little muppet's got a good face for radio.'

Laurenia sniggered.

'Once I find out who it is and expose their little game, my resignation papers will be on Ginny's desk faster than she can say Rocky's Rhymes are dead, but not until then.'

'Well, look at this.' Laurenia opened her phone and scrolled through Rocky's page until she reached some photos of a sunny reflection in a loch with hills all around it.

'Most of the pictures on the page are gifs or graphics of weather maps and his poems. These are the only pictures I've seen that look real,' she said.

'Yeah, but that doesn't tell me who it is.'

'Someone will be able to identify those hills, won't they? Don't you have the power of e-Broadcast Scotland behind you?'

'You think?'

'Yeah. It actually looks like Loch Briar to me but I guess loads of lochs look similar.'

'It kind of does, but it could be anywhere. I might see if anyone's up for a bit of investigating.'

'Good plan. Now, let's eat, then we can chat about the review meeting, and I'll show you some pictures of the facility I found for Toby. Just think, it won't be long until you'll have your house back to yourself.'

'True.' He rubbed his fingertips together. When his mum had died leaving an incapable husband with their children, Marcus had stepped in and offered up his house to his younger siblings. What a culture shock it had been. A sure way of killing off his love life. What woman wanted to come back to a house full of irritable teenagers? All he'd wanted for years was his life back. One by one, his siblings had flown the nest. Now Toby was due to go and an odd sense of disquiet slipped over Marcus. What would he do with himself? How could he reclaim his old life? Did he want to? It would be so odd coming home to an empty house.

Everything was changing. He pushed away the thoughts that pressed heavily on his chest and narrowed his eyes as his focus switched back to Rocky Rainman. Nothing could stop him brooding over him. His blood simmered and he balled his fists. Why did the dude have it in for him? How he'd love to turn up at his door, whip off the mask and let the world see who was behind the online hate campaign.

As Laurenia chatted about her plans and the kids, his brain fast forwarded to a point in the future. Rocky Rainman was exposed, the nastiness had died down, and Marcus was back to being number one weatherman. As soon as that happened, he'd consider other options. No way was he leaving under a black cloud. The top slot called. Once he'd regained that, the world was his. He could sidestep into presenting and take his popularity with him. He'd add his unmasking of Rocky to his CV and send his ratings off the charts. As soon as Rocky's followers realised their champion was some phoney hanging off others' coattails, it would all disappear. Life could go back to normal.

Sort of.

After years of caring for his siblings, it would be strange with them gone. Normal was something he'd lost long ago and he wasn't sure where to find it again, or if he really wanted to.

Chapter Five

Willow

Gentle breeze, tempera-
tures high, no chance of
rain and a clear blue sky.

Willow checked the weather charts again, peering in to make sure she'd read the data correctly. This had been much easier on the multiple monitors at e-Broadcast Scotland. On her own humble laptop, it wasn't quite so good but she made do.

Her parents might not have forgiven her completely for moving so far away but their generous housewarming gift of a meteorology set had gone a long way. She ruffled Marshmallow, the fluffy white cat, and smiled. She'd accomplished her dream of becoming a weather girl... albeit in disguise, but nonetheless it was proof dreams could come true. She stuck a virtual finger up at Marcus Bowman. How could she ever forgive his vitriolic words from last year? If she hadn't heard them with her own ears, she wouldn't have believed it. He called her so many things – unqualified, a girl just out of school, someone 'like that' and a ticky box. *Well, screw him.*

Ginny had accepted her resignation with only a brief email. Willow had expected nothing less. She barely registered on Ginny's recognition scale and as Ginny had never even made Willow's contract permanent – instead renewing her temporary status over and over – Willow didn't have to work notice. Polly had messaged her saying she was sorry she'd gone and wondered why. Willow couldn't bring herself to tell any of them what she'd heard and claimed she was leaving as she needed a change of direction, which was partially true. She'd apologised to her uncle Jonathan for resigning after he'd kindly helped her get the job in the first place but she didn't dare let on what Marcus had said. She didn't want him starting on her uncle too. Jonathan's help had never been anything other than kindness but she could almost hear Marcus calling nepotism.

She made a quick post for social media, starting with a few rhyming words to catch people's attention, then sent it. Sure, it was a gimmick but she'd learned that much from working in a newsroom; catching people's attention was ninety-nine per cent of the battle. She grabbed her bag ready for the short commute up the path to the old schoolhouse where she worked.

This was the change of direction she'd made and really she had Marcus to thank for it. After hearing him drag her down, she'd realised it was time to take control of her life. After quitting, she'd only confessed the truth to one person: her wonderful cousin, Hayley. Always sympathetic, Hayley had listened with no judgement, then just two days later had messaged to tell Willow about a job opportunity in the small town of Glenbriar. Willow had gone for it and never looked back.

Her parents were horrified. The new job meant moving to Highland Perthshire. At first, she'd thought she might stay with Hayley in Glenbriar but the job had accommodation for workers and Willow had taken the plunge. Why not? It was about time she at least tried to live on her own and here was the perfect place. She could be alone but never far from help.

She breathed in the warm, scented air. Bees hummed in the flowers along the side of the path, shaded by the tall trees. The peace and tranquillity were just idyllic. A giggle escaped her as her mind wandered to the latest storm surrounding Rocky and Marcus Bowman. How funny the way Marcus had taken her predictions for a few days of exceptionally hot weather. His smug remarks about Rocky being 'an enthusiastic amateur' were being bandied around social media, played back in gifs and on reels with fake captions. Well, he could just wait and see. Rocky Rainman said there would be heat, so there would be. She was convinced and unlike Marcus she wasn't bound by TV contracts. Her forecasts could be as outrageous as she wanted, though she made sure they were as accurate as possible.

Up ahead was the stone-built Victorian-era schoolhouse that had once served as the teacher's accommodation and primary school for the village of Clachnabronnachan a few miles north of Glenbriar. The school had closed in the late eighties and pupils were now bussed into Glenbriar Primary School. A local couple had bought it to run as a home for young adults with additional needs and, during the summer, as a retreat for families with teenagers with support needs. Willow's job was mostly admin, though she didn't mind helping out if they needed her for other jobs.

She opened the side door into a small hallway that even now had heavy wood panelling lined with rows of pegs, where once pupils would have hung coats and bags.

'Good morning, Willow.' A cheery grin greeted her. Marion Corbett always had a bright smile. It shone from her wise face, her large round glasses propped on her nose and long silver hair flowing around her shoulders. Her ankle-length floral skirt looked as bright as the gardens she tended with the residents and kept perfect all year round.

Willow hung her bag on one of the hooks. 'Morning.'

'Lovely day, isn't it?' Marion said.

'Gorgeous.'

'I have a very good feeling about today.' Marion brought her hands together under her chin like she was praying. 'It bodes well for the future.'

That was good news because Marion had been worried for a while now. They hadn't had much interest in new residents for a while, to the point where Marion and her husband, Barry, were seriously considering putting up prices for the ones they had. But they didn't want to. They'd always been generous, but this was their livelihood... And now Willow's. Once the summer retreats were done, only a handful of people were returning to stay.

'A couple have just phoned asking if they can have a look around today with a young man named Toby Bowman.'

Like an arrow had been unleashed by said bowman and hit her in the chest, Willow flinched. The name did that to her. Marcus Bowman might be a class-A arsehole but the thought of him made her heart flicker. Still, Bowman was just a name. Anyone could be called Bowman, though she wasn't sure she'd ever met anyone else with that surname.

'And guess what?' Marion's smile was broad and her hands were almost shaking. 'The person who called was one Marcus Bowman.'

Willow gulped. Ok. Not just some random person with the surname Bowman. Someone who was related to Marcus Bow-man and surely it was too ridiculous that there was more than one of them. And he had a family. Polly had seen them. Maybe she was right and his divorce had been nothing but show. Willow wanted to curl into a ball and cry. How could she admit how much her foolish heart craved Marcus Bowman? And how could she cope with seeing him again? Possibly having to come into close contact with his child every day?

'Willow? Are you all right? Do you need to sit down?'

'I'm fine. Totally fine. So... Marcus Bowman. As in the TV weatherman.'

'I'm sure it was him. It sounded like his voice. Wouldn't that be great if we could get him? Think of the publicity.'

'I doubt he'd want it public that his son was here.' He'd always been so private about his personal life. It was probably his worst nightmare that someone would find out the whereabouts of his children. Possibly his second worse. Was he more paranoid people would discover he had a child with additional needs? *His comments about me said it all.* Maybe that was why he hid him away. Was that why he was looking for a facility so far from Glasgow?

'That's true, but it would be good to have some celebrity backing. If we had a big name shouting about us, it might attract more people.'

'Hmm. He's not that big a name.' Willow grabbed her crutch and made her way into the office.

'He is,' Marion said. 'Especially since that TV series started. He has quite a following, you know. Such a lovely voice, and very nice eyes. In fact, he's very handsome altogether. It's the smile that does it. So charming.'

And fake. Willow didn't say it aloud. How could she burst Marion's bubble? One thing was certain though. She didn't want to see him. 'I used to work with him.'

'Oh, I forgot. You were at e-Broadcast Scotland. My goodness, do you think that's why he chose here?'

I doubt it. He hates me.

'Does he know you work here?'

'I don't really know him that well. In fact. I'd rather not see him. I always found him a bit intimidating.'

'Oh dear. That's a shame. But don't worry. I'll show him around and you can stay in the office. Having said that, if he's intimidating, I might find Barry and get him to come with me.'

'Well, he's like six foot five or something, so when you're my height, even just the size of him is intimidating.' And hot. Or it had been until she found out what a bastard he was.

Marion was a woman on a mission all morning, sprucing the place up and rushing around, putting vases of flowers on the windowsill with Paige, one of the residents. 'Careful you don't spill any water,' Marion instructed.

Paige sat a large vase on a table near the door. 'Nice, huh?'

'Lovely,' Willow said, peering out of the office door. As soon as Marcus appeared, she'd be shutting that door and hiding. But Paige was sweet and Willow liked chatting with her. Paige's language skills were poor but she was affectionate, kind, and always desperate to help. She loved plaiting Willow's hair or putting it in crazy updos. She was the same age as Willow but mentally a lot younger. It didn't stop Willow from considering her a friend.

Time ticked on and Willow's eyes constantly leapt to the window. At eleven o'clock sharp, a large black car with tinted windows pulled up. Her heart thumped so hard it almost leapt out of her chest. The passenger door opened and an absolutely stunning woman got out. She looked like a model, tall and tanned, with long glossy dark hair, pinned off her face by a large pair of sunglasses.

When the driver's door opened, Willow almost fainted. She'd forgotten just how tall and handsome Marcus Bowman was in the flesh. He opened the back door and a younger man got out; he looked no more than twelve, though Willow knew he must be at least sixteen if he was going to be coming here. Very skinny, he had hair longer than average that hung around his face in layered waves. Marcus took his hand and leaned down to speak to him, perhaps telling him to calm down as the boy was bouncing up and down. Marcus and the woman barely looked old enough to be his parents. They must have had him when they were really young.

The door to the office clicked open and Willow jumped. 'Paige. You gave me a fright.'

Paige put her finger to her lips. 'Shh. Look.' She parked herself on the window ledge and pointed outside. 'He on the telly, you know.'

'Yes, I do know that.'

'He's nice.'

Willow sighed. Yup. So everyone thought.

Voices in the corridor made her heart quicken. Marion sounded delirious and there was Marcus's low rumbling tone. Willow half closed her eyes, remembering how that voice used to talk to her, show her charts, and ask for assistance while pretending not to. If only Marcus knew he'd taught Rocky Rainman loads without meaning to. That satisfaction almost made up for the hurt he'd inflicted on her.

'Can I do your hair?' Paige asked.

'Ok. Just for a little while.'

Paige jumped up and took hold of Willow's long hair. Gently, she separated it and wound it into plaits. Willow exhaled slowly. *What am I going to do?*

If Marcus Bowman sent his son here, surely this wouldn't be his only visit? The day would surely come that she'd have to see him again. She half wished he would choose somewhere else, but they needed the money. Two residents weren't enough to pay for the upkeep of this place. They needed Marcus Bowman to choose them.

Chapter Six

Marcus

November

Marcus sighed as Ginny waffled through the latest production meeting. Why did he even have to attend? His job was the same no matter what cack stories they decided to churn out this week.

'Now, here's a strange one,' Ginny said, scrolling down her iPad screen and bringing Marcus bumping back to the table. 'Does anyone remember little Willow? The girl who used to work in the newsroom.'

Marcus stopped tapping his stylus and looked up as a few people acquiesced with vague grunts. How could he forget her? Sometimes he saw her face in his dreams. That pretty smile, rosy cheeks and over-long hair.

'I got a very random email from someone who works with her. Apparently, they run a facility for children with disabilities but the funding has run out and they might have to close. She wants us to run a story on the facility and get them publicity. Seems a bit too provincial for us. It's in a place called... Let me see... Glenbriar. Never heard of it. Somewhere in Perthshire.'

'Wait a second,' Marcus said. 'What's the name of the facility?'

'Utterly unpronounceable. The Old Schoolhouse residential care facility at Clach... na—'

'Clachnabronnachan.'

'Yes. Really trips off the tongue, doesn't it?' Ginny frowned and gave him a quizzical look, no doubt wondering how the hell he knew how to pronounce it, but she didn't ask. She pouted at her screen. 'So, we'll scrap that one.'

Marcus frowned. He'd been to visit the place in June. But Willow didn't work there... Did she? If she did, he hadn't seen her. It'd been a pleasant building in a beautiful location and seemed ideal, except poor Toby had been plagued by anxiety ever since. Instead of a simple transition, he'd got so panicky Marcus had decided against sending him. The trouble was, he couldn't stay at home on his own either. Laurenia was at her wit's end. She wanted to move back to Perthshire but that increased Toby's anxiety. Although he couldn't say many words, he communicated enough to let them all know he wanted his family altogether and he wanted to be with them.

The schoolhouse was under threat of closure, was it? An edge of guilt crept through Marcus's chest like a cold front moving across the Atlantic. If he'd sent Toby, they would have had more money. Was that why they'd applied to Ginny? Were they hoping he'd get to hear of it? And what about Willow?

Talk about confusing.

'Right, moving on.' Ginny tapped her iPad.

'No, hang on,' Marcus said. 'Surely that would be a nice little Christmas story.'

'Welcome to the meeting, Father Christmas.' Ginny peered at him over her red glasses. 'I didn't have you pegged for the Hallmark type.'

He cast her a look. She could be such a snarky bitch. 'People lap that kind of stuff up at Christmas, you know they do.'

'Indeed, I do. So, anybody fancy it?'

Most people shook their heads or kept their gazes low.

'Well, Marcus.' She arched her perfectly shaped eyebrow. 'Looks like you'll have to do it yourself.'

'Why?'

'Well, after all, you're the presenter of *Destination Forecast*. Who better than our very own celebrity weatherman?'

He flicked her a fake one-sided smile. 'I'm not sure I'm right for this story.' Seeing Willow again was a double-edged sword. Part of him wanted to but the other part knew he shouldn't. She'd consumed his mind too much when she'd been here. Her leaving had been for the best. Also, it would be awkward after he'd chosen not to send Toby there.

'Why not? Don't you have enough Christmas jumpers? I'm sure the viewers would love some wood chopping scenes. Can anyone lend him a flannel shirt?'

'Not even vaguely amusing, Ginny.'

She considered him and they locked eyes. Once upon a time, he'd have gone for a woman like her. Older women in power were his catnip, and she was attractive, but he knew better these days. 'I'll decide who does the story if we take it on. And you're quite right, it would be good to get a human-interest story at this time of year.'

December

'I can't believe you're going away again.' Laurenia let out a sigh and held her hand to her forehead.

'I'm sorry,' Marcus said. 'I really am, but I haven't got a choice.' Ginny had pulled rank and decided he was doing the schoolhouse story whether or not he wanted to, but not for the reasons he'd initially hoped for. She'd jumped on the Rocky Rainman bandwagon when someone had identified one of his photographs as being from the Glenbriar area. Now Marcus was on a snooping mission as well as having to do the report on the schoolhouse. The chance to uncover Rocky was a delicious thought, but the circumstances felt wrong. Maybe he was being sentimental, but bringing down Rocky's world at Christmas seemed cruel. Or was it karma?

'I'll be back for Christmas,' he said.

'You better be.' Laurenia shook her head. 'I'll need help with wrapping and prepping.'

'Don't worry. It's not that far and it's only for a few days. I promise I'll be back.'

He understood her panic. Her husband had been landed with the Christmas shift this year and she was gutted her two girls wouldn't have their dad at home. Having their uncle was second best but better than nothing. All of their siblings wanted to come home too, so it was going to be full on and Laurenia would get the brunt of it as usual.

But that wasn't her only issue with him being away. Once again, she'd be left with Toby and his needs. Marcus had hired a carer who came in during the day when Laurenia needed space and time to spend with her own children. But with Marcus away, Laurenia had to have Toby living with her and he was hard work.

'Bye.' Marcus waved into the living room.

Toby got to his feet, ran across the room and jumped on him, tears rolling down his face. 'I... Noo...' His cries wrenched Marcus's heart out.

'Toby, get down.' Laurenia tried to prise him away. 'He'll be back soon.'

'Hey. Leave him a minute,' Marcus said and Laurenia let go. He lifted Toby, who clung around his neck like a lemur. 'Look, it's ok.' He held him and let him sob on his shoulder, ignoring the flood of tears soaking into his shirt. He could change that in a second. 'Just take it easy,' he said quietly in Toby's ear. 'I'm not going for long this time. Just a few days. And I'm not far away. New Zealand was a long way away, but Glenbriar is just a hundred miles away.'

'Hundred?' Toby said.

'I know it sounds far but I can get back in a couple of hours, so it's not really. Now, you go cuddle up by the fire and keep warm. Look after Emily and Freya. And behave. Ok?'

'Ok.' Toby let Marcus put him down and Laurenia took hold of his hand.

Marcus closed the door, raced upstairs for a dry shirt, then left by the side door. He jumped into his Maserati and took several deep breaths as he rolled down the driveway and onto the street. If some solution would just present itself, he'd be delighted, but Toby wasn't a problem to be solved. He was a person – a loving, kind and sensitive person, who needed a lot of support and it was proving more than challenging.

The car was loaded with work suits and portable recording devices, so Marcus could send in reports from the schoolhouse. Ginny insisted he didn't need a camera operator, just good Wi-Fi and a remote control. Everything was a cost cutting measure – or it was when it suited her. So no camera operator and, instead of a hotel, he had to stay in the schoolhouse. They would, of course, give him a room for free in return for the story. *Whatever!* It was only for three nights and he'd seen the accommodation in the summer and it looked perfectly pleasant. He had a funny feeling Ginny was giving him this job as a punishment. She hated the idea of him getting paid to go jet-setting around the world. No doubt the idea of him being stuck in the back of beyond in a bed full of bugs was a cheap thrill for her.

He cranked up the gears and headed out of Glasgow. Despite being raised in a small town, he'd spent all his adult life in the city. But deep down, he yearned for something more, although he couldn't quite put his finger on what it was.

He put on the radio and listened to his e-Broadcast Scotland colleagues chatting. He'd been on TV almost every day of his adult life, something nobody could have predicted when he was growing up. The incident that got him into broadcasting was one of the shadier parts of his life. His colleagues and other journalists frequently approached him, asking for an inside report on Scotland's favourite weather presenter, or second favourite these days. But it wasn't happening. None of those hacks were getting a piece of him. He'd heard every rumour going: he was gay, he was married with a secret wife and family, he was married with more than one secret wife and family, he was a player, he was celibate... You name it, he was it.

His phone rang. Ginny.

'Hello,' he answered.

'Where are you?'

'On my way to the schoolhouse.'

Surely she hadn't forgotten already.

'Obviously,' she said, 'but where exactly are you?'

'Just leaving Glasgow.'

'Hmm.' The tap of her pen pounded like a nail gun against his head. 'Are you going to be there in time to make the afternoon forecast?'

'I'm not doing the afternoon forecast. Sadie's on today.'

'Sadie's called in sick. You'll have to do it. Even if you're not there in time, stop somewhere pretty and film something. We'll load the sat screens.'

'Seriously? I haven't had a chance to look at the data,' he protested.

'Make something up then. Use that famous experience and knowledge of yours.'

'That isn't how it works.'

'You told me yourself the value of experience in this job. Predicting the forecast is a matter of understanding the climate more than anything else is what you said.'

'That is not what I said.' He ground his teeth. Of course, understanding climatology and its local and regional effects was important, but that didn't mean he could just invent the forecast. 'What do you want me to say? Based on this day last year being like this and the year before like that, I'll draw the average and voila?'

'If that's how it works, then yes,' she replied.

'No, it isn't, and I bloody won't.'

Rocky and his cronies would have a field day.

'Right now, I don't care what you say as long as it's vaguely plausible. I'm trying to get someone on standby but no one's available. If we don't get something on air, half our viewers will turn to that bloody Rainman character. So do the report.'

'Yes, ma'am.'

She ended the call, and Marcus gritted his teeth at the steady flow of traffic in front of him. Bang went his peaceful day.

Glenbriar was a pleasant little town and when he arrived just after two, daylight was still holding. Places he remembered from his childhood looked the same but different. His family had lived in the council houses, hidden behind the main streets with their fancy shops, twinkling Christmas lights and old stone Victorian buildings.

He checked the time. Already later than he should be if he was going to get this report done. He nipped down a side street and pulled into a carpark near a footbridge across the River Briar. This was a pretty little spot. On the other side of the river was a restaurant called the Cross Keys. It was lit up with fairy lights decked around the stone walls and the outdoor seating area that was like a viewing deck over the river. When he was a child, that building was boarded up and derelict. Now it had been done up beautifully.

There was a park with drab wintery trees that would do for a nondescript backdrop. Marcus pulled out the bag of recording equipment, hooked it up to his phone, and extended the tripod legs. Twenty-odd years ago, if someone had told him one day he would be doing this, he'd have thought they were insane. But here he was, as cool as you like, sporting his smart winter coat and telling the camera today's weather forecast, grinning like the Cheshire Cat on LSD.

By the time he was done, darkness had almost descended and the carpark was lit up with orange streetlights. The one above his car buzzed and flickered enough to induce epilepsy. The Cross Keys now looked like a boat lit up at the side of the river.

As he drove through Glenbriar, lights twinkled all around him. Every street lamp had a swirly silver decoration glittering from it and the shop windows glowed with Christmas trees and wintery scenes.

Further on, the houses became fewer but each one he passed had a colourful tree at the window like a welcoming beacon waiting for the owners to come home. Or maybe they were already inside, keeping warm by the fire, cuddled up with loved ones, watching TV or reading stories. So what if it was a phoney ideal? He liked it. The warmth of knowing that these were people's homes seeped into his heart, filling him with thoughts of Toby and Laurenia, his other siblings and his nieces. His sadly departed mother and his estranged father were there too. The ideal family didn't exist for him but he tried his best to make things work. None of it had been ideal for Laurenia either. Whatever happened, she had to come back here after Christmas. That was what she wanted and that was what she was going to get. His Christmas present to her would be to set her free.

That was the real him, not the emotionless weather-predicting machine the public saw. His heart was full of people they knew nothing about. People he wanted the world for. He'd never wanted kids of his own. Seeing his mother struggling with so many had put him off. But when everyone left, his life would be so lonely, and he still had so much to give – to the right people.

The lights faded as he left the town. Darkness consumed everything. Where he knew there were hills and woodlands, he could see nothing. He passed a cottage and spied a house up on the hill. Soon he'd be there. The journey had passed quickly and he hadn't allowed himself time to dwell on what might happen when he arrived and who he might meet. But at some point, he was going to see Willow, and that made his insides tense like he was being compressed. *This is not like me. Must stay in control.* He took a deep breath. Marcus Bowman was the king of control. He could do this. Easy.

CHAPTER SEVEN

Willow

A cold front approaches,
bringing changeable days.
Some stormy nights in this
wintery phase...

Where were Marion and Barry? Willow flexed her fingers and peered from the office window into the darkness beyond. She couldn't see a thing. They were supposed to be back by now. A reporter from e-Broadcast Scotland was arriving soon and Marion and Barry were meant to be here to greet them. Who would it be? Someone she remembered from the newsroom days? Would they remember her?

'Where are they?' she muttered to Marshmallow, who was curled up in her basket in the corner. It was after four and Willow wanted to go back to her little house and rest her weary legs but she couldn't leave until Marion and Barry were back.

Headlights flashed around the corner and her chest lightened. *They're back.* Phew. She shifted away from the window and made her way slowly towards the hall. Marshmallow jumped from her basket and followed. The Christmas tree lights flashed intermittently, providing a pleasant ambient glow, better than the old school strip lights. Willow unlocked the interior glass door between the hall and a small porch. She always locked it when she was here on her own in the dark.

Moments later, a tall, hulking shadow of a figure strode across the car park, visible through the mottled window on the front door in the glow of the outside light. Fingers shaking, Willow wanted to turn the key and lock out whoever it was. Her pulse was racing as the figure reached the porch doorstep. She recoiled into the hall and was on the verge of screaming when the door opened and she looked up. Her eyes linked with a face that was oh so familiar. She stumbled back into the hallway.

Marcus Bowman.

Willow couldn't move a muscle, and it had nothing to do with her cerebral palsy and everything to do with the man who'd just walked into the foyer. What was he doing here? He was a weatherman, not a reporter. Why had they sent him? At one time in her life, she would have gone all aflutter seeing him, but her heart was as stone cold and frozen as the rest of her. She'd been cross enough that Marion had approached e-Broadcast Scotland and name-dropped her to get publicity, but now this.

Her eyelids were the first part to regain conscious movement, and she blinked rapidly, processing the whole unbelievable scenario. But Marcus Bowman was unique, and there was no getting away from the fact that it was him. And he was here, staring at her like she had grown an extra leg – something that might be useful round about now because she was getting weak-kneed.

'Hello, Willow,' he said.

'Um, hi.' She swallowed and made an effort to move forward. 'Can I help you?'

'Possibly. Are you the receptionist here?'

'Kind of.'

'Well, I'm here to do your report on this place. Where's Marion?'

My report? She didn't look at him as she edged away. She couldn't. When she looked at him, stuff happened inside her – body sensations she couldn't control. She didn't want that to happen because she couldn't stand him. She hated what he was. Never should she have been swayed by his handsome face and sexy body. That's how easy she was. She'd been willing to forgive his brashness when he was vaguely nice to her, but that was just evidence of what a hot and cold guy he was.

'She isn't back yet,' she said. 'And it isn't "my" report. I had nothing to do with it. I didn't even know she'd contacted e-Broadcast Scotland until after she'd done it.' She still couldn't look at him.

'Fair enough. So... Where is she?'

'She and Barry have been away all day visiting her sister.'

'I see. Well, I guess I'll have to wait.' He glanced around the hallway. 'What brought you to be working here? I always wondered where you went after you left us.'

Like she believed that. He wouldn't have given her a second thought the minute she walked out of the door. The only mystery was why he'd given her a birthday present. *Maybe just trying to butter me up so I wouldn't suspect he was the one who blocked my promotion.* He'd flicked on the charm, just like he did for the camera every day of his life. An Oscar-winning performance every moment.

'I moved on.' She glanced at him and blinked. Was he x-raying her? His gaze was intense.

'This is quite a change. What happened?'

Was he seriously asking her that? Of course, he didn't know that she left because of his disrespect, but to play the smarm like this was making her skin crawl.

'I just wanted a change. You're in room three. It has a woodland view. I hope it's to your liking.' She had to look at him as she spoke, otherwise, she risked being as rude as him. His face was unbearable. He was like a handsome, confident Roman commander, and she was nothing but a slave in his eyes.

'I'm sure it will be.' He held her gaze, and her lungs hiccupped. If she took a breath now, she'd inhale more of his fragrance, the scent that infiltrated her brain and took her to crazy places. As she passed him the key, her damn hand shook. It did that sometimes because of the CP, but this time it was all him. Did he know it?

His hand brushed hers as he took the key, and stupidly, she dropped it. He picked it up off the floor before she could even give it a second thought and looped the keyring around his finger.

'So. We, um, don't normally let the residents lock their doors, but as you're a guest...' She cleared her throat.

He brushed lint from the lapel of his dark wool coat. 'And are there any residents here just now?'

Willow shook her head. 'The last one left last month.' She twirled her hair around her finger. Paige leaving had been so sad but she'd moved into sheltered accommodation where she had more space and freedom now she was older. Willow missed her so badly. 'We have a family on a retreat though.' Normally they only ran retreats during the summer but they had to do something or the money would run out.

'Hmm. Ok. Do you think they'd let me interview them?'

'Possibly.'

His gaze was unnerving now. Willow was used to people staring. Going through school with a myriad of walking aids was the start, then doctors and physios observing her like some kind of science experiment. Even walking down the street, people threw her looks. Their eyes roamed over her splints and onto legs that would never be perfectly straight. Sometimes she saw pity in their faces, other times distaste mixed with relief that it wasn't them. But none of that was what she was reading from Marcus. His deep brown irises burned a hole in her soul. What was going on? He lowered his head briefly and rubbed his thumb along his lower lip, the key still dangling. 'Can I interview you too? Tomorrow obviously.'

'I, um. I suppose so.'

'Great. And is there food here? Or do I need to go back into town?'

'I can get you something from the kitchen.'

'Thank you. I'll get my bags and drop them upstairs, then come back for food.'

'Do you need a hand with anything?' She asked out of politeness, but she hoped he'd say no. Doing the stairs too often was painful.

'No, thank you,' he said.

Once he was safely out of sight, Willow properly breathed. Where the hell was Marion? She couldn't endure much more of this on her own.

She waited in the kitchen, pottering about but not really too sure what she was doing. Barry usually cooked meals and prepared food, though he wasn't precious about anything and he never minded if people needed midnight snacks. Marcus was longer than she expected before he appeared. *Holy crap*, he was gorgeous in dark jeans and a ribbed cream sweater. It showed off his tanned neck and hands. Did he do sunbeds? Or was that still the *Destination Forecast* effect?

'What can I get you?' she asked, moving into the common room that they used as a dining room and lounge.

He tugged up his sleeves and leaned his crossed forearms on a high-backed chair. 'What do you have?'

'There's steak pie I could heat up.'

'Sounds great. Are you having anything?' he asked.

'What?'

'Well, as you're the only other person here, it feels rude to be eating if you're not.'

She turned away. *WTAF?* Why was he being nice? Sleazy more like. Do NOT be taken in, she warned herself. It happened before and she didn't need that again. 'I'll eat later when I go home.' She went back to the kitchen. Her legs were killing her and her treacherous stomach rumbled. She'd love the steak pie, but she was not eating with him. Nope.

When it was heated, she ported it through and placed it on the table. 'Do you want anything to drink with that?'

'Just water, please. But let me get it.'

'No. I can do it.' She bloody well would too. She didn't need his phoney pity.

Marcus tapped his finger on the table when she returned. 'I was really surprised when you left us. You were good at your job.'

She banged his glass down in front of him. 'Not what you said at the time.'

'Pardon?' He gripped his fork and frowned.

'I know what some people thought of me.' Her hands were shaking almost uncontrollably and she pushed her hair behind her ears because she needed to steady them somehow. But she couldn't let him off the hook. She wanted him to know she'd heard every word of his vitriol. 'You in particular.' She shouldn't speak to a guest like this. Marion would be so cross. She might have blown their chance for free publicity.

'I don't follow.' He leaned back and cinched his shoulders. 'Did I ever say you weren't good at your job?'

'Not to my face. But I heard you talking to Ginny.'

His frown deepened and he ran his fingertip around the rim of his glass. She needed to sit down. Her legs were achy and her head spinning. Just saying these things was increasing her heartrate to risky levels and he still had power. The power of taking away what they needed. And looking too frigging hot.

'I'm not sure what you heard. I don't recall ever talking to Ginny about you.'

He wouldn't, would he? She was an insignificant speck in his illustrious career. She leaned on the chair and took a long sigh.

'Why don't you just sit down? I don't bite.'

'Pardon? You want me to sit with you?'

'Only if you want to.' He gestured to the chair she was leaning on. There was no denying how much she wanted to sit, so she pulled it back and lowered herself into it.

'This must be quite a change for you.' He stabbed his steak pie and sawed off a corner of pastry.

'Everyone is very friendly here. We're like a big family.'

'That does sound appealing. There's nothing better than being surrounded by family.'

She pulled a face. How could she help it? For him, of all people, to come out with a crack like that.

'I take it your family don't mind you being here alone?' she asked. 'I mean, you must be away a lot with all your TV shows.'

He took a slow sip of his drink, his eyes ever so slightly wavering over her face. 'I am, yes. And they do mind. They get very upset when I leave, but it's my job. This is how I make money.'

'Didn't they want to come with you?'

'One of them did.'

'Just your wife? Or one of your kids?'

He raised an eyebrow. 'I don't have a wife or kids.'

Willow frowned. Was he lying to her face? 'No kids? But you came here in the summer with your son. I saw him and your wife. And Polly saw you with a woman and three kids.' The words poured out before she could stop them.

'Did she now? Well, doesn't everyone know everything about me? But nope, you've all got it wrong. I have no kids of my own. The woman you saw me with was my sister. I assume that's who Polly saw too. She has two daughters.'

'And what about Toby?'

'He's my brother.'

'Wait... Your brother?'

'I'm one of seven.' He leaned forward and grabbed his glass. 'I never talk about this stuff. I'm not sure how you've got it out of me so quickly. What have you put in this drink?'

Willow had lost the power of speech as she tried to fit together all the missing numbers he'd just handed her. 'Why did you want Toby to come here?'

'Because he has global learning difficulties and growth issues. My sister does the majority of his care and she wants to move back to this area. But the idea of leaving Glasgow – and me – was too traumatic for him.'

'Oh dear. Don't you have parents?'

Marcus smirked. 'You're very inquisitive, aren't you? My mama died some years back. My father is incompetent and I never see him. That's pretty much my life story. Just don't go selling it.'

'I won't.' She swallowed. The most private man in the universe had just opened up to her. And she believed him. His demeanour said it was true. 'I'm sorry. I just assumed. I shouldn't have.'

'I wouldn't worry about it.' He took a mouthful of food. 'People assume a lot about me.'

'I should know better.' Christ, people assumed all sorts about her or asked questions that left her speechless. *Can't you be cured? Are you happy? Can you have a normal job? Are you allowed to drive? Can you have sex?* All of them left a bitter taste. Maybe the last one most of all – physically she could, but finding someone who wanted to was hard. So often potential dates viewed her as physically fragile or damaged and didn't know how to act around her.

'Tell me,' he said. 'What was it you heard me saying to Ginny that made you believe I thought you were incompetent? I honestly can't remember ever saying anything bad about you.'

She gave a half shrug. It was painful just thinking about it. Here was a man she was deeply attracted to on a raw, uncontrollable level. So attracted it hurt in places she didn't normally hurt. But then she remembered that conversation and bile rose in her stomach. She didn't want to repeat it, but why lie to save him? He should be the one to suffer from it, not her. 'You gave her a list of reasons why I shouldn't be employed there, what made me wrong for the job, how I was unqualified and I only got in because of my family connections, and how I was just there to tick a box.'

Marcus shook his head and his eyes narrowed. 'I never said anything like that.'

'Are you calling me a liar now?'

'I just know I never spoke about you like that. I wouldn't have.'

'Yes, you did and I heard you. I was outside Ginny's office and your voice... Well, it was obviously you.'

'Something's gone wrong here.'

Now she knew he was lying because no one could fake his voice.

'When was this?'

She didn't want to say the day she left. Why give him the satisfaction of knowing it was him that sounded the final bell? 'I can't remember.'

He frowned for a moment and downed the dregs in his glass. 'Was this around Valentine's Day when Sadie came to look around?'

Her cheeks heated at the memory of that day. 'Around about then, I think.'

'I remember having a heated conversation with Ginny about Sadie.'

'What about?'

'I was pissed off that Ginny was about to hand her a job on a plate without even interviewing her. I don't remember exactly what I said, but if that's what you heard, then I wasn't talking about you. I swear on my sister's life, I never spoke to Ginny about you and I never said anything to anyone about you not being good at your job or being there just to tick a box. It's not something I would ever have said about you.'

She fiddled with a lock of hair, twirling it tight around her finger. Had she been totally wrong about him? About everything? She'd overreacted completely and not even considered he might have been talking about someone else. This was what he did to her. He caused such a powerful emotional reaction in her that she lost control. Or maybe secretly she'd wanted an excuse to leave. She'd panicked she'd never have got the forecasting job, but instead of facing her fears, she'd run at the first sign of trouble and Marcus had given her the excuse she needed.

But what about Rocky Rainman? Her insides squirmed. She hadn't started the Rocky persona to get at Marcus but there was no getting away from the fact she'd been an active part of that not-so-friendly rivalry.

'You were great at what you did. You helped me out loads of times. I was surprised when you left. It's not the same without you. I mean, for starters, there's no one left who'll tidy my shelves.' He smiled and it was a real smile that brightened his whole face. Her pulse rocketed and banged in her eardrums. What the hell was she going to do now? She'd been so wrong. Had she walked away from the chance of a real forecasting job? And did the guy she was infatuated with actually value her in a way she'd never dreamed possible?

CHAPTER EIGHT

Marcus

Willow's smile was too adorable, perched between shock and delight. Her two front teeth rested on her lower lip as she nipped it. Marcus had an urge to lean over and kiss her, but he mastered it. Christ, he had to. But it was hard. His eyes were irresistibly drawn to her. Dangerously so. Because he wanted her. *Stop now.* She was too young for him, and her boyfriend was probably at home, desperate for her to get back to his arms – who could blame him?

'I hope…' his words trailed off and he tapped the rim of his empty glass.

'Hope what?' she asked.

He took a mouthful of food and chewed it carefully. 'I hope you didn't leave because of what I said to Ginny. I'd hate to think—'

'Of course I didn't.' She got to her feet with a sharp exhale and lifted his glass. She was hurting. Something in her eyes told him. He'd seen it in his mum for years as she struggled with rheumatoid arthritis. But he also knew she wouldn't want him to draw attention to it or patronise her with meaningless words. He also couldn't rule out it was possibly her emotions hurting her. If she'd thought he'd spoken to Ginny about her, not Sadie, no wonder she was upset. He hadn't minced his words, but why would she think it was about her? Then again, why wouldn't she? That newsroom was cutthroat.

He ate quietly until he spotted her coming back from the kitchen. 'You were lucky to escape,' he said. 'e-Broadcast Scotland is full of backstabbing. I'm sorry you thought I was like that.'

'I... I shouldn't have. I guess it's just easier to believe people don't like you than...'

He nodded, not wanting to read too much into what the alternative was.

'I thought you'd leave yourself now you do the TV shows.'

'Do you watch *Destination Forecast*?' He leaned on his hand, his eyes connecting with hers. *Go on, say yes, and make my day.* Was it wrong that sometimes, when he'd spoken to the camera, he imagined her watching?

She propped her elbows on the table and rested her chin on her hands, not quite touching him, but close enough to raise the fine hairs on his neck. 'I might have seen one or two.'

'I'm honoured.'

'Marion loves them.'

Ah yes, of course, she was much more the average age of his audience.

'I don't know why you didn't do TV from the start. Why did you go into weather presenting at all?'

'Because of my qualifications. I was originally chasing a different career but I got talent spotted soon after I finished university.' That was the glossed-over and polite version. Not the one explaining how he'd shagged his way into both university and up the career ladder. Women in power often had a soft spot for him and he knew exactly how to play on it.

'That was lucky.'

'I guess.'

'Why did you decide to do this story?'

He rubbed his chin and considered her carefully. 'I didn't. Ginny sent me.'

'Oh. I thought it was because... Well, because you'd thought about sending Toby here.'

'I'm happy to do it.' Maybe that was stretching the truth, but now he was here and looking into those eyes, he couldn't think of anywhere he'd rather be. 'I like what you're doing here.'

'I'm not doing anything. It's all Marion and Barry. I just do the admin and help with little jobs.'

'I bet they appreciate it.'

She gave a half smile, her cheeks still a little too pink. What did that mean? Anything? Was she flustered? Too hot? Or in pain?

'Why do you need three days? Marion thought it was something you might do in an afternoon.'

'Well…' Marcus tapped his finger on the table. 'Can you keep a secret?'

'It's my speciality.'

He finished another mouthful before saying, 'Ginny wants me to do some snooping about for Rocky Rainman.'

Willow's eyes widened. 'What?'

'Haven't you heard of him?'

'I have, but…' Her brow furrowed. 'Why would you come here to find him?'

'Good question. Ginny had some inside info that some of the pictures he's posted on social media were taken in this area.'

'Really?'

'Yes. So, she wants me to use this as an opportunity to do some digging, though I'm to be discreet, so don't tell anyone.' He gave her a hard look. 'Promise?'

'Yeah… Ok.' She sucked on her lower lip again, and Marcus looked away. When she did that, he got an overpowering urge to suck on it too.

'How will you investigate?'

'I'll find some local people to ask and see where I get.'

'Right.' She nodded. 'That sounds like an interesting project.'

'We'll see. I don't suppose you know anything about him?'

She gave a little shake of her head and her forehead creased. It was obvious now she was really hurting.

'Are you ok?'

'Yeah, fine. What will you do if you find Rocky Rainman?'

'Expose him and string him and his poetry out for the crows.'

'Really? Is he that bad?'

'Are you having me on? He's an online bully and I'd like nothing better than to shut down his little operation and let everyone see what a lowlife he is.'

'But... I mean, is that why you're really here?'

'Part of it. I'm still going to do a great report on this place, so don't worry. Ginny wants me to do both. She thinks it'll boost the ratings. But if I'm honest, I want to expose him for the phoney he is. He's always bringing me down and undermining me. I read things in his posts that make me feel like he's got a vendetta against me. Once his cover's blown, he won't be so cocky. I can't wait to have the satisfaction of pulling off his mask and letting the world know he's just some sad individual.'

Willow looked away and sighed. 'I, um...' She turned back to him. 'Should message Marion and see if she's ok.' She glanced at her phone. 'Oh here.'

'What is it?'

'There's a message from Marion.' She read it with a growing frown. 'Barry slipped on the ice when they were out with Marion's sister and they're in the A&E in Inverness.'

'Inverness?'

Willow looked up. 'That's too far for them to be back tonight. Marion says sorry she won't be here to see you but you can still stay and do the report if you want.'

'Of course I do.'

'I'm not sure what I should do. They live here, so they're always about in case there's a problem. I don't live here.'

'Where do you live?'

'Well, it's not far. Just in one of the little houses down the track, but what if the guests need something? Or you?'

'I'll be fine. And why don't you just go and tell the guests? Give them your number and they can call if there's anything urgent, though I don't expect there will be.'

'I'll call Marion and see what she wants me to do.'

Willow thumbed away at her phone; her brow furrowed as she held it to her ear. She was so young, fresh faced and uncertain. The protector in him wanted to leap up and make sure she didn't have to worry about anything, but she was capable. She didn't need a saviour.

'Hi. How's Barry? ... Everything's fine here.'

Marcus listened to Willow's side of the conversation.

'Ok. I'll let them know and I'll ask one of them to lock up.'

Marcus raised his hand, indicating he would do that and she gave him a brief smile. When she ended the call, she stared at the blank screen for a moment. 'Marion wants me to tell the guests I won't be in the building overnight. And... well, are you happy to lock up before you go to bed? I have a key to get back in in the morning.'

'Sure, no worries. Are the other guests in?'

'No, they're not back yet. I'll wait.'

'Are you sure? I'll be here anyway if you want to go home.'

'No, I'm good.' She got to her feet. 'But I guess I should make myself something to eat. Do you want anything else?'

'This was fine, thanks. I'm quite done.' He watched her leave for the kitchen again, then wandered into the lounge area and sat on an armchair next to the log fire.

Willow returned with a plate some minutes later.

'Shall I throw some more logs on here?' Marcus asked.

'Yeah, please. I might sit over there. It's warmer.'

She made her way slowly across the room, her limp very obvious though she clearly was trying to keep as upright as she could. 'Here.' Marcus pulled over a side table so she could put her plate on it and she collapsed into the seat.

'Thanks. My walking always looks worse than it is,' she muttered. 'I'm used to it, you know.'

'If you want help with anything, just say. I know you're perfectly capable but I really don't mind. It's tiring working all day. Some days, I'm so drained when I get home. That's usually the days Toby's full of energy and wants to wrestle me. He's just a big kid and I try to be there for him.'

Willow smiled as she tucked into her dinner.

He never told anyone shit like this but she was just so easy to chat to. Something about her was trustworthy and he was convinced she wouldn't gossip.

After she'd eaten, noises in the corridor announced the other guests' return. Willow dragged herself up and went to talk to them. Marcus waited, stretching his legs out and crossing his ankles, watching the fire dance. If Toby had given this place a go, he would have loved it.

Willow returned. 'They're not going out again, so I can lock up when I leave.'

'Are you going right now?' He glanced up at her tiny, slender figure in the doorway.

'Yes.'

'And you're planning to walk down a dark path on your own?'

She gave a half shrug. 'I do it all the time.'

His protective side roared into action again. He wanted to walk her down and make sure she was ok. Not because her legs were in splints or because he deemed her helpless – he knew she could look after herself – but it was windy out there and dark. Who knew what might be lurking by the track?

'I'm sure you do,' he said, pushing the crazy thoughts away. It wasn't like wolves still roamed the Highlands. 'And... Is it just you? Or do other people live there too?'

'Why do you want to know?' She pulled out her phone and checked it. 'If I say just me, how do I know you're not a mad stalker?'

'You don't.' He got to his feet and moved closer to her. She was so small next to him he towered over her. Thinking he might appear overbearing, he stopped a little way off. Her mouth twitched and she looked away. Did she think he was recoiling? Far from it. His impulses pulled him closer, not further away, but maybe that made him a creepy stalker after all.

'Exactly.'

He followed her as she headed for the door. 'I give you my word of honour I'm not a stalker. I'll happily walk down with you if you'd like company and I could do with fresh air.'

'It's blowing a hoolie out there. You'll get more than fresh air. Honestly, I'm fine. I do this every day. I don't need someone holding my hand.'

'I'm well aware of that. Sorry. Like I said, I'm the eldest of seven. I can't help having a protective side. I hope someone's waiting with the heating on when you get down there.'

'Nope, no one's waiting. I live by myself in an old prefab in the woods that feels as flimsy as cardboard. I'm sorry if your protective side doesn't like it, but as I've been doing it for the past year, I think I can handle tonight as well.' She folded her arms, almost daring him to spar with her.

'Yeah. Just ignore me, pretend I didn't barge in and trample over your life like an elephant in a flower field.'

A little smile played at the corner of her lips. 'I appreciate your concern. Sleep well and remember to lock up.'

'Thanks. You take care, and I'll see you in the morning.'

He pulled the common room door shut behind him.

'Yeah, see you.'

As she took out her phone, she brushed him accidentally on the arm. Electricity crackled between them. She must have felt it too. The look on her face said she did.

'Night.' He followed her to the door, watching as she pulled on a coat, grabbed a crutch, and headed into the darkness. This was insane. She had him all hot and sweaty just thinking about her. And freaking out on her behalf, though she was right. She did this all the time and it was nothing to do with him.

Branches creaked beyond in the darkness. Was it that crazy to think one might blow off and hit her? What if a tree fell?

And since when was he such a worrier?

It only usually happened in relation to his family – people he really cared for.

He barely restrained the urge to go after her. It was rare for him to be attracted to people younger than him. But there had been always something about her. When they worked together, it would have been completely inappropriate to get involved with a colleague and she'd let him know she was unavailable. But there were times he'd been sure she was watching him. Her desk had been just far enough behind his that he couldn't look at her without making it blatantly obvious but he could sense it. Was it her who sent that Valentine card? An unspoken attraction lingered between them. He felt it again now. He'd always been happiest when their shifts coincided and she could sit by him, help him out, chat and just be there – a sunny presence in his grey cloudy day.

Upstairs, he opened his room and turned on the bedside lamp. It was a pleasant, if plain, bedroom with grey and white décor and slightly old-fashioned floral cushions and curtains. He drew them back and peered into the heavy darkness. Was Willow out there somewhere? Hopefully she was ok. Trees creaked and swished in the wind. He crossed his arms over his chest, hauled his sweater over his head and sat on the end of the bed. What chance of waking up tomorrow morning and discovering he didn't feel a thing for her? That would be helpful, if unlikely. He leaned his elbows on his knees, ruffled his hair then clutched his head. He'd forecast an unsettled day but there was no way he would have predicted feelings like this.

CHAPTER NINE

Willow

*Take care folks, when
you're out today, a storm
is on its way! Batten the
hatches, one and all, slates
might fly, and trees may
fall...*

Posting weather updates as Rocky Rainman always had a clandestine feel about it, but tonight it was worse because of who was up at the old schoolhouse. Willow was edgy enough knowing Marcus was so close, but he was actually here to expose her under the guise of the report. 'Oh god,' she said, sending off the post and snuggling with Marshmallow. 'What am I going to do?'

What had she already done? Misjudged him and made a complete mess of things. Now he saw Rocky as nothing but an online bully. She should never have let it get so out of hand. How could she stop it? She wanted to keep on forecasting but not hurt Marcus. What would he say if she confessed?

Maybe she could do some posts about how much she admired Marcus. Would her followers lay off him then? Perhaps confessing after that wouldn't be so bad.

She lay awake, listening to the wind whistling over the roof of the odd little bungalow where she lived. It was dated and basic. Built in the eighties when the schoolhouse had first opened but not upgraded since, it had only just stood the test of time. And in this wind, there was a real danger of a wall collapsing. They were paper thin. The thought didn't help her drift off to sleep. Neither did waking dreams of Marcus and how she'd misjudged him. After two years of thinking he was an arse, she was having to readjust everything.

In tonight's post, she hadn't mentioned him or made any of the little digs she sometimes did. *Why did I ever do that?* Now she knew the truth, she saw how unfair it was. Marcus hadn't pissed all over her career prospects. Did he even know she'd applied for the job? She'd exacted revenge on an innocent man. Not just an innocent man, a man she'd always held a candle for. Tonight he'd let her know he'd always valued her and look at how she'd repaid him. Her insides burned at the thought like a bad case of indigestion, and she couldn't close her eyes.

Wednesday dawned just as blustery as she'd forecasted. She cringed at a particularly ferocious gust overhead as she dragged a brush through her long hair. The sound of trees swaying around was ominous.

Marcus being here was just temporary but it had cleared up something in her mind. She wouldn't make any more personal remarks about him and maybe she could try some friendly ones... Perhaps a Christmas truce that would lead to an end of hostility. Didn't change the fact she'd already been part of what he was calling cyberbullying. She cast her brush aside and loosened the cuff on her jumper; her skin felt prickly, like guilt mites were nibbling at it. She'd never meant it to be bullying – a bit of competition at most.

Now all she had to do was get through a few days of his snooping and try to put some Christmas sparkle into the Rocky/Marcus relationship. That might be enough to stop him wanting to unmask Rocky and make him see they could happily co-exist. He wouldn't guess it was her and there was no need to confess right now. Maybe in the future when they were online friends – if that was possible – she could confess and he would be far enough away from the rivalry to be angry. She could certainly try. Hopefully Rocky's followers would copy her lead, though haters would always hate, but she couldn't change everyone.

And if he stopped being mad with Rocky, she could steer his focus to the story he was meant to be here for.

Top of Form

Her heart did a little hiccup as she reminded herself that Marcus was only there for a few days. For Rocky Rainman, it was a relief, but for Willow Roxburgh, it was painful. Seeing him last night had reconnected some scattered fragments of her soul. Memories she had shoved away after overhearing his chat with Ginny resurfaced. Those chats they used to have, the sarky, cheeky way he'd rib her, the times he trusted her with information or showed her interesting things on the charts all rose to the forefront. And of course, he gave her a book and suggested she was a genius.

Why had she ever thought he was the enemy? Because, like she started to tell him last night, it was so much easier to believe people *didn't* like her. Now where did it leave her? What did it mean? That Marcus *did* like her? Had he always liked her?

Mustn't jump to conclusions this time – good or bad.

She'd done enough damage doing that already. Now she just had to be calm.

Three days. Just three days.

If she could keep him focused on the story of the retreat for those days and start making some friendly posts packed with Christmas cheer for Marcus Bowman, hopefully that would be enough. Anything else her heart fancied would just have to stay firmly locked away in the imagination drawer.

Willow tickled Marshmallow under the chin before she dragged herself to her feet from the end of her bed. Barry would normally be about to make breakfasts but Marion had messaged in a flap saying they'd spent so long in A&E that they were all knackered. Barry had to be rechecked as he might need surgery.

It sounded awful. Willow could sympathise only too well. She'd had so many hospital visits as a child she'd lost count. The least she could do was help out, so she'd messaged Marion and told her not to worry. *I've got this.*

Now she needed to prove she was worthy of Marion's relieved response. She grabbed her coat and scarf, winding it tight up to her chin. Yesterday had been a long and tough day on her feet and she was grateful for her crutches. She lifted one and stared at it. She didn't like self-pity, and she was lucky really, but sometimes she couldn't help wondering. If she didn't need splints and crutches, would things have been different? Maybe she'd have had more dating success. Or was it her own fear holding her back? Did she always think people wouldn't like her and not give them a chance – as she'd done disastrously with Marcus? Not that *dating* him had ever been a serious option. That Valentine card had been nothing short of ridiculous. She hadn't seriously expected anything to come of it.

Grabbing the other crutch, she opened the door to darkness and more roaring gusts. Marshmallow darted out and led the way up the path. That cat wasn't daft; she knew Willow would get a cosy fire going in the hotel lounge, and Marion didn't mind her sneaking home with Willow on an evening. She went wherever she knew she'd get the most cuddles.

'Just keep out of the kitchen,' Willow reminded her as they battled up the path. The health and safety inspectors wouldn't appreciate that. Marion freaked constantly that they'd turn up unannounced and find something that would shut them down. Barry always reminded her there was little danger of that since they'd always passed the inspections without any issues.

The trees whipped around like crazy, and the only light was from Willow's phone, but it was just a hop, skip, and a jump to the side door of the schoolhouse. Clinging to her crutches, she felt one mighty gust could blow her over or a tree branch might crack off and hit her. Her chest sagged with relief when she reached the door and unlocked it. Finding the light switches in the dark was a pain. She was used to Marion and Barry being there before her. Juggling the keys and her lit phone, she fumbled around, until she got them and flicked them all on. She pushed the door for Marshmallow to go into the common room, and the cat slunk to her favourite spot beside a large pot plant and curled up under it.

Before Willow had even taken off her coat, footsteps on the stairs caught her attention. Something about the heavy thud told her who it was. She slipped her scarf and coat off and flattened her hair before turning to see Marcus at the bottom of the stairs.

'Morning.' His lips quirked slightly at the corners, so he was almost smiling. He was the tallest man she'd ever met, with shoulders so broad he could probably lay her out flat across them. Not really, obviously, but his tailored wool coat magnified their breadth more than usual. And that was saying something because he always looked muscular and strong. If she'd crushed on him before, it was back with a vengeance. Her mind would take a trip with him anywhere, but that's all it would ever be. Nothing real.

'You survived the night,' he said.

'Without any creepy stalkers at the window, yes.' She blinked under his powerful stare.

He smirked and adjusted his lapels. 'Good.'

'Are you going out?'

'Just to do the forecast. I wasn't meant to be doing this as well, but there seems to be a bout of winter vomiting in the office, so it's either this or I return to the studio, which I'd rather not do. I'm on air in half an hour, so I've got to set up the equipment.'

'Do you need help with that?'

'Um.' He gave her an appraising look. She wouldn't be offended if he said no. She was used to it. People took one look at her and thought she'd be more of a hindrance. Or was that her mind playing tricks on her again? Maybe she expected people to think like that and didn't give them a chance. She was learning a lot about herself and it didn't sit well. Her chest was tight and her head full of thoughts and ideas she wasn't sure what to do with.

She'd already started moving towards the kitchen when Marcus replied. 'Do you have time?'

'How do you mean?'

'It would be helpful if you could set the camera in position. That would save me nipping back and forward three hundred times to get the right angle, but if you're busy, it's not a problem.'

'I'm sure I can spare a few minutes,' she said. Her chest loosened and her heart felt full as she grabbed the scarf and coat from the hooks and lifted a crutch. She shot a glance at Marcus who was crouched down, stroking Marshmallow, who'd snuck back out, sniffing out cuddles as only she could.

As he got to his feet, his eyes settled on Willow's. His lips lifted into a full smile and she melted in his presence.

'So, what's the forecast?' she asked. Would it be the same as Rocky's?

'Wet and stormy mostly. Definitely for up here.'

He got that right. She unlocked the front door and pushed it open.

'Christ, the wind,' he said. 'That's going to take a few trampoline casualties today.'

'Yeah, it's fierce,' she agreed, adjusting her crutches for the stairs.

He waited for her. 'I'm not sure where best to do this,' he said.

'It's dark anyway. No one will see anything much.'

'True. But I need to be close to a light.'

'There's a lamp in the staff carpark.'

'If the light's on my face, what will be in the background?'

'Just trees really.'

'That would work then.' He kept pace with her as they crossed the car park to the spot she thought would work. Her legs didn't go very fast. Was she moving too slowly? He didn't seem bothered, and he was a great windbreak. His gladiator shoulders took the brunt of it.

When he put his bag down and squatted to open it, Willow got the full blast and it knocked her momentarily off balance. He glanced up but didn't say anything.

'Is that all filming equipment?' she asked, peering over his shoulder.

'Yup. My own personal studio in a bag.'

'And you know how to work it all?'

'Yeah. I did a crash course in computer technology.'

She wasn't sure if he was joking or not.

If she was brave, she'd have a setup like this and do live forecasts, but the thought made her wince. Maybe Marcus had inadvertently saved her skin last year. The likelihood of her getting that job was tiny, but if she had, she would have caved on the first day. She was petrified of being on screen. Only now she started to realise her true reason for leaving e-Broadcast Scotland. If she'd just done it without harming Marcus in the process. Or at least given him a chance to explain. A pain rose up her throat and she swallowed it down. She wanted to reach out to him and say sorry for all Rocky's doings that had upset him but she needed him to do the report. Marion and Barry were counting on it. If he discovered she was Rocky Rainman now, that was the story he'd want to focus on and he might be so angry he'd refuse to say anything favourable about the retreat. How could she risk it?

Just keep quiet for now.

'So, if we set up the tripod here, I'll stand over there and you can manoeuvre it into position.'

'Ok.'

He extended the tripod legs and placed it in front of her. 'Can you wind the upper section to about there?' He wavered his hand over the top of it. It wasn't the easiest move with her crutches in tow, but she did it. He was fiddling with a camera, and as soon as she had the tripod at the right height, he clipped the camera onto the top.

She clutched the camera and angled it, getting the feel for how it moved.

'Right.' He straightened his already perfect tie, lapels and cuffs, then ran his hand across his hair. 'Let's try here.' He stood in the beam of the lantern-style lamp. 'How does this look?'

Honest answer? He was gorgeous. She had such limited experience with dating she couldn't imagine herself ever finding anyone half as attractive as him. 'Um... good,' she said, looking through the viewer. 'Should I take a picture so you can see?'

'Yes, good idea.' He pulled one of his charming TV smiles, and she pushed the button hard to stop her hand shaking. She'd like to pass it off as part of her condition, but it was purely him.

He stalked over, and she stepped back for him to check the picture. His hand brushed hers as he held the camera, and she whipped it away like he'd burned her.

'Perfect,' he said, looking down at her. 'Thanks.'

She swept some tangled strands of hair from her mouth and squinted at him. 'No worries. But won't it blow over if we let it go?'

He lifted his hand from the camera. 'It might. It's weighted and it's well balanced, but that wind is hellish.'

'I don't mind waiting,' she said. 'I could hold it. You wouldn't want it toppling in the middle of your report.'

'I definitely don't want that. But are you sure that's ok?'

She gave a little shrug. 'Depends how long it'll take. I should be doing breakfasts but it's only you and one other family. They haven't been down before eight all week, so I've still got fifty minutes.'

'I'll be on just after the seven thirty news bulletin. Fifteen minutes yet.'

'I'll wait.' She had a crazy zing inside – she'd do anything to spend some more time with him.

'You're a superstar.' He gave her a gentle pat on the shoulder. 'I appreciate this. I owe you.'

'Really, it's fine.' His touch had almost made her pass out. 'How does all this work?'

'Through the Wi-Fi.' He hooked up his phone to the camera, put in an earpiece and clipped a microphone to his lapel. 'I have a remote that works the camera once everything is set up, though they can adjust it remotely too. It's amazing what technology can do these days.'

'It really is.'

'Here we go.' He gave her a little wink and she almost keeled over again... The wind had nothing to do with it this time.

Seconds later, he was chatting to Ginny and Willow hovered by the tripod, making sure it stayed in place.

'Ok, we're ready.' He got into position and Willow held the camera in place. How could he do this? He looked like the camera was his best friend and they were just going to have a chat. She couldn't hear what was going on in his earpiece, so when he spoke, it was disjointed and she had to guess what was being said in the studio. 'Yes, I'm live from Highland Perthshire and I couldn't have picked a more blustery day for it.'

She was invisible. Marcus smiled at the camera and gave his forecast with his usual charm. As soon as it was done, he ripped off the microphone. 'Let's get inside,' he said. 'Before we freeze.' He tugged out the earpiece and crouched to unzip the bag.

'Should I take this off?' Willow asked, still gripping the camera.

He jumped up and took hold of it. 'No, you go and sort the breakfast. I wouldn't like you to be late on my account. Those guests are bound to come down early if you're not there. It's sod's law.'

'Ok.'

'Thanks again,' he said. 'I really appreciate it.'

'Anytime.' She drew up her shoulders and smiled. Even though it was crazy, she meant it. She would help him with anything.

It was a struggle to get to the front door in the wind and she was missing the Marcus windbreak. The fairy lights over the front door of the schoolhouse swayed around, still flashing a somewhat manic rhythm. Inside, it was deadly quiet. The guests weren't in the common room. She flicked on the Christmas tree lights and put on classical radio. A soft Christmas carol played in the background. *Very festive.* She smiled as she opened the kitchen and emptied the dishwasher. With so few people, there wasn't much to get ready. At ten past eight, the family appeared: two parents and a son around fifteen, wearing a set of ear defenders. Willow went out to take their breakfast order.

'Two boiled eggs,' the mum said. 'And... Oh... Who's that?' she added quietly.

Willow looked over her shoulder. Marcus sidled in. If he was trying to look incognito, he could forget it. He was like an Italian supermodel in his sharp white shirt and black jeans. Her desperate heart and body would lay herself on a plate for him but even the idea made her shudder. She could only imagine the kind of woman he liked. And she didn't dare imagine the reality of being with him. Her romantic encounters to date had been various degrees of failure and *that* wasn't her imagination – unfortunately. Her sexual experience was literally painful and completely humiliating. No way did she ever want that with Marcus. While he was a fantasy, he was safe, and she could be someone else. Not Rocky Rainman but a projected version of Willow Roxburgh –

one who was confident in her own skin and, for all he knew, a sex goddess with a string of boyfriends behind her.

'He's a guest,' she replied, realising the mum was waiting for an answer.

'He looks like that man from the TV... What's his name?' She snapped her fingers as if to summon the answer.

'What would you like with your eggs?' Willow said.

'Oh um... Pancakes please.'

'Boiled eggs and pancakes?' Ok, weird combination, but who was she to judge? 'And your son?' She took their order and strolled over to Marcus, trying to hide her limp, hold herself tall and look like someone he might find attractive. 'And what can I get you?'

'I feel bad about you having to wait on me like this.' He smiled and it was that real smile again. The one that reduced her to melted ice-cream. 'I can get something myself.'

'No. It's fine. Only staff are supposed to be in the kitchen.' Even though she wasn't one of them normally. She usually left this to Barry.

'Well, if you insist. I fancy...' His eyes lingered over her and her heart skipped a beat. She was already weak from his smile. That look wasn't helping. 'Eggs, sausages, bacon. I don't like beans.'

'Tomatoes?'

'Yes, ok. But don't cook them, please.'

She almost let out a laugh as she scribbled it down. Not because his order was any weirder than boiled eggs and pancakes, but because the nervous tension in her body was looking for an escape route. 'Ok, uncooked tomatoes, eggs, sausages and bacon?'

'And toast, please. And coffee, very strong.'

'Suits you.' She cringed inwardly. Was that any worse than if she'd just let her laugh tumble out loud? She glanced up from the notepad. 'I mean...'

He was grinning and he leaned back, shaking his head. His tanned cheeks glowed. 'I get what you mean. I look like someone who needs a lot of coffee to get through the day and you're not wrong.'

That wasn't what she meant at all but she wasn't going to let on and she had a sneaky suspicion he knew full well what she was really thinking. He could lift her like a feather in the wind. His shirt was open enough to tease her with the promise of sculpted abs and well-toned muscles, now famous from his shirtless dips in *Destination Forecast*. Her eyes feasted on it and her lungs contracted sharply.

'I'll bring it shortly.' She needed to get away. Now she'd spied his chest, her imagination had gone into overdrive. She wanted to see more, touch it, feel it against her own, but what could she give him in return? A man who'd gone to that much trouble over his body surely wanted someone with an equally fine one in return. Willow got a lot of exercise doing this job and her waistline wasn't bad. She'd say she was a column when it came to body shape... except instead of being straight up and down, she was more like the Leaning Tower of Pisa. Where his body was likely covered in flawless skin, she had scars running the length of her legs from childhood operations where her bones were broken and put back in place. It wasn't something he needed or would want to see.

She pulled out a frying pan and landed it on the worktop with a clatter. Why was she thinking these things? It wasn't like it was ever going to happen anyway. For all she knew, he was with someone. He'd said he didn't have a wife, but he was bound to have a girlfriend. Guys like him didn't stay single for long or they stayed single and played the field. She didn't want to be his latest conquest… Or did she? Maybe that would be a diversion like she'd never had in her life.

'Just stop thinking about it,' she muttered.

There was probably a queue waiting to catch him. And even without that kind of competition, there was one very large factor going against her.

She was Rocky Rainman.

Chapter Ten

Marcus

Marcus took a mouthful of toast and chewed it very deliberately, staring out the window at the swaying trees as light slowly dawned. Without turning to face the family across the room, he knew they were watching. This was part and parcel of his life. Whenever he went out, he got it. Sometimes people approached him and wanted to talk weather or ask him about *Destination Forecast*. Other times he got asked to sign things or make on-the-spot forecasts. It got tiring and if he was out with his family, he had to resort to baseball caps and keep away from overcrowded places. With Toby in tow, that made sense anyway. Being under public scrutiny was never what Marcus wanted. A nebulous idea of packing it all in and riding horses, walking dogs and spending time with his family reared up in front of him. But surely that was lying down for Rocky Rainman? No way was Marcus Bowman allowing Rocky to get on top of him.

Willow slipped in the door and sidled over to his table. 'Was that ok?' She lifted his empty plate.

'Great, thanks.'

She magnetically attracted his gaze. It was more powerful than the moon pulling the tides. She was gorgeous in a natural and gentle way. The women he usually dated were so different from this fresh-faced beauty. She had barely any make-up on but her clothes were smart; the bright pink top and the abstract print scarf had a bohemian quirkiness about them that was all her.

His heart ached to stay close to her, even for a little while, but he couldn't. She may be spoken for and he had interviews lined up in the village he couldn't ignore. Ginny had emailed him the name of a local worthy, who'd apparently messaged e-Broadcast Scotland frequently over the years with various non-newsworthy stories or complaining about apparent inaccuracies. He may have a good ear to the ground for gossip. Marcus was to approach him on the pretext of discussing local people's views on the impact of The Old Schoolhouse in the village and how its closure would affect the community. Somehow, he then had to work in a conversation about Rocky Rainman.

He scraped back his seat and got to his feet. 'I'm off to meet someone called Malcolm McManus, who apparently is the man in the know around here.'

Willow smirked and looked at the carpet.

'What?'

'Nothing.' She held her fingers to her lips like she was trying to stifle a giggle.

'What is so funny?' He placed a hand on his hip.

'He's a total gossip but whether he talks any sense is debatable.' Her big doe eyes peered out from beneath long lashes and her cheeky smile grew. 'My cousin told me he got kicked off a local community group for dodgy dealings, and I think his wife was arrested for something, but he's still got his finger in every pie.'

'Great.' He rolled his eyes.

'I thought you wanted to interview the guests... And me.'

'I do but I don't want to spring it on them. I'll arrange a time with them. Maybe this evening. And when would suit you?'

'Just whenever. I'm going to be about all day.'

'Great. Well, I'll catch you later. If this Malcolm is a gossip, then he'll hopefully have lots to say about how wonderful this place is.'

'Maybe.' She cinched her shoulders and raised her eyebrows, then ran her gaze down his face and over his chest, lingering there for a moment. His stomach flip-flopped as if he were a fifteen-year-old with a crush on the cutest girl in the class, not a thirty-seven-year-old who should know better.

He cleared his throat, interrupting her body-scan. 'I'll let you know later. And thanks for breakfast.' He patted her on the shoulder but quickly withdrew his hand; the urge to touch her was too strong. She blinked and twirled her hair around her finger.

He headed out. Was he crazy to imagine she felt the same buzz as him? He shouldn't be encouraging it or even entertaining the idea.

Once he was out in the fresh air, the icy wind knocked the fluff out of his brain, and he focused on the task at hand.

He drove a mile along the country road where the satnav told him Malcolm's house was situated and turned into a small cul-de-sac with a tiny green in the middle and a collection of about eight houses surrounding it. A Christmas tree twinkled in the centre of the green and a couple of people with dogs stood chatting on the far side.

Marcus's jaw dropped when he saw the house in the corner all lit up like the Blackpool Illuminations. That was it? It looked like they were advertising the tackiest Christmas possible. It was made a hundred times worse as the garden was an utter disaster zone. Piles of crap were heaped around and the decorations were balanced on top of them. More mess spilled out onto the street too: old palettes, broken machinery, paint cans, oil drums, stuff he couldn't even guess the function of. A mass of trailing Christmas lights flashed around the perimeter even though it was broad daylight; they were looped over the junk piles like old ropes in a harbour. What the hell was this? Such a mess. He wanted to turn round and go straight back to the schoolhouse, or his safe, clean desk. His fingers clamped his nose as he got out. The smell was like diesel mingled with fertiliser. It made him retch. For a place in a beautiful setting like this, it was a disgrace. Rolling hills formed the backdrop with green fields and wintery trees to the front. The other people in the street must spit blood about this mess. *I know I would.* The other houses were all painted white with neat, well-kept gardens and tasteful wreaths on the doors or carefully arranged string lights on their fences.

The house door opened before Marcus reached the thing he now saw was a gate hidden among the detritus. A short, very obese man staggered down the front step, followed by an equally proportioned woman. The man was smiling and looked jovial, but the woman had a harsh expression. She folded her arms across a chest that could double as a shelf. Not someone to cross then.

'Hello,' the man said. 'Are you Marcus?'

'I am.' He reluctantly took his hand away from his face.

'Malcolm.' The man stretched out his hand.

Marcus shook it very briefly. Malcolm's fingernails were black with diesel oil. The urge to wash his hands clawed at Marcus's insides.

'And the wife, Brenda.'

'Hi.' Marcus nodded. She didn't offer him her hand.

'So, you're up here about The Old Schoolhouse, aye?' Malcolm said.

'Yes. That's right. Do you mind if I ask a few questions?'

'Fire away.'

'Can you tell me about the positive impact the schoolhouse facility has on the community and a bit about how you would feel if it closed?'

'Are we getting filmed doing this?' Brenda asked.

'Not at the moment.' Who'd want to see this on TV?

'I thought we were getting on the telly.'

'There might be that possibility depending on what you have to tell me,' Marcus lied. No way was he bringing a film crew to this disaster zone.

'Well, The Old Schoolhouse has been open for a long time,' Malcolm said. 'You know it used to be Clachnabronnachan school? The kids used to walk from here. Quite a way. My mother was a teacher there before it closed.'

And she clearly hadn't taught her son much about clearing up. Marcus listened to them waffle and pretended to be taking lots of notes, though really he was just wishing he could get back to the schoolhouse.

'By the way,' he said, hoping this sounded like a flyaway question. 'Have you heard of the internet weather forecaster Rocky Rainman?'

'Aye, I have. He does good forecasts. Why?'

Marcus's gaze shifted, travelling over the debris. None of this looked like forecasting equipment, but was it possible that Malcolm was the Rainman? Marcus always imagined him being some alternative individual, and Malcolm seemed to fit the bill. 'What is it you do here? You're not into a bit of weather forecasting on the side, are you?'

Malcolm laughed. 'No, I wouldn't know where to start. I'm a handyman and I do odd jobs.'

'And we run our own business,' Brenda said. 'We have a salvage yard.'

'Er, ok.' Nothing here looked particularly salvageable and why would anyone do business with people who lived like this? One look at the place and Marcus would scarper before they got a whiff of his money.

'And I'm chairman of the local Highland Games Committee.' Malcolm grinned a crooked smile, looking mighty proud of himself.

'Are you?' Was this the role he'd been kicked out of, according to Willow? Had he been reinstated and that was why he was looking so smug?

'We've been on committees in the town for a long time,' Brenda said, pulling an obviously phony smile. 'When you've lived in a place so long, one thing leads to another. I started off helping out at the school when the kids were younger, and then I was asked to run a club, then something else, and before you know it, we're running the Highland games, and it's no small task, let me tell you.'

'Sounds like you're very generous with your time,' Marcus said, though he remembered Willow had also said this woman had been arrested and she definitely had an intimidating air.

'It's all for the community,' Malcolm said. 'Though it's not how it used to be. Incomers and young folks these days don't know how things work.'

Marcus nodded and looked around. At least they knew how to keep their gardens tidy.

A creaking sound behind a pile of junk made Marcus look over. An ancient caravan was almost hidden in the mess. The door opened and a young woman emerged. She had long, curly, flaming red hair and stopped dead when she saw Marcus.

'Get inside,' Brenda said to her. 'There's an order on the worktop and I need it for tomorrow so you better hurry up.'

'Ok,' the young woman said and scooted in the main door of the house behind Malcolm.

Was that their daughter? What was she doing in that caravan? Weather forecasting maybe? Could she be behind the rainman persona? Maybe it wasn't a man at all. Several new questions formed in Marcus's mind but he didn't know for sure if he was even in the right place yet.

'I heard a rumour that Rocky Rainman lives up this way,' he said. 'You wouldn't know anything about that, would you? Or know how I can get in touch with him?'

Malcolm scratched his thick neck and glanced at Brenda. 'Is that so?'

'First I've heard,' Brenda said. 'Is that his real name?'

'I doubt it,' Marcus said. 'But no one knows his real name. That's the problem. It's difficult to locate him.'

'Aye,' Malcolm said. 'What about Ross McPherson?'

Brenda nodded. 'Aye, good point. He's a weirdo.'

'Who's that?' Marcus asked.

'He has a farm down the way, keeps horses. Always thought there was something not quite right about him.'

Marcus raised his eyebrow. That was rich coming from someone whose garden looked like a landfill site. 'And is there any reason to suspect he might be Rocky Rainman?'

'Aye,' Brenda said. 'He has some big satellite thing in his back garden. I bet that's what he was doing with it.'

'Ok. Interesting.' Marcus looked back at the caravan. Was it equally as interesting that there could be a weather station set up in there? It could be full of screens and equipment for all he knew. Was this a double bluff? Was Brenda saying they had an 'order for tomorrow' a code to let the young woman know they needed an updated forecast? Or had he just taken an idea and run wild with it?

'I can give you directions,' Malcolm said.

'Pardon? Oh, to the farm? I'd appreciate that. And thanks for your information on the schoolhouse. Very interesting.'

A short drive brought him to the farm. He pulled up outside it. This was like the place of his dreams. A gorgeous old stone farmhouse sat proudly on the side of the road with a tidy, if wintery, garden and fields beyond. Some new looking buildings, possibly stables, were set a little further up a minor road leading towards a hill. Gorgeous. He spent a few seconds just soaking it in before getting out of the car. *Here goes nothing*. In the window, a Christmas tree twinkled and seemed to welcome him. He knocked under a large wreath of real holly, evergreens and berries, then waited, rubbing his hands as cold air whooshed by.

A middle-aged woman answered. 'Oh goodness,' she said. 'Are you Marcus Bowman from the TV? You're his double.'

'I am Marcus Bowman.'

Her hand leapt to her chest. 'What are you doing here? Is this some kind of Jeremy Beadle thing? Are there cameras around the corner?'

'No, nothing like that. I'm looking to talk to Ross McPherson. I'm reporting on a local weatherman and I was told Ross is something of an enthusiast.'

'My husband, Ross?'

'I assume so.'

She shook her head. 'He couldn't even predict tomorrow's date, never mind the weather. Not Ross.'

'I heard he keeps satellite equipment in the garden.'

She chuckled. 'Hardly. He had some solar panels he rigged up to try and cut down on fuel bills but I don't think that makes him a weatherman. I'm not sure those solar panels even work.'

Marcus ran his hand over his head and sighed. Was it possible this was the guy and he somehow kept it quiet from his wife? Having his own satellite equipment seemed very extreme when almost all the information could be found online. Then again, an enthusiast would want to do everything 'properly'.

'Ross is just up there with the horses,' she said. 'You can ask him yourself if you don't believe me. I'll take you, come on.' She grabbed a coat and walked with him along the mud-covered road towards a field. It was exposed and wind whistled past, ruffling the grass in the field. To their left was the wooden building Marcus had guessed was a stable block.

'Ross!' she called.

A man with a shock of fluffy white hair looked out. 'Yes, dear.'

She marched up to him and mumbled something, presumably explaining who Marcus was. Ross burst out laughing.

'Nice to meet you,' he said. 'But I'm not a weatherman.'

'Pleased to meet you too,' Marcus shook his hand. 'And you're definitely not Rocky Rainman?'

'Ah, the internet weather person. No, that's not me.'

'And you don't know who he is or where I could find him?'

'Sorry, no.'

Marcus blinked and turned his attention to the horses. Three heads peered over the stable doors.

'They don't like this wind,' Ross said. 'I come out to chat to them and let them know everything will be fine.'

'They're stunning.' Marcus stroked the closest one's nose. 'I love horses. I always wanted to learn to ride, but it's more my niece's domain now than mine.' Toby might enjoy it too. If he was to agree to coming to live at the schoolhouse, Marcus could bring him here to ride.

'I could teach you,' Ross said. 'I do lessons for adults. That's Mist, he's a good lad, but wind spooks him. Have you ridden before?'

'Only once as a child. Pony trekking. Nothing exciting.'

'Feel free to book in for a lesson.'

'I'd love to but I'm only here for a few days.' If he did it next year, maybe he could ride with Toby. This could be something they did together.

'Well, it's a quiet time of year. If you change your mind, give me a call. I have the barn set up for indoor sessions, so we can stay dry.'

'Sounds delightful.' He just wasn't sure he had time this week. 'If I get some spare time, I'll be in touch.'

When the goodbyes were said and done and Marcus was on his way back to the hotel, he smirked to himself. A vision of him riding alongside Toby and his nieces played in his head. It was perfect. Almost. If he could just add Willow to that scene. Or was that just madness, even in his dreams?

Willow was in the office, clicking away at a computer screen. Marcus's heart swooped as she looked up and their gazes met. He leant on the doorway and smiled. Looped strings weighed down by several Christmas cards hung around the whole room and a little fibre optic tree twinkled intermittently at the window.

'Hi,' she said. 'How did you get on with Malcolm?'

'I don't think much of his house.'

She minimised her screen and gave him her full attention. 'I've heard it's a bit of a mess.'

'That's an understatement.'

Willow gave him an almost shy smile. 'I bet. But I never like to say too much about him or his wife. Marion and Barry are very friendly with them.'

'Do they have a daughter?'

'Marion and Barry?'

'No, Malcolm and his wife.'

Willow shook her head. 'I don't think so. They have kids but I think they only have boys.'

'I saw a young woman coming out of a caravan. I thought she was maybe their daughter.'

'I think they have a lodger. I heard Marion talking about her.'

'I hope they don't make her lodge in that caravan. It looked barely a step up from a cardboard box.'

'It wouldn't surprise me. I doubt their house has any spare room.'

'True. Anyway, they sent me to see a man called Ross McPherson, who they thought might be the Rainman.'

'Ross? He's a sweet man.'

'You know him?'

'Yes. I go riding with him sometimes and Marion often takes the residents and guests pony trekking there. He's a big supporter of the schoolhouse.'

'I didn't know you could ride.'

'You don't know anything about me,' she said, and there was defiance in her tone. 'Why wouldn't I be able to ride?'

'That's not what I said. I just didn't realise.' He hadn't meant anything by it, but he understood why she was touchy about it. 'I think it's great. I've always wanted to learn. Ross suggested I book a lesson.'

'And did you?'

'I don't know if I'll have time... and, truth be told, I'm a bit nervous.'

'Why?'

'Because horses don't have brakes.'

She giggled. 'I'm sure he'd lead you if you asked. He's great with the people who come here.'

'I wish I'd interviewed him about the schoolhouse.' Rather than obsessing over the idea of finding Rocky Rainman.

'I'm sure he wouldn't mind if you went back. It isn't far.'

'I think I will, but not until tomorrow. I'll give him a call.' Maybe he'd do a lesson while he was there. He'd like to ask Willow to come with him but there were a hundred and one reasons not to, so he didn't.

'You didn't find the Rainman then?' she muttered.

'Nope.'

'Why do you care so much about him?'

He straightened up and sighed. Wind howled past the door, rattling the glass and the handles. The predicted storm had arrived. 'Because Rocky's a bully and I don't like it. It's someone who's made this personal and they're trying to take me down. But they've got an unfair advantage. Maybe I'm being too sensitive but I'd rather have it straight out and face the competition head-on.' He ran his hand over his head. 'I guess I have an inbuilt need to prove myself.'

'Surely you've already done that? You're a famous weatherman.'

'Yeah, but it never stops. I've always had the need to do better, even when—'

CRASH. They both jumped.

'What the hell was that?' Willow's hand leapt to her chest.

It was louder than bins blowing over, a slate hitting a car or anything else he could think of.

'A window breaking?'

'Oh no.' She got up from her seat and grabbed her crutch. 'I think it came from that way.' She pointed to the side door and he followed her out.

'Oh my god.' Her hand leapt to her mouth. Marcus followed her sightline along a short track into the woods, where an outdated building stood in a clearing. A tree had uprooted and crashed through the roof.

'That's not where you live, is it?'

She nodded her head.

CHAPTER ELEVEN

Willow

*Sorry folks, the weather's
dire... Coorie doon by the
cosy fire*

Willow stared at the mangled mess of the tree sticking out of the now buckled roof and her heart hammered almost as loud as the wind.

'Thank god you weren't in there,' Marcus said, voicing almost her exact thoughts. Hers only differed in her gratitude that Marshmallow wasn't in there either and that she'd brought her laptop out with her that morning.

'Yeah,' Willow agreed, running through a mental assessment of what was in there and if it was anything she needed urgently and if so, how would she get it out? She tried not to imagine what might have happened if the tree had fallen overnight when she was in bed. A tremor ran through her at the thought.

'And no one else is in there?' he asked.

'Not that I know of.'

He stepped closer and placed his arm around her shoulder. Willow froze. She wasn't used to physical contact. People didn't normally hug her. They saw her as someone fragile who might be damaged at the slightest touch, so they kept their distance. And this wasn't just some random person. This was Marcus Bowman, the man she dreamt about. Was it weird to like the sense of safety? Did that make her a needy damsel? She'd never seen herself like that but, right now, she soaked up the warm, reassuring sensation. Her heartbeat slowly returned to normal, though she didn't examine the panicky might-have-beens flying around her head. He increased the pressure a little on her upper arm, perhaps in response to her yielding into him.

'What a nightmare,' he said. 'I'm so glad you're Ok. But all your clothes and belongings must be in there.'

'They are. But there's not a lot I can do about it.'

'Christ. What a horrific thing to happen.' He let go of her arm and rubbed his forehead. She shivered as he moved off. 'Is there someone you can call? What are you going to do?'

She took a deep breath. 'Not panic, I guess. Worse things happen at sea, so my mum always says. No one's hurt. I'll need to call Marion and let her know the building's damaged.'

'Never mind the building. Let her know you're ok. And suggest she get better safety checks done in the future before offering accommodation to workers.'

'No one could have predicted that. It was a freak accident.' Thank god it happened when no one was inside though.

Her whole life had been so sheltered she wasn't sure where to start. Would insurance cover this? How would she find the numbers to call? Marcus stared at her, his eye contact strong and reassuring. Her heart leaped. Her body and soul ached to be near him. A connection to him tugged at her. She couldn't explain it, but it was hollow because nothing could come of it. He didn't belong with her, no matter how much she craved him.

'You're taking this really well. Better than I would in your situation,' he said. 'Just let me know what you want me to do. I'm happy to help if I can.'

It was her turn to smile. 'Thanks. Let me call Marion, and I'll let you know.'

'Sounds like a plan. Have you heard from her today?' he asked, giving the fallen tree one last dirty look, before they returned to the warmth of the schoolhouse.

'Yes. Barry's going in for surgery on his wrist, so they won't be back for a day or two yet.'

'Oh. Well, they're lucky to have you here.'

'Are they? Even though I'm clueless.'

'I don't believe that.'

'Thanks... I think.'

'Listen, are you going to be ok on your own for a bit? I need to check the charts and sort out the next forecast.' They'd reached the entrance hall.

'Of course.' She couldn't exactly say she'd rather he hung around with her all day. If she kept busy she hopefully wouldn't dwell too much on her near miss.

'Ok. I'll be in the common room. When you're off the call, let me know what she said.'

'It's fine. You're a guest. You don't have to help.'

'I want to,' he said. 'That's a horrible thing to happen to your home. I don't want you to face it alone. And anyway, I owe you.'

'How do you work that out?'

'You helped me with filming this morning. Shout me if you need anything, ok? I insist.'

'Ok.'

He disappeared through the doors, and Willow called Marion.

'Oh my god. No. Are you ok? Thank god you weren't in there. Oh help, what shall we do?' Marion said. 'How can we get back to sort it out immediately?'

'Hey,' Willow said. 'Don't panic. There's nothing different you could do, even if you were here. And it's not a good idea travelling in this weather unless you absolutely have to. You might get stuck. Trees are down, rivers have burst their banks, roads are closed, and snow's on its way.' Yup, she had to face this without them.

'You sound like a weather forecaster.' Marion chuckled. 'Marcus Bowman must be rubbing off on you.'

If only. Willow smirked to herself.

'How's he getting on anyway?'

'Fine. He's been doing some interviews.'

'That's good. Now, you make sure you sleep in one of the guest rooms tonight,' Marion insisted. 'And you can borrow my clothes, or there are spares in the cupboard at the top of the stairs.' Residents often left things and Marion kept everything just in case anyone ever needed anything – and that moment had arrived. 'Take anything you like. I'm just so relieved you weren't in there. I can hardly believe it.'

Once Willow had found all the insurance details in the files, she gave them to Marion. Willow would have made the calls but Marion suspected they would only talk to the policy holder.

The guest family returned from their day out, soaked through, and went to dry out before their interview with him.

Willow had just finished chatting with them when the phone rang.

'Hi, Willow.' It was Marion again. 'I just remembered. The guests who are staying, it's their son's birthday and Barry was going to make them a fancy restaurant style meal. They can't normally take him out. It's difficult for them as the lad has ASD. He doesn't do well in crowded places. I feel so bad letting them down.'

'Don't worry,' Willow said, though tension was creeping into her chest again. 'I'm sure I'll figure something out.'

'Oh, would you? That would be wonderful. There's plenty in the store cupboard and the fridge. I think Barry was going to make them a mini menu and everything. If only we'd been more organised and prepped it before we left.'

'I'll think of something.' Though she wasn't exactly sure what and she'd never been much of a cook.

She put down the phone and rested her face in her hands. This day was going from bad to worse. But before she turned her mind to dinner plans, she needed to make a forecast. Rainman's followers were clamouring for storm updates. She opened her laptop and pulled up the charts. This was where she could lose herself for hours. Using the online draw tool, she circled the eye of the storm and showed its trajectory. Cross-referencing data and building her own interpretation took time, but her earlier predictions were still accurate. She only needed to tweak a few things.

'Hey.'

Marcus was resting on the doorframe. Willow quickly min-imised her screen.

'Is everything ok?' he asked.

'Kind of. I've sorted the tree, though no one can get out to cut it for a day or two. An engineer from the electricity company is coming later to shut off the electrics and there's no gas out here, so that's not an issue.'

'I'm sorry,' he said. 'Is there anything important in there?'

'Not really. Just my clothes and... well, my medication.' She'd forgotten about that until now. The pain meds and muscle relaxants were useful on busy days, but she could live without them if she had to.

'Is it something I can get for you?'

'You can't go in there. It's too dangerous.'

'I mean from a chemist or somewhere. I could drive into Glenbriar just now.'

She shook her head, though she couldn't express her gratitude. 'It's on prescription. I'll have to call up and arrange for more, and I can't do that right now.'

'Why not?'

'I need to work out what to do for tonight's meal. Marion just called.' Willow let out a sigh. 'She and Barry promised the guests a restaurant-style meal with a menu and everything. They aren't able to go out often, so it was a treat for them. I'm not a great cook so it'll have to be something simple that looks good... They aren't exactly going to have a lot of options from my repertoire.'

'I could help with that,' Marcus said. 'I enjoy cooking.'

'Do you?' She couldn't imagine him liking anything that might get messy. Her kitchen always looked like a hurricane had whipped through when she was done cooking.

'Absolutely. My mama was Italian, and she taught me some great recipes. I'm sure I can sort something out. I'll play chef for the night.'

'Oh, wow. Great.' She nodded slowly, scanning him over. Her blood heated as it pumped fast through her veins. Part Italian explained his Roman looks. She couldn't take her eyes off him.

Her fingers twitched and burned with the desire to touch him. She'd love to know what his body would feel like against hers, not that she'd ever find out.

'I need to do another forecast in half an hour. Maybe you could help me out again?' he said.

'Sure.' It was the least she could do, though guilt seared through her chest when she remembered what she'd just been doing. Would there be any harm in telling Marcus it was her he was looking for? Except she couldn't risk him refusing to do the report or painting the schoolhouse in a bad light.

'Amazing. I'm glad you're back in my life, even if it's only for a few days.' He nodded, looking pensive. 'You always bring the sunshine.'

Do I? Her mouth jammed, and she just stared. She'd heard Marcus turn on the charm for the camera, but what he'd just said was... well, a compliment. *And I'll take it.* She doubted it would have been forthcoming if he knew he had just called Rocky Rainman the sunshine in his life.

'Let's get this forecast done,' he said. 'Then you can lead me to the kitchen.' He folded up his sleeves, displaying his beautifully muscular forearms. Willow grabbed a lock of hair and twisted it around her finger. Did he have any idea what he did to her? What would he think if he knew what went through her head every time she saw him?

Top of Form

Chapter Twelve

Marcus

'Maybe I should give up TV forecasting and do cooking instead,' Marcus suggested to Willow as she handed him a black apron. 'I could give Gino D'Acampo a run for his money, no?'

Willow's doe eyes scanned him down and he waited for her assessment. He'd always kept himself in shape. Had to look good on camera, didn't he? His body had got him the job in the first place. And there was satisfaction in reading articles about the 'hottest weatherman on TV'. Rocky Rainman couldn't have anything to rival this. If he did, surely he'd want to show it off. But with Willow doing the looking, it was like being interrogated. Did she like what she saw? Marcus was heading for the big four O. When he hit in three years' time, would e-Broadcast replace him with someone younger to keep tugging in the viewers?

'You could give all the TV chefs some stiff competition, but only if you can actually cook.' She half-frowned as he pulled the apron over his head. He'd be a liar to say it wouldn't please him if she admired his body, but hopefully she had more sense than to dream of someone like him in the long term. His lifestyle came with built-in problems. His ex-wife couldn't cope with the pressure and the publicity. Did Willow want a life like that? He doubted it. She deserved a nice, normal guy nearer her own age. She'd already opted to move somewhere quiet and his life was rarely that, even if he moved on from forecasting and concentrated on presenting, he'd be in the public eye.

His relationship history saddled him with more baggage than the carousel at Gatwick and the tabloids would love to get their hands on the details. What would she make of it if she knew how he'd slept his way up the career ladder? If only Rocky Rainman was a single woman. Marcus smirked. How the hell had he made his way to thoughts of sleeping with his nemesis just to get one over on him? That would be more than somewhat extreme.

'Show us what you're made of, maestro,' Willow said.

He blew a chef's kiss towards her. 'Molto bene.'

'Bless you,' she said.

He chuckled and tied the apron strap at the back. 'Let's see what we have then. Are they expecting à la carte? Or can I just make a big pot of Bolognese and be done with?'

'They should have some options, if it's to be like a restaurant. How about you tell me a few things you could make quickly?'

'No pressure then.' He opened the fridge.

'I would have thought this would be easy for you,' she said. 'Surely being on camera is worse.'

'I've had a lot of practice on camera. I've been doing it for long enough.' He sifted through the various packets, cobbling together ideas about what he could make with them. It reminded him of *Ready Steady Cook*.

'You must have been good to start with if you got talent spotted.'

He cringed behind the fridge door where she couldn't see him. Had she read his mind from moments ago? The talents he had didn't qualify him for TV. What a hypocrite he'd become, getting pissed off about Princess Sadie when his lucky break was just as bad, if not worse, than hers. He was a fine one to get on his high horse about undermining his profession. The only difference was, he had qualifications. But he'd definitely jumped on a lucky springboard... or two. Usually very attractive, older ones.

'Ok, here are some ideas.' He chose not to reply to her about the talent spotting. It was a Marcus Bowman speciality, bullishly ignoring tough questions.

'Let me get something to write with and I can make a menu.' She pulled open a drawer and raked about.

He checked out the ovens, hoping to god he could figure out how everything worked.

'Ok, tell me what you can do.' She poised with a pen and a folded piece of paper.

He cast her a quick glance. Honestly, right now, he was so hot for her he would do anything she wanted. That would be one of the craziest moves of his life, and he'd made a fair few of them in his life, sleeping with TV producers and influential women. He cleared his throat. 'Ok. I've got beef.'

'You certainly do,' she said and he gaped at her.

'Eh... Pardon?'

Her cheeks coloured and she seemed to diminish as if wanting the floor to swallow her. Poor girl. He wasn't a guy she needed to fall for. He'd be nothing but bad news for her, but she set fires burning in him. Would it be so bad to quench them in the only way he knew how?

'Nothing,' she said, all innocence again.

'I can make Italian beef.' He ignored her smirk as she wrote it down. 'Spaghetti al pomodoro which is a vegetarian option and...' He checked the fridge again. 'How about good old acqua pazza for the fish?'

'How do you spell that and what is it?'

'Poached fish with white wine and tomato sauce on crostini with roasted vegetables.'

She peered up at him and raised an eyebrow. 'Seriously? This is amazing. Barry would have done a choice of steak pie or pasta.'

'Now you tell me.'

'Sorry. But this is going to be better than anything we've ever had,' she said. 'I better not tell him.'

'Reserve judgement until it's cooked.'

'I'll type this up and make it into a fancy menu.' She straightened from her leaning post on the worktop. 'You realise you have to cook something for me too... and yourself.'

'Of course.' He locked eyes with her. 'What do you fancy?'

Her cheeks coloured slightly, which could have been the heat from the oven he'd just switched on. 'I'm not usually a fan of beef,' she said, 'But Italian beef sounds tasty.'

Christ, she was as bad as him. 'I hope you'll find it to your liking.'

'Hmm. I might be safer sticking to fish. I like the sound of that too,'

He nodded. 'That's a better plan.'

She waved the piece of paper and left to type it.

Marcus leant back on the work surface and inhaled a long, slow breath. What a day. Willow had made a lucky escape from that bungalow. Christ. If she'd been in there when... It didn't bear thinking about. An engineer had turned up and gone in wearing a hardhat to turn off the power. He'd said there wasn't too much damage inside other than a large crack in the ceiling. Most of the damage was confined to the roof and presumably the attic space. But Marcus's mind eased at the thought of Willow being safe in the schoolhouse and not stuck out in the woods on her own.

He raked his fingers through his hair. Why was he getting so involved? This wasn't like him. He had enough going on of his own. His life was a mess at the best of times, he was just great at putting a shine on it and making himself appear the consummate professional. Look at his career. He had the perfect home, evenings in the gym, and a smart car to boot. Who could ask for more? *Normal people, that's who.* Normal people who carried on normal relationships. Not people who had other commitments thrust unexpectedly on them. He wasn't complaining. He loved his family, and they were his priority, but since he'd become their guardian, it had left little time for dating. And in a way it was a relief. He had a habit of falling for older women. Women who liked his body and his money. Maybe if they'd just agreed to sex and some expensive dates, they could have bypassed several stages of angst, dispensed with the fake, and not ended up in a twisted vine of lies. Because all the serious ones had lied and hurt him in some way or another. When he put in the effort to make a deeper connection only for them to cut him, it was painful. His marriage had fallen apart. Firstly because of the media pressure on his ex and then his family had moved in with him. How could he risk something similar happening again? Chains and an iron portcullis surrounded his heart, keeping his love-life restrained. Usually he could deal with it even if his body and soul were starved.

'Right, food.' He rubbed his face, massaging sense into his brain. First, he'd have to prep some basic ingredients. He scrubbed his hands, then started dicing onions into perfectly sized pieces.

Tempus fugit once he got going and Willow came in with the order.

'They're very excited about the menu,' she said. 'You've made their week.'

'Great. Now, I just have to cook it.' He had one of every dish to do, plus one for himself and one for Willow. It was only five meals but it got unbelievably hot in the kitchen once the oven fired up. He wiped his brow with the back of his arm. No way could he do this every day. The mess building around him put him on edge and he started shoving some of the sauce-covered utensils into the washer.

'Here, I'll do that,' Willow said, coming in the doors behind. 'I know how much you love mess.'

Maybe his expression told her he was on the verge of a breakdown. 'Yeah.'

She grabbed a handful of plates. Somehow she was a dab hand at doing everything efficiently, even when she had her crutches. He guessed she'd got used to it over the years but he still couldn't help admiring it.

'I might have made enough to feed us for the next several days. I haven't got quantities down to a fine art yet.'

'It smells delicious.' She raised her eyes to him and blinked. Those long eyelashes were especially appealing. Everything about Willow was appealing and he needed to remind himself he was trying not to notice.

'Thanks.' He moved away, lifting a pot from the stove. 'I hope the presentation is as good as the smell. I don't want it looking like a dog's dinner.'

'Here.' She grabbed two plates and laid them on the work surface. He dished out the food, squinting as he leaned down, attempting to make it look tempting.

'It's great,' she said. 'Let's just hope I don't drop them on the way to the table.'

'Yeah, make sure you don't.' He narrowed his eyes at her, half joking but *please god, don't.*

'I'll do my best.' She pulled a half shrug. Should he offer to help? She may have a disability in the technical sense but she did a perfect job of not letting it rule her life. Ever since he'd known her, he'd seen a smiley, friendly, and smart woman. She didn't need some heroic man leaping in to save the day. She had this. It was a fine line between giving help and being a patronising twat. He held open the door for her and she gave him a little grin as she headed into the dining room.

A few moments of calm were in order and he wiped the surfaces and took a breather from the cooking mania. Willow was back within moments.

'Is everything ok?' He spun around, expecting to see uneaten food and have her tell him the guests thought it looked dreadful.

'Perfect,' she said. 'They're overjoyed. I'll give them a few minutes before I check on them again. They told me they haven't eaten out with their son for a long time, so this is a real treat for them.'

'Yeah. That must be hard.'

'Does Toby react badly to lots of people too?'

'No, he's usually ok as long as he's with someone familiar, though he can get a bit overexcited. He loves food, which is just one of the conundrums that is Toby. For someone who eats as well as him, it's always been a puzzle why his growth isn't great. It's always been put down to hormones. But, yeah, we've had him out to meals when he's smashed things, not because he's bad, just because he's so excited to see his pizza he can't control his emotions. But then I'm a bit like that when it comes to pizza too. Who isn't?' He winked and she let out a little giggle.

'So... um, what happened to your parents? Am I allowed to ask?'

'My father is still alive, though we never see him. He's a lazy man and he ran my mama into the ground for years. She had chronic fatigue alongside her rheumatoid arthritis but she still went out to work and ran after him more than any of us kids. He was always "ill" and needing her, though truly he never had anything wrong with him. He didn't work and he didn't care about anything except where his next meal was coming from.'

'Oh. That's not good.'

'Too right, it isn't. My mama wasn't that old when she died but she looked twenty years older than she was.' His jaw hardened. A bitter taste formed in his mouth whenever he thought of the way his father had treated his mama and showed no remorse now. His father's only regret was that he'd had to cook his own meals once she was gone. No concern for the kids she left behind. 'Mama was a great cook,' he said, trying to lighten his mind. 'I used to help her. I'm the oldest. It was expected that I would help with the youngers and cooking was the bit I liked most.'

'My mum never let me cook… Not on my own anyway. She liked doing cookery with me but I think she was terrified I would burn the house down.'

'Was that likely?' He drew his head back.

'No. But she… you know.' With a semi-shrug, she looked at her left foot, which turned in at a sharp angle. 'She never thought I was capable of anything.'

'She must be really proud now. You've always worked hard, yeah?'

'I try.'

'Exactly, and you've not burnt anything down yet.'

'I'm sure she is proud when she's not panicking about me.' She smiled and tossed back her head of long blonde hair. It was tied back but half of it had escaped and hung around her ears in messy waves. He'd like to stroke it out of her face, sweep it behind her shoulders, dip in and… never mind. *Must banish these thoughts.* 'I'm sure your mama would be very proud of you if she was still here.'

'Yeah. I guess she would be.' Normally, he'd have shut down or cut off this conversation long before now. For anyone else in the world, he would, but Willow was different. He liked talking to her and what harm could it do telling her about himself? 'What about you? Any siblings?'

'No,' she said. 'I don't have anyone, just cousins. I think... Well, it wasn't easy when I was younger.'

'Yeah.' Marcus leaned back on the work surface and glanced at the floor. He couldn't imagine what she went through as a child. Toby didn't have many physical issues, except being on the small side and needing growth hormones. But if the amount of appointments he had to attend were anything to go by – not to mention the specialists he had to see about his learning and developmental delays – then he bet she'd had ten times as many.

'I should check the guests,' she said.

Marcus carried on the kitchen clear up until she came back beaming from ear to ear.

'They loved it,' she said. 'It was the best meal they've ever had apparently.'

'Seriously?'

'You're just over talented.'

'Hardly, but thanks.'

'The mum wants to know if you're single.'

'Are you kidding? She's married and her husband's sitting right across from her.'

Willow giggled. 'I know but he can't cook for toffee – so she says.'

'Aw man. She sounds like a case. Tell her I'm—'

'Married?' She arched an eyebrow. 'I think she'll have guessed you're not unless your divorce was fake.'

'No, that was very real.'

'And it's obvious you haven't remarried.'

'Is it?'

'Well, yeah. I mean, who'd marry someone like you, who's so obviously let himself go?'

'Oh, haha.' Marcus fake clapped. 'You get the prize for wisecrack of the day. You're right up there with David.'

'Lucky me. So you'll not be wanting a sneaky liaison with her later.'

'Er no. If you're trying to set me up with someone, then maybe don't choose married women.'

'Isn't she a bit old for you anyway?'

He gave a little shrug. She didn't need to know he'd always preferred older women... Until she came along. 'Maybe you should leave me to get a date myself, then.'

'Oh, I don't doubt you're very good at that.'

'Hmm.' He sighed. 'Most of them only want... Never mind.'

Willow's eyes gaped. 'Want what?' Her voice was little more than a whisper.

'Nothing. Just thinking aloud.' He rubbed his forehead. 'Ignore me. Stupid thing to say. I've been burned a lot by women, that's all. I must have mug written across my face because I seem to pick up the ones who lie to me about god knows what. Maybe to impress me or bed me or whatever. Who knows? It wears thin after a while.'

She teased a lock of hair over her shoulder and twisted it around her index finger, not meeting his eyes.

'Why are we talking about this? I didn't mean to sound so callous, sorry.'

'It's ok,' she said. 'I think I should check the guests. They'll probably be finished.'

'And let them know the celibate chef is perfectly happy on his own.'

She smiled as she left and he breathed a sigh of relief. This was why he didn't normally talk about himself. When he did, it frustrated him and he ended up saying something he regretted.

Willow returned with the empty plates and placed them on the worktop with a triumphant grin. Leaning over, she braced herself for a moment. All this walking and standing must be hurting her. She wasn't using her crutch when she went into the dining room. Probably because it was easier carrying plates with her hands free.

'All ok, yeah?' He stepped up beside her, close enough to take her arm or for her to take his if she wanted to.

'They loved it.' She straightened up with a sharp breath she expertly masked with a smile. 'I can't thank you enough.'

'No need. You helped me with the filming.'

'That was easy compared to this.'

'Not really. This wasn't too hard and it was quite enjoyable.'

She smiled at him and they held eye contact. His pheromones were nudging him closer, shoving him down a wholly inappropriate road. He took a half step back and the moment passed. She looked away with an odd expression, a rueful smirk perhaps. 'I'll just get their puddings,' she said.

'Thank goodness for frozen desserts.'

'Totally. Though I still think you missed a trick with the cooking. You could add it to your TV repertoire.'

'Maybe. I could set myself up as l'arciere di cucina.'

'What does that mean?'

'The cooking bowman. I could be an anonymous sensation like my dear pal, Rocky.'

'Oh... him.'

'Yup. Him. And I'm still no closer to finding him.'

Willow blinked and opened her mouth like she was about to say something. Marcus frowned as the moment lengthened, then she gave him a brief smile and left with the desserts.

Marcus leant back against the worktop and ran his hand over his chin. What had that look meant? Did he dare wonder what she was thinking? If it was anything like what was going on in his head, it was probably better if he didn't.

Chapter Thirteen

Starting bright and chilly
for most, then later on a
touch of frost.

Willow sat on the end of her bed, massaging her left thigh. By the time she'd lain down last night, her legs had been killing her. The schoolhouse had no bedrooms on the ground floor, so she had no choice but to do the stairs.

Pipes creaked and clanked as the heating came on. She shivered a little. Maybe it was a throwback to her childhood, but the idea of being close to Marcus and the other guests was reassuring. Being out in the now damaged staff bungalow had never been that great – more like something she forced herself to do to prove she could. There was no denying it was a lot comfier being in the main building. Safer too. She hadn't dared tell her parents what had happened with the tree. Her mum might actually have a heart attack. She panicked about Willow doing simple things. The bungalow's roof falling in might tip her over the edge.

Maybe it was a miracle she hadn't had nightmares about collapsing ceilings. Or maybe it was purely the Marcus effect in action. He was all she could think about. She lifted an oversized cream sweater she'd found in the cupboard and pulled it on.

Marcus Bowman.

He consumed every thought, whether awake or asleep. He'd been a superstar last night. Hot as always, turning her insides to mush. But the Rocky Rainman stuff was getting out of hand. *Just ride this wave for another few days and make sure he gives us a good report.* But what then? She liked Marcus's company so much she shivered at the prospect of losing it.

They'd had a moment last night, a brief one, where she'd almost confessed. She wanted to. But she couldn't. Just like she couldn't wholly believe the connection between them was anything more than just normal man-to-woman interactions. She closed her eyes, trying to remember how it felt when he'd put his arm around her. How could she recreate the wonderful physical sensation? She liked hugging but she only very rarely did it... Only with her parents and Hayley. She couldn't just march up to Marcus and ask for a hug. *Must accept he doesn't look at me the same way I look at him.* He was the oldest of seven siblings. He was used to looking out for people, and that was all he was doing for her, nothing more. *Not the man for me, plain and simple.* Because no matter how much she fancied him, if it came to the crunch, she wouldn't have a clue what to do. Her dating and bedroom experience was so shit.

Her chest burned and she got to her feet, tugging the hem of the sweater over her leggings. *Do not let him see what an innocent I am.* There was no need for him to know.

She had to make breakfasts. All these extra tasks were exhausting. When the schoolhouse was busier, they employed cooks and cleaners, but with so little money to spare, Marion and Barry were doing the brunt of it alone. Willow switched on the lights in the kitchen. A faint smell of the garlic from the night before still lingered, despite her and Marcus scrubbing it and putting on all the fans. Bacon and eggs were about as far as her culinary skills went. Marcus made cooking look easy... and sexy. She just scraped by on the bare minimum.

Barry always checked the fridge temperature and recorded it in the logbook. She should do the same in case the health and safety inspector turned up, as Marion always feared. Apparently the inspection was due at some point in the next few months, but Barry pooh-poohed it, saying they were notoriously late for these things.

A knock on the door startled her. Marcus's head poked around. 'Good morning. Am I allowed in when I'm not cooking?'

'Probably not.'

'Thought not.'

'Why do you want to come in? Do you need help with the filming?' She crossed her fingers behind her back. Please, let him want me.

'Kind of. I'm not doing the early forecast today.' He pushed the door wide and came in fully. Everything about him was perfect, like he'd been made over by a team of stylists. His thick black sweater looked cosy but slick at the same time, his jeans were perfectly fitted and he oozed Armani-style sex appeal. 'I'm doing the lunchtime forecast and I thought I might ring Ross McPherson and ask if I can do it from his farm. It would look awesome with the hills behind and maybe some horses running about. I could interview him at the same time.'

'Sounds great.'

'You want to come with me?'

'I can't really leave here.'

'Not even for a couple of hours?'

'Would it take that long?'

'I thought I might take Ross up on the riding lesson... Maybe you'd like to do it too? I wouldn't feel so freaked out if you were with me.'

'Really?' She swallowed.

'Definitely. You know what you're doing with horses. I don't have a clue. I like them but they sense my fear.'

She pressed her fingers to her lips, covering a laugh. Marcus didn't look like he'd be afraid of anything.

'Well, ok. I guess Marion wouldn't mind as long as I get the work done.' And as she was doing the extra time with breakfasts and dinner, it surely wouldn't be a problem.

'Great.' Marcus smiled that delectable smile and she melted into a pool of goo.

A completely different day to the one she'd forecast now loomed ahead. She was going somewhere with Marcus. He had a very slick car, a Maserati no less, black and shiny. *Oh my god.* She'd never been in anything even half this fancy.

He zipped off down the road smooth as you like and she cast him a little look. He was made for a car like this. The leather interiors and flashy, spaceship-style dashboard suited his immaculate persona to a T. He touched a button and warmth emitted from the seat. Her messy little car with its mucky mats and wind-down back windows probably suited her just as much.

'I haven't ridden for a while,' she said. All her gear – none of it particularly professional or stylish – was in her tree-demolished bungalow and she couldn't get it. Ross would have to lend them hats.

'Remember, I haven't done this since I went pony-trekking. And that was over twenty years ago. Maybe closer to thirty.'

'Ok, you win.'

'Good. I always like to.'

'If it comes to a race today though, your luck's out.' She cast him a defiant look and his lips curled up.

'Lovin' the fighting talk, but we'll see.'

'Yes, we will.' She hoped she sounded confident because she didn't see herself beating him at anything if he put his mind to it. Her body could be so unpredictable and restrictive that she just muddled along with what it decided to do at any given time. Riding was something she enjoyed and could do well, but she hadn't fitted it into her life as much as she would have liked.

The lower levels of Ross's farm were green and horses grazed in their paddock. Behind, the mountains loomed with white peaks, both intimidating and stunning as a backdrop.

'This is perfect, isn't it?' Marcus said.

'It's a beautiful place,' Willow agreed.

Ross greeted them cheerfully and gave Willow's hand an extra squeeze.

'I've missed seeing you. Must have been the summer since you were last here,' Ross said.

'I've been so busy, but I really should make more time,' Willow replied.

'You're so good with the horses. You're always welcome.'

Marcus set up his equipment. It wasn't a live broadcast, so it wasn't as critical. If something went massively wrong, they could change it, but he wanted to get it done and dusted.

'Then we can ride.' He quirked his eyebrow a little as he steadied the camera on the tripod.

Willow couldn't wait to get back in the saddle.

Marcus warmed up his smile, straightening his tie and flicking the lapels of his coat. It was his usual routine. He was so OCD sometimes. Willow hoped he had something less glam to wear for the riding. He wouldn't want that coat smelling of horse.

'Ok, shoot,' he said.

She made a pistol with her fingers and aimed it at him. 'Ok, Tonto.'

His grin doubled into a laugh, showing his white teeth to the full. She might need a seat quite soon. Her legs often turned to jelly even without him, but he sped up the process alarmingly.

After the report was a wrap, he brought Ross in beside him and talked to him about The Old Schoolhouse. Willow fixed her gaze on them, her fingers absently caressing her breastbone through her pink puffa jacket. How did he make it look so effortless? He was made to be on screen. His words flowed without any sign of a script and it all seemed so natural.

He closed the interview by thanking Ross, then edged in beside Willow to watch the playback on the camera and check everything was fine. How tall he was next to her. She leaned closer, pulling it off as her wonky body, but really his warm woodsy scent lured her towards him, and being so close ignited a belly fire deep inside.

'Good,' he said. 'Now, let me pack this stuff away and get my other jacket, then we can ride.'

Willow bit back all the puns about Italian stallions that kept invading her head and left him to put away the camera. She ambled over to chat to Ross.

'All very interesting, this, isn't it? And hopefully it'll do some good. I'd be very sad if the schoolhouse had to close after everything Barry and Marion have done there. How is Barry? Have you heard any updates?'

'His surgery went fine but Marion doesn't want to do anything rash. She wants him to rest for at least a day, so I said I'd keep things ticking over as best I can until they're back.'

'Ah, good for you. Give us a ring if you need anything.'

'Thank you. I'm ok just now.' A brief vision of the fallen tree flashed in her mind, but it wasn't causing anyone immediate harm. 'We only have one family staying and they're checking out tomorrow. Then Marcus is going the day after that.' Her chest prickled as she said the words. He'd be gone so soon. And he might want to leave earlier as the forecast was wintery... He would most certainly know the dangers of a heavy snowfall in a highland glen.

When he returned, he was in a casual jacket and thick boots. He now resembled a hillwalker, the smart type who bought brand new equipment to look the part but got lost after half an hour on the trails.

'Come on then,' Ross said. 'Let's find horses for you.'

They followed him into the small stable. Someone had hung stocking-shaped hay bags on the doors. 'That's cute,' Willow said.

'Ah, Lena does it,' Ross said. 'The grandkids like to think Santa delivers some extra hay for the horses on Christmas Eve.'

'I quite like it too.'

Ross chuckled. 'This is Mist.' He rubbed the large grey on its sturdy neck. 'He'll do nicely for you, Marcus.'

'I remember him,' Marcus said. 'He doesn't like the high winds. But, my word, he's huge.'

Willow looked him up and down. 'You're not exactly pint-sized yourself.'

He nodded. 'Fair point.'

'He's very good natured,' Ross said. 'Now, Willow. Would you like to have Commodore again?'

'Definitely.' She stroked the beautiful grey and he stood placidly.

'Excellent, let's get them out then.'

Bending and lifting were two things Willow found really difficult, but Marcus looked in his element, helping Ross with the saddles and chatting with him like they were old friends. She was convinced this was real and not the act he put on for the cameras. She remembered her first time riding when she was eight and she'd been petrified. Being petrified was pretty much a permanent state of mind for her at that age, especially in unfamiliar situations. Her mum transmitted her fears by osmosis. On one hand, she wanted Willow to be like everyone else and have just as many new experiences. On the other, she protected her so much from any kind of danger she never learned to take risks. The only reason she allowed Willow to ride was because one of her physios told her riding had a positive impact on children with cerebral palsy. Willow wasn't sure it made a huge difference to her muscle tone or provided the miracle cure her mum would have liked but it gave her something positive and joyful to take part in. Horses weren't saddled with human prejudices. When she was riding, nobody knew she was in splints, had a turned in foot, needed crutches to get around or a wheelchair if she was going far. She was just a girl riding a horse.

In the place she learned to ride, they were all set up with hoists and staff to manoeuvre riders of all abilities into place but Ross's farm wasn't so well equipped. She wasn't too bothered normally. He had a ramp outside and from there she could get on, though it wasn't a very graceful sight and she'd prefer not to appear like a clumsy fool in front of Marcus. He probably wouldn't mind. But she'd like this to be spectacular, not pathetic; the beginning of what should be a beautiful moment.

He looked over at her and smiled. She grinned at his riding hat. Most people looked like twats in them but somehow he managed to pull off the look. Mist was saddled up and Ross adjusted the bridle.

'Your steed awaits, topolina,' Marcus said.

'Top-oh-what?' Willow made her way over, all too aware of her crutch as it dragged through the straw. Heat flooded her cheeks. What now? Could she wait until he was out before she attempted to mount?

Marcus smiled. 'It's an Italian nickname. It suits you.'

'Hang on,' Ross said. 'I almost forgot. I got these handy steps. You'll like them.'

She appreciated the thought but she doubted they'd make this any less ridiculous. Marcus was watching her. She wasn't looking directly back but his eyes were boring into her. He'd be wondering how she was going to do this. As if a magical elf was going to pop out of a chimney, scoop her up and drop her into place.

Ross returned with some wooden steps and Willow swallowed. No way were they high enough.

'I don't think that'll work.'

'No?' Ross frowned at the steps.

'It might.' Marcus led Commodore alongside them. He passed the reins to Ross and climbed to the top step. For him, it would be a simple leg over. 'Well, Cinders, would you like a hand?'

Her eyes widened and she tightened her chin strap. 'What?' Did he mean he was going to lift her? She might die if he touched her. It was what she wanted but at the same time what she dreaded.

'I think Prince Charming is going to sweep you off your feet,' Ross said with a wide grin.

Marcus was half-smiling but his eyes were steely, like the Roman general he was in Willow's fantasies. She walked slowly towards the steps, using her crutch to help her up. She couldn't look at Marcus even when she was at the top, almost touching him. He took her crutch and passed it to Ross.

'You'll have to turn around,' he said, moving to the very edge of the step to give her space and gently taking hold of her upper arms. His touch was so light she barely noticed, but it was there and just as well. If she fainted, he would have had to catch her. She glanced up and caught his eyes. His pupils were wide and inky black. His face was the most appealing shape she could imagine, narrow with chiselled cheekbones and a firm jaw. She turned slowly, and he kept his loose hold on her. With him behind her, she felt wholly in his power. She couldn't watch what he was doing, she just had to trust him.

'Ready?' he asked.

'I think so.'

She expected it to be as ungainly as every other way, but it was so quick she barely had time to think. One second his hands had slipped under her arms, the next she was in the saddle. It was easy, like when her parents lifted her as a child. Marcus was obviously tall and powerfully built, but how strong must he be?

'All ok?' He stepped down one, so they were eye to eye.

'Good. Thanks.'

'No bother. Just watch the fun when I try to get onto Mist. I can see why they named him that. I bet his head's in it most of the time.'

'Good name for a weatherman's horse, though,' she said. Thank god, she'd regained the power of speech and didn't sound like a blithering idiot.

'Ha! Very true.' He strutted over to Mist.

Ross adjusted the stirrups on her feet. 'This guy is great,' he said, grinning over at Marcus. 'I love him on TV, and he's even better in real life.'

'Yeah,' Willow agreed, though there were several people working at e-Broadcast Scotland who wouldn't.

Marcus made one dud attempt at mounting and laughed it off. Mist was so placid, standing by as though everything was normal. Ross started them off in the arena, which was beautifully laid out for indoor lessons with benches around the edge, by showing Marcus how to go, stop and steer. Willow used the time to practise on Commodore. Being back in the saddle was like a second home and felt so natural. Marcus was a quick learner.

Once Ross was satisfied they could manage, he led Marcus out of the barn towards the track.

'Are you alright there, Willow?' Ross called.

'Yes, thanks.' She eased Commodore forward so he was level with Mist. 'The forecast is good today,' she said. 'Bright and cold, but no frost or ice until this evening, so we should be fine just now.'

'Talk about stealing my thunder,' Marcus said.

Oops. She hadn't thought that through but he was smirking.

'You just looked out of your depth,' Willow said.

He cast her a look and she was convinced he remembered saying something similar to her in the newsroom once.

'Like you would in a puddle,' she added.

'You are so damn cheeky.'

She grinned at him, then they both laughed. Ross shook his head, chuckling.

Willow rode ahead, loving the freedom and being so high up. 'How do you feel?' Ross asked Marcus from behind.

'Great.'

'Would you like to go a little on your own?'

'Yeah. That'd be cool.'

Ross unclipped the lead rope. 'Just take it easy.'

Willow waited as Mist plodded up the path.

'This is amazing. What a beautiful horse.' He gave Mist an affectionate rub. They stopped at a gate. In the field beyond was a barn which had seen better days and had a partially caved roof. 'A fixer upper for someone brave.'

'Or mad.' Willow pulled a face at it. 'Cute location though.'

'Perfect for a horse lover.'

'Who doesn't mind getting wet or living in fear of having the roof collapsing on their head.'

Marcus shuddered. 'Terrifying to think that nearly happened to you.'

'Don't remind me. I'm amazed I haven't had nightmares about it.'

'I have,' he said.

'Have you?'

Ross caught up before Marcus could reply. 'Let me help you turn the horse.' He took Mist's bridle, gently steering him around. 'You did well.'

'Thanks,' Marcus said. 'I promised Willow a run for her money.'

Ross chuckled. 'For a first timer, you're doing great.'

Riding back down the path filled Willow with delight. So Marcus had nightmares about the roof caving on her... Did that mean he'd dreamt about her? She cast a look at him and he beamed back at her.

'I could do this every day,' she said.

They followed Ross back towards the barn and he opened the doors to let them in. Willow's gaze was drawn to the far corner where there was a storage area for equipment. At the back was something she hadn't noticed when they were practising. 'Is that a carriage?'

'Certainly is,' Ross said. 'I picked it up a while back. It was in a terrible state but I've been doing it up. I'll need to take it for a test run soon.'

'Wow. I'd love to go in that,' she said. 'It looks so Christmassy too, like something out of an old film.'

'Very cute,' Marcus said. 'Is this something you're going to do? Carriage tours of the area?'

'Oh no,' Ross chuckled. 'I just enjoy tinkering, and maybe I'll do the odd ride or two at the Highland games and that kind of thing.'

'I'll be first in the queue,' Willow said, stifling a yawn. She was exhausted, but not in the dragging fatigued way of a long day on her feet. This was happy tired.

They ambled back to the stables, and Ross led them towards the stalls.

'What goes up must come down,' Marcus said. 'Does Cinders want a lift down from her steed?'

'Oh... I guess.'

He dismounted and lavished some attention on Mist as Willow rode Commodore up to the mounting block. Ross took off her stirrups then went to Mist to undo his saddle. Willow stroked Commodore's mane as Marcus approached. He hopped up onto the top step and smiled.

'Shall we?' He put his hands forward and she rotated slightly.

Oh god. This time, he was going to take her from the front. He waited, his eyes on her.

'Um, yes.'

He slid his hands around her waist and she braced herself on his shoulders. Nothing changed in his expression as he lifted her up and off like she weighed absolutely nothing, and his eyes didn't leave hers. Her heart drummed a thunderous pulse in her ears at the crackling intimacy running along an invisible power line between them. Her leg caught on the saddle but he gently moved it before setting her on her feet. He didn't let go. Where was her crutch? She didn't know where Ross put it, but she needed to ground herself with normal and mundane thoughts.

Marcus looked away first, turning to face the steps, still holding Willow with one hand. His grip was firm and gentle at the same time. She knew he wouldn't let her fall; she was quite safe. He guided her down and she leaned on him.

'Thanks. I'm ok.' Though she'd rather he didn't let go. She was shaky, and with his hold, it was so much easier and warmer.

'I know.' He stopped at the bottom, still supporting her. 'That was the best morning I've had in years.'

'Was it?'

'God, yes.'

She'd enjoyed it too but didn't expect him to be this excited about it – not OCD Marcus with his love of smart suits and immaculate haircuts. When he took off his hat, his hair was flat. He ruffled up and it suited him. Now he was rugged and verging on a bit of rough. Just a little more stubble and he could trade Armani model for The North Face. She would browse their site all day if he was their cover guy.

Her crutch was up against the wall, not far off. Marcus spotted it at the same time as she did and without a word, he walked towards it, gently keeping his hand on her back. The sensation of being protected by him was overwhelming.

'I wish I had this on my doorstep,' he said.

She took her crutch and his hand fell away, leaving her a little giddy in mind, not body. 'Come back and visit another time.'

'Yeah. I will.'

She was pretty sure he wouldn't. She caught his eye and tried to smile. A pang struck her heart. This was a fun little interlude in her normal existence but it couldn't last much longer. Marcus was a celebrity with a city lifestyle to match.

They said goodbye to Ross and the horses and Marcus drove back. They talked a little but were mostly easy with their own thoughts. Willow was still imagining him modelling menswear, starting with padded coats and thermals and continuing until he was lounging on a chaise in nothing but a loincloth, seductively eating grapes.

She cleared her throat – and her head – spotting an unfamiliar car in the otherwise deserted car park. On the front step stood a woman with a clipboard, frowning through the glass window.

'I think that might be someone from the insurance company about the tree.'

'I'll let you out at the door,' Marcus said, pulling up.

Willow wriggled out in her usual clumsy fashion. The woman's attention was now on her and she frowned as Willow dragged herself onto her crutch and headed towards her.

Marcus drove off to park.

'Can I help you?' Willow said. 'Are you here about the tree?'

'No. I'm from the council health and safety team. I'm here to carry out a kitchen inspection.'

Holy shit. Willow's heart plummeted into her stomach.

CHAPTER FOURTEEN

Marcus

In his rear-view mirror, Marcus watched Willow talking to the woman at the front door. A prickle of curiosity niggled him. But did he really care who it was? Normally, he'd get out of the car, march through the front door, and straight to his room without bothering about anyone he happened to pass by. He'd learned to desensitise himself to other people's problems – he had enough of his own. It was easier like that, keeping his head down. Running the risk of people recognising him and having to engage in mindless small talk or dodge unwelcome personal questions took its toll. Call it anti-social, call it rude, call it whatever, but it was a defence mechanism. Letting people in had never been simple for him and shutting them out solved his problems.

But already he'd told Willow things about himself that he rarely told anyone. Something about her made him drop his guard. Could he afford to let that continue? Pushing her away made more sense, but could he do it? He reverse-parked into a space, still watching as Willow unlocked the door with shaky fingers. *What if she's the one you're waiting for?* Was he waiting for someone? Maybe he was, but he hadn't admitted it for fear of it never happening. Could she be the elusive woman he finally made a connection with? The one his soul was drawn to. Someone open and honest.

What's got into me? He never normally even entertained thoughts like this.

He opened the car door once Willow and the woman had gone inside. Confusing emotions raked his mind like they had been doing all day. Lifting her off the horse was a moment of charged electricity. He couldn't deny how much he enjoyed holding her like that even for a few seconds... And the way she looked at him. He shuddered. Where was all this going?

Zapping the car shut, he nipped to the front door. Hopefully, Willow and the woman had gone off to discuss the tree and he could get to the common room unseen, work on the report, and get the footage off to Ginny.

Worst luck, they were still in the foyer. The woman had a phone pressed to her ear. As Marcus clicked the door shut, she lowered it and ended the call.

'Excuse me,' the woman said, putting the phone away. 'Now...' She glanced at Willow, then Marcus, and her eyes flickered with the usual recognition. 'Are you two the owners? Mr and Mrs Corbett?'

'No,' Willow said. 'They're not here. I'm looking after the place.'

The woman's eyes leapt back to Marcus.

'I'm just visiting.'

'Oh, right. Do I know you from somewhere? Do you work for the Council?'

'No, sorry.' He gave a little shrug. 'I should go and leave you to discuss the tree.'

'What is this about a tree?' the woman said, half-smiling, half-frowning. 'I'm here to inspect the kitchen. I'm from the Environmental Health Department in the council.'

'The kitchen?' Marcus's focus darted to Willow, and she met his gaze with a helpless expression. He guessed she was as clueless about health and safety procedures as he was. But, shit, he'd prepared the food yesterday and hadn't even thought about health and safety. There must be protocols and policies, but he was damned if he knew what they were. All the leftover food he'd made was in boxes in the fridge. Should it be labelled? Tested? He ran his hand over his jaw. 'Has someone complained?' he asked.

'No,' the woman said. 'We do spot checks every year.'

'Marion said it was due soon,' Willow said.

'Well, it's overdue, truth be told. We're behind in our schedule and we've been focused on larger facilities first, but I'm here now.' The woman smiled at Willow and Marcus. 'Now, can I see the kitchen?'

Willow threw Marcus a wide-eyed look behind the woman's back. Now was the time for him to head straight for his room or disappear through the common room doors and leave her to it. Normally, it wouldn't bother him in the slightest. It was none of his business. But, hell, this time it was. He'd helped out last night, and if something was wrong, it was his fault. And more to the point, he liked Willow. He wanted to stand by her and support her through this. She shouldn't have to face this alone. They were in this together.

'You know when I said I was a visitor?' He caught up with the woman.

'Yes.' She squinted at him over the top of her glasses.

'I'm also a friend... of the family, the owners, you know?'

'That's nice.'

'Sometimes I help out when it's busy. So, I'll come with you too.'

'It's ok,' Willow muttered aside. 'You don't have to.' But her expression said otherwise. Her eyes were wide and unblinking.

'I missed your name,' Marcus said to the woman.

'Nicola Ballantyne.' She pushed the doors to the kitchen.

Marcus hung back for a second, keeping his eyes on her, then beckoning Willow over. She edged up close.

'What?' she whispered.

'I cocked up last night, didn't I?' He hunched down, so he was level with her ear. 'All that food's in the fridge with no labels or anything.'

'Shit.' She covered her mouth. 'Oh no!' She froze with an expression of horror. He followed her sightline as a fluffy tail disappeared through the door. 'Marshmallow!' she hissed. 'If Nicola sees her, we're screwed.'

'Go in and talk to her,' Marcus muttered. 'I'll try to get Marshmallow out.'

He let Willow in before him. Nicola had her clipboard on the work surface and was ticking boxes. 'Can I see the temperature control book, please?'

Willow seemed to know what she was talking about and lifted a red folder from a shelf. As she presented it to Nicola, Marcus edged around the stainless-steel prep table to where a fluffy white tail twitched. If its owner was eyeing a mouse, they were doubly screwed. Mice in the kitchen surely equalled an instant fail.

Trying to keep a low profile when he was six foot five was always a struggle but trying to do it in a compact kitchen with an eagle-eyed inspector was almost impossible. And what the hell was he actually supposed to do? Pick up the cat? He'd never picked up a cat before. *How do you...?* This was going to be impossible. Amber eyes glared at him and the end of a tail twitched. Marcus smiled hopefully and Marshmallow meowed. 'Shhh,' he mouthed through gritted teeth, throwing up his hands.

'And who is in charge of the food prep?' Nicola asked. Marcus cringed and crept further around the table, beckoning to the cat. Marshmallow looked at him like he was deranged and right now, she had a point.

'Barry, the owner,' Willow said. 'But he's had a fall and is in hospital, so I'm covering and yesterday, we had... a visiting cook.'

'Ok.' Nicola made a note on a clipboard. 'Can I see the food storage area? Then I'll look in the fridge.'

'The larder is in here.' Willow opened a door off the side of the room and Nicola disappeared inside.

Marcus lunged for the cat and it jumped onto the prep table. 'Fuck's sake.'

'Here.' Willow propped her crutch on the table, grabbed Marshmallow, and chucked her out of the door. 'You're in trouble,' she muttered after her. 'Quick.' She grabbed a roll of what looked like yellow tape from a box on a shelf next to the folders and thrust it at Marcus. 'Can you write on these what's in the boxes in the fridge and a date for when they should be eaten – tomorrow probably. We didn't test the food temperature either.'

'Shit. I hope no one gets salmonella.' Marcus grabbed the yellow roll of food labels and started scribbling.

'Oh, god, don't say that.' Willow peeled the labels as soon as he'd written them and with trembling fingers, stuck them onto the boxes. Nicola was still shuffling about in the cupboard. They didn't have long.

'Bloody hell.' Marcus scrawled as fast as he could. Willow shoved the last label on and closed the fridge door as Nicola came out. Marcus thrust the labels inside his jacket and folded his arms.

Nicola opened the fridge and scanned through it, making notes on her clipboard. 'This looks fine,' she said. 'When you have a visiting cook, you should always ensure they've read the guidelines and are adhering to them. Not recording a food temperature can be enough to shut you down if there's a serious outbreak of food poisoning.'

Willow bit her lip and Marcus's heart went out to her. This was his fault but she'd get the brunt of it. How would Marion and Barry take this? Surely they couldn't blame her if they failed? She'd only done her best.

'If this is the food cooked yesterday, it should be discarded. If it hasn't been cooked to temperature, then it's unsafe.'

'It was cooked to the correct temperature,' Marcus said. 'It just wasn't recorded.'

'That's impossible to know without an accurate probe test,' Nicola said. 'And as far as we know, this wasn't carried out.'

'Right.' *That's my tail shoved firmly between my legs.*

'So... Are we going to be shut down?' Willow chewed on a cuticle.

'I shouldn't think so,' Nicola said. 'I'll have to mark you down for it, and I'll need you to contact everyone who ate here and check none of them are unwell. Please call me when you have this information. I'll send my report within a few weeks and make it a requirement for more robust procedures for visiting cooks to be put in place and to ensure they have access to the guidelines. I'll move your next inspection forward to ensure this is implemented.'

'Ok,' Willow said. 'Is there anything else you need to see?'

'No. That's all. Everything else is in good order.'

Willow showed her out, and Marcus flopped onto a padded bench in the foyer next to the twinkling Christmas tree.

'Oh god.' Willow returned and slumped down beside him. 'What a nightmare. I thought she was going to shut us down. How would I have explained that to Barry?'

Marcus stretched his legs and crossed them at the ankles, then leaned his head against the wall. 'I'm so sorry.' He rolled his head to look at her. 'That was all my fault. I didn't think to check regulations or anything like that.'

She turned to face him, resting her head on the wall too. They were face to face, only inches away, close enough for their breath to mingle in the void between them.

'It was as much my fault,' she said quietly. 'Why didn't I think to call Barry and ask about the procedures? I remember him talking about the probe and temperature controls before but it wasn't really my job. I've occasionally helped with breakfasts and lunches when it's busy but Barry was always there to do all the other bits.' She let out a long sigh. 'What a nightmare. How can so much happen in just a few days? I wish... I don't know.'

'Hey.' He gave her a little nudge. 'Don't worry too much. You did your best. How much worse would it have been if that family hadn't got their special meal? The inspection's done. Just check none of the family got food poisoning, which I'm confident they haven't, and everything will be fine.'

'It just feels a bit crap. I have one job, and I screw up.'

'It's not one job, Willow. It's not even the job you're here to do. You've been doing everybody's job plus helping me, plus dealing with acts of god. It's been a tough shift.'

'I shouldn't have gone riding, should I? That was crazy. I should have stayed here and got stuff done.'

'Look, I'm sorry if I dragged you away. I shouldn't have, but don't beat yourself up. You deserve a break.' His hand strayed toward hers, and he was seized by the need to hold it. Gently, he took it. Her pupils dilated, reflecting the dancing colours on the Christmas tree lights. 'Life is a learning curve. You've done your best in a tricky situation.'

Slowly her gaze travelled from his face to their linked hands, and she twirled a lock of hair between her fingertips. Her shoulders sagged. 'I took this job because it gave me a chance to do something different, something for myself, but now I've messed up.'

'You haven't.' He watched her closely until she looked back. Her lips were so close he could almost feel them on his.

She sighed. 'I just want to—'

The front door opened, and he leaped back so quickly he knocked a side table and almost toppled the Christmas tree. He grabbed a branch and steadied it just as Willow took hold of her crutch and pulled herself to her feet. The family had returned from their outing. When they entered, they brought a blast of cold air with them.

'How are you feeling?' Willow asked.

'Very well, thank you,' the man said. 'We've had a lovely walk but it's very chilly now.'

'Can I just check none of you have food poisoning symptoms?'

'Nothing, why?'

'We had a health and safety inspection and yesterday's food temperature wasn't recorded. It's probably nothing to worry about but we have to check and make you aware.'

'We're all fine, thanks and the food last night was delicious,' the mum said.

'Great. Well, let me know if anything changes. Why not go and warm up in the common room?'

The woman smiled on the way past, steering her son towards the stairs. 'Hello again.' She smiled at Marcus as he replaced a fallen bauble on the tree. 'When will your report go out about this place? It's such a godsend. I'd be gutted if it closed.'

'I'm going to work on it now. It'll be next week before the full report is out.'

'And were you also our chef last night?' the dad asked.

Marcus nodded. 'The one who didn't record the temperatures, yes.'

They all chuckled.

'A man of many talents.' The mum beamed.

'Well, I don't know about that.'

'It's true,' Willow said.

Marcus half coughed a smile and tugged his neckline. 'Um, thanks. I should get going. I need to upload the footage of today's interviews.'

'Of course,' the mum said. 'We'll let you get on. You'll be pleased to know we're picking up a fish supper tonight, so you won't have to cook us anything.'

'Probably safer. I think I'm officially sacked. But it was my pleasure cooking for you.'

The mum's smile was radiant as they headed up the stairs. Willow caught Marcus's eye and a tremor of unspoken desire surged between them. He glanced away and edged towards the common room door before the urge sunk in or nudged him to make a move he might regret. Now was the time to put some distance between Willow and him before his hormones pushed him over a cliff.

CHAPTER FIFTEEN

Willow

> *Cold fronts are moving*
> *far out in the ocean... If*
> *they collide over us, we'll*
> *have a snow commotion!*

Willow returned to the office and tried to focus on the jobs she was supposed to be doing – the ones she should have been doing when she was out riding horses and gallivanting with Marcus. *Seriously, what am I playing at?*

But she couldn't concentrate. Her mind kept wandering. *Must phone the health and safety inspector and tell her the family are ok.* She lifted her phone and waited but it rang off, so she left a quick message.

She then fired off a text to Hayley with shaky fingers because she needed to vent.

WILLOW: Omg... had a really bad day. Barry and Marion are away and the H&S inspector showed up. Got into trouble because I let a guest cook dinner last night. Eek. Xx

She also had to call Marion and update her but that call rang off too. Willow forced her head down and got back to the admin work she was paid to do. But she just couldn't concentrate. She pulled out her phone again and messaged her mum. Now wasn't the time to tell her about the fallen-in roof. There may never be a time for that. Instead, she asked her if she and dad were planning on coming for Christmas. They weren't great travellers and never liked to drive too far. Mum wasn't fond of public transport either, which meant getting anywhere was always a big task.

I could always go to Glasgow. That hadn't been an appealing option last year but if Marcus was going to be there... She almost laughed out loud. Like she'd ever see him again after his time here was done. All she'd do in Glasgow would be to pine and watch reruns of *Destination Forecast*, wishing she'd bump into him on trips to see the lights at George Square.

Her mum's icon appeared and three dots bounced up and down for a long time before a reply pinged through.

MUM: we'd love to come to see you for Christmas, but travelling in December is always risky. I'm not sure it's sensible to make firm plans until nearer the time. We should wait until we see the forecast. I adore Marcus Bowman. He was on TV the other day and I thought he said he was at the Schoolhouse where you worked

*but your dad was talking and I didn't catch the whole thing. Was
he there? XX*

Willow pulled a face. Her mum liked Marcus better than
Rocky Rainman... Shocking! Not that she knew who he really
was.

Such a shame her parents had to live so far away. How much
nicer it would be if they were just down the road and she could
drop in and visit them. Even her mum would be able to drive
from Glenbriar to the schoolhouse.

Later in the afternoon, the front door clicked open and a
cheery voice called out, 'Helloooo!'

Willow got to her feet, recognising Hayley's voice. Hayley
burst in before Willow had reached the office door.

'Willow.' Hayley pulled her in for a hug.

'What are you doing here?' Willow relaxed into the hug for a
moment. Hayley wasn't much older than her, but she was taller
and her hold was comforting and very welcome. She'd always
been the best cousin.

'I got your message and I suddenly realised I hadn't been to
see you for ages. I was doing a home job for a lady outside the
village who's not been very well and can't get into the salon. We
don't normally but she's a longstanding client, so for a one off,
you know, especially at Christmas.' She stepped back and gently
pulled out Willow's long hair. 'You could do with a trim yourself.
But anyway, it was just a couple of minutes out of the way to get

here, so I thought I'd nip in and see you. Where are Marion and Barry?'

'They were visiting relatives in Inverness and Barry fell and broke his wrist. He had to have surgery. I'm not sure when they'll be back but I'm so out of my depth.'

'Aw, sweet Willow, my beauty.' Hayley clutched Willow's face and took a long look at her. Ironic really that she chose to call Willow a beauty when she was gorgeous herself with long, glossy chestnut hair – always immaculate, of course, seeing as she was a hairdresser – and equally dark eyes with luscious lashes to boot. 'I'm sure you're doing your best. Why did you let a guest cook?' She grinned. 'Wouldn't it have been better to do it yourself?'

'Frying eggs and bacon is my limit. Cooking a fancy meal from scratch is beyond me.' Even lifting heavy pots was a struggle.

'So, what's happening? Are they shutting you down?'

'No. The inspector is making recommendations. I hope Barry and Marion aren't too angry. Marion isn't picking up the phone.'

'But the people who ate the food aren't ill or anything, are they?'

'No, they seemed fine. I just feel like I've messed up.'

Hayley cocked her head to the side, her twinkling eyes full of sympathy. 'These things always feel worse straight after they've happened but try not to worry.'

Willow dragged in a sigh. The health and safety inspection was just the tip of the iceberg of niggling thoughts. Hayley was the only person in the world Willow had ever told about Marcus...

Mostly about how she'd overheard his conversation with Ginny. She'd omitted mentioning the Valentine card. But Hayley was quick to pick up on vibes and guessed Willow had deeper feelings than the ones she'd confessed to. Hayley's anger on Willow's behalf was always welcome but what would she think now if Willow told her it had all been a mistake and Marcus was here, right now? Not only that but he was the chef and they'd been riding together? Technically, she was supposed to be working, and this didn't seem the right time for a big confession, especially when she didn't really know how she felt herself.

With Marcus safely out of the way, there was no need to mention him, and it gave her libido a chance to cool down. She wasn't used to getting wound up around people and the lines were getting blurrier by the second. After the euphoria of the ride, going straight to the inspection was quite a slap.

'A tree fell on the bungalow yesterday too and smashed the roof.'

'What?' Hayley gaped at her. 'That's even worse than an inspection. You could have been killed.'

'I wasn't in it when it happened and an emergency engineer had to go in yesterday and turn off the power. He said nothing heavy had fallen in the rooms. It's not safe to enter though now the structure's been damaged.' Willow shrugged. 'All my stuff's in there. I'm having to wear old clothes from the spares' cupboard.'

'Never mind about your clothes. Just thank heavens you're safe.' Hayley pulled her in for another hug. 'I'll bring you some spare clothes up at the weekend.'

'It's all happening this week.'

Hayley looked out the window. 'What does Scotland's favourite weather presenter tell us about the snow?'

'Shh,' Willow said. Hayley was the only person who knew her secret but she didn't know that Scotland's second favourite weather presenter was in the same building.

'No one's listening.' Hayley grinned and checked her phone. 'Rocky hasn't made a forecast for a while.'

'Rocky's been busy.' Hundreds of notifications had pinged in from followers but for some reason it felt duplicitous forecasting with Marcus here, plus she wanted to think of a way of saying something nice about him. Marcus was a good weather presenter, really good. He might look like a frontman who had a team of researchers telling him what to say, but he wasn't. Willow had seen him at work, and he knew his stuff, but he was bound by the restrictions of TV. He couldn't be controversial or put himself on the line. She was free to do what she wanted. If she made a prediction and it was wrong, she gave herself a low score and told the punters she must try harder. So far, it hadn't happened often.

She'd stuck her neck out, saying they'd have snow by the end of the week, and she stood by it. A low-pressure zone was moving across the Atlantic that could go anywhere. But she had a good feeling it was coming their way, and if it collided with the one hastening in from the east, they were in for a load of snow. She was sure Marcus had seen the signs too, but it was simply a possibility for him, not a dead cert.

'Snow's on its way,' she said. 'It'll be here possibly by tomorrow night and definitely by Saturday morning.'

'Oh no, I'm working on Saturday.'

'Sorry.' Willow smiled.

'I should get back.' Hayley checked her phone again. 'I have an evening appointment – someone off to a Christmas party, lucky thing.' She kissed Willow's forehead. 'If it's not too snowy at the weekend, I'll nip up with the clothes. Keep messaging me, my beauty, and let me know you're ok.'

'I will.'

'You're the best cousin in the world.' Hayley hugged her tight.

'Am I?' Willow let out a little laugh. 'Even better than that cousin on your dad's side?'

Hayley giggled. 'Aidan? Well, I love him too but in a totally different way. And he's still in Canada, so he's totally useless for cousinly hugs.'

'Well, I'll have to do then.'

'You definitely will. In fact, when I come up at the weekend, I'll tell you some crazy gossip about Aidan.'

'Can't wait.' Willow waved her off. Normally she loved Hayley's gossip about everyone but this time, she didn't feel quite as intrigued as usual.

She couldn't shake the heavy doom that one of the guests would fall ill. After the triumphs of Marcus's gorgeous dinner, it seemed so unfair. She slumped into the seat at her desk and stared at the screen until the words fuzzed and merged. The happy-tired feeling from this morning had completely worn off, and all-consuming fatigue had taken over. Her mind crawled over a mountain of thoughts. She needed to make sure the guests got an early breakfast the next day as they were leaving. She was expecting someone to cut the tree. And there was Marcus. He was right there, wading to the forefront of her brain. A few hours ago, they were sitting in the foyer on the bench, so very close. Willow wanted to tell him everything, her dreams and how she wished to be a forecaster like him. But all she could think about was how close his lips had been and how strong his hand felt as he held hers. Wildly beautiful imaginings took over her brain for a second, and she visualised a world where none of the constraints of the real world existed. She could ride off into the sunset with Marcus and everything would be fine.

But it wasn't real. *Ugh!*

'Hey.'

She jumped. Speaking of the devil, Marcus stood at the office door.

'Everything ok?' Willow asked. He didn't look like he had had an onset of vomiting, so that was a good start.

'Fine. My weather report from this morning has gone out, but I've got a live to do shortly.'

'And you want me to help?'

'Is that ok? I feel bad always asking you.'

'It's fine. I could do with a break.' Which was stupid, as she'd done nothing much other than list all the things she should be doing.

'Is that inspection still bothering you?'

'Yes.' She got to her feet. 'It's so frustrating. And I can't stop thinking that one of the guests will get ill, and the schoolhouse will get closed down because of me.'

'Because of us,' Marcus said. 'If it comes to an investigation, I'll put my hands up and let everyone know it was me.'

'There's no point. Why ruin your career too? What's the point when we might be closing, anyway?'

'I'm working on that. If I can help keep this place open, I will.'

'I wish I'd called Barry and asked for advice.' She always made stupid mistakes. 'This is partly why my parents wrapped me in cotton wool for so long. I'm a bloody liability.'

'That's not true. Sounds like they wanted to protect you. The world's a harsh place.'

She let out a sigh.

'Were Marion and Barry angry with you?'

'I haven't got hold of them yet, but Marion never really gets mad about anything. Barry can get a bit grumpy occasionally but he's usually calm and kind.'

'Well then, you shouldn't worry. They'll appreciate everything you've done. Come on, let's get some air and try to forget about it.'

Willow followed him out, ignoring the tired pains creeping up her legs. Her meds were in the unsafe accommodation and she hadn't phoned up for new ones. What had she done, other than moon over Marcus? *What's the matter with me?* She was a total novice around guys but that wouldn't change unless she did something about it. What would someone with more confidence do with a guy they fancied? Because let's be real, she'd fancied Marcus for ages. Should she have flirted with him? Made a move? What kind of move? They were almost all alone in the schoolhouse – a place with several spare bedrooms. If that wasn't the prime site for a one-night stand or two, then what was?

Cringeworthy visions of her trying to pull off something like that played before her. Nope. She couldn't. She could barely bring herself to imagine a physical encounter between them that wasn't humiliating for her and completely off-putting for him.

'Ok,' Marcus said, shattering her musings. 'It's Baltic, now.' He rubbed his hands together. 'I'm live in fifteen, so let's get set up.'

Willow knew the drill now and could get the camera on the tripod while he wired himself up. He was super suave in his long black wool coat as he went through his routine of loosening up his smile and straightening his tie and lapels. Maybe it was how he dispelled nerves before he went on air, though he always looked like the pinnacle of confidence and ease. She didn't interrupt him.

He pressed in his earpiece. 'Ready,' he said, nodding at Willow to put on the camera. He ran the sound and visual checks while Willow watched and listened. She'd never tire of just looking at him – the weather god.

'Thank you, David,' he said and Willow knew that was him live. 'Yes, I'm still in Highland Perthshire. It's already dark as you can see and we're fast approaching the shortest day. This far north, the daylight hours are shorter in winter. And it's going to be a cold and crisp night for most Highland areas tonight with a widespread frost for everywhere above Perth as you'll see on your screen.'

Willow peered around to check the wireless mini-screen attached to the camera, where Marcus could see everything that was on the viewer's screens. Somehow, the technicians in the studio could flip seamlessly from that to his incoming feed. It was all beyond her how they did it.

What would it be like to stand on his side and do a live forecast? She remembered pretending to do it in her parent's house as a child and them laughing at how cute it sounded. But when she attempted to talk on camera these days, she got tongue-tied and her voice sounded odd. No one would want to listen to her bumbling on. If she'd set herself up as Willow Roxburgh's weather and done live reports, she'd never have got the following Rocky did. How could she compete with the might of Marcus?

People tuned in as much to see his smile and melt in his sex appeal as to listen to the forecast.

Marcus continued his broadcast and it sounded as accurate and conservative as ever. She couldn't hear what was being said in his earpiece as he answered some questions from the presenter, but she didn't mind. The lovesick fool in her was captivated by his face, just like his viewers.

'I don't generally look at his reports,' Marcus said and Willow's chest tightened. How obvious whose reports he was talking about. 'Since his snow forecast, I haven't heard much. There's still a weather front in the Atlantic that I'm keeping an eye on but it could have dispersed by the time it reaches here. There's another front moving in the opposite direction and if these two fronts collide, then we're talking about a white out. In meteorological terms, they're still a long way off and lots can change. There is a possibility of snow for some areas this week but that's all I'm saying.'

He finished off then ripped out his earpiece.

'I wish that dick would stop asking me about Rocky Rainman on air. He knows I hate him.'

Willow cringed behind the camera as she loosened it from the tripod. Marcus may not know she was Rocky Rainman, but she still felt the verbal punch to her ego.

'I don't know who he is, but I'd like nothing better than to sink his little operation,' Marcus continued.

'Is he really doing you any harm?' Willow asked quietly.

'He's undermining me and my profession. His bullying makes me look like a rookie or a thicko. People think I'm a coward because I won't make a big hotshot prediction, but it's not that simple. I'm not an entertainer. This is my job. I could make wild forecasts based on my experience, and they might be right ninety per cent of the time, but that isn't the point. I hate how he's turned my job into a circus and a fucking competition.'

Well, that was a fairly comprehensive rant. While she'd been angry with Marcus when she first started the idea, she didn't do it to discredit or undermine him. In fact, her followers had started it. She'd added funny asides and in-jokes if she predicted something Marcus missed, but she shouldn't have. It had got out of hand. She saw that now.

Confessing was out of the question. How could she when he'd just vowed to help save the schoolhouse? As she looked at him, she saw murder in his eyes, reflected in the streetlamp's glow. No way would he take a confession well.

'I think he's got wind of me being after him,' he said as he packed away the camera.

'What makes you think that?'

'Because he's pissed off. E-Broadcast admins have been monitoring his accounts, and there hasn't been much activity according to David.'

'Really?'

'Apparently he's usually very active when the weather is this changeable. Maybe I've scared him into submission and for good.

Pathetic little tit.' He bundled the equipment into his bag and zapped open his car boot.

Willow narrowed her eyes at him. This was the rude and ugly Marcus who used to inhabit the newsroom they worked in – the one who got everyone's backs up. Even though he didn't know who he was talking to, it still niggled at her.

But she couldn't really blame him. As soon as they got in, Rocky Rainman would have a forecast and some kind words for Marcus Bowman... Hopefully that would start to placate him a little and the thaw would begin.

CHAPTER SIXTEEN

Willow

Rocky's been quiet, but never fear. Now he's back with updates here... Christmas is coming and so is the snow. Tomorrow evening, just so you know. Over the countryside and over the town; there's gonna be a midwinter snowdown!

Willow typed in her forecast, then added:

And remember folks, it's Christmastime.
That means parties, mince pies and wine.
It's also a time for love and good cheer.
Let's all be friends for the rest of the year.
I sense a change, a really good omen...

We should all be kind to Marcus Bowman!

Would that do any good? Time would tell. Willow pinched some of the food Marcus had cooked the day before and heated it in the microwave. No way was she throwing it out. She was sure he cooked it fine by normal standards. Her cooking wasn't up to much and she was too exhausted to think about meals. As she waited for it to heat, she went to the common room to check if Marcus wanted anything. She approached him hesitantly. Her leg muscles tensed even more as she got closer. Was he still in a vile mood?

'Hey. I'm making some dinner. Well, heating the leftovers. Can I get you anything?'

'Rocky Rainman's head on a stick.' He lounged back on the armchair he was sitting in and steepled his fingers.

Ok. Still angry then.

'I'm not sure I can do that.'

'Just when I hoped he'd buggered off, here he is.' He waved his phone about.

Willow tried to smile but didn't quite meet his eye. How could she look at him when he was being so insulting?

'And what the hell is this? He's even got a poem about me.'

'Oh? Isn't that good?'

'Good? Have you seen it? It's a total piss-take. His followers are having a field day. "I'll be kind to Marky-boy even though he can't predict a fart after a night on the beans. All hail the rainman." What utter dumbfuckery.'

'If he's asking people to be nice, isn't that good? It sounds like he's trying to make peace.'

'Yeah, right.' He smacked his palm on the arm of the chair. 'I'm sick of him.'

'Maybe some food would help?' Heat stung the back of her neck as guilt attacked her skin. She didn't want to hurt Marcus like this but she couldn't give up forecasting. Not now. Obviously her idea had completely backfired. Maybe she should go for a more direct appeal to her followers.

'Yeah, ok, thanks. Just whatever's left,' he said. 'And is there any more wine stashed away? Other than the one I cooked with yesterday?'

'I'm not sure. I'll have a look.' But she raised her eyebrow. Was brooding with a bottle of wine a good idea?

The guests had got their chippy tea and gone straight to their room for an early night as they were leaving the next morning. Willow served Marcus his food before withdrawing to the kitchen. She'd eat in there and avoid further confrontation.

As she finished, the kitchen door opened, and Marcus came in with his plate. 'Why are you in here?'

'Thought I'd leave you in peace.'

'Right.' He put down the plate and frowned. 'I wouldn't have minded.'

Willow's back felt doubled up as she got to her feet. She needed to lie down soon but she couldn't ignore him.

'Are you ok?' He eyed her over.

'Fine.' What a lie. Every step she took was an effort. She staggered across the kitchen with her plate.

'Listen, I know it's not my business, but can't you take ibuprofen or something until you can get your regular medication?'

Shit. It must be really obvious. How bad did it look? 'I'm fine.'

He arched an eyebrow. 'Why not join me with some wine? It's lonely drinking by myself.'

She swallowed. 'Well, ok. Just a small one.' She didn't want to admit that he was one of the few people who'd ever noticed when she was hurting. Hayley could spot the signs and occasionally Marion, but other people just thought it was what she looked like all the time. The chronic pain that went with cerebral palsy was often overlooked. Then again, she hadn't helped herself that day with all the rushing about. She couldn't even resign herself to her wheelchair as it was folded up in the staff bungalow, possibly crushed under rubble if the ceiling had caved under the weight of the tree. She wasn't stupid enough to go and look. Her new meds were on their way but she couldn't get to the chemist until the next morning, so this was her for the rest of the night.

'Would you like anything else?' She pulled out her brightest smile.

Marcus ran his forefinger along the worktop, then looked up at her. 'Just your company. Come sit by the fire with me.'

Her eyes almost popped out. 'Are you... Well, serious?'

'It's my middle name. I'm always serious. Come on. Let's get you a wine and put the seal on a crazy day. Horses, health inspectors and horrid weathermen.'

'Are you talking about yourself with the horrid weathermen?' Willow grabbed a spare glass and followed him out of the kitchen.

'Totally.' He lifted the bottle of wine on the table and poured a measure into hers.

She wasn't a big drinker, but why not? The numbing powers of alcohol were legendary after all.

'To an insane day.' Marcus raised his glass and clinked it on hers.

She hesitated, then swigged some back before moving to a seat by the fire. Blissful warmth penetrated her body as she slouched in an armchair and took a sip. Marcus stretched his long legs in front of him and crossed his ankles.

'Did you put the fire on?' She took another sip.

'Yeah. I hope that was ok.'

'Fine. Rather you than me. I find it so awkward. You know, with all the bending.'

'Sure.' His eyes didn't leave hers for a long moment and her heart rate increased.

'I could do with a footstool.' She glanced around. There was one in here somewhere. She spotted it near the window and made to get up.

'Stay.' Marcus leapt to his feet. 'Allow me, topolina.'

'Tell me what that means. It better not be something cheeky.'

'It's not. Now, here you go.' He dropped the stool at her feet. 'Shall I?' He scooped his arm under her ankles. She'd barely given a nod when he gently raised her legs and pushed the stool under her. Her heart missed several beats and she held her breath. Did he have any idea what he did to her? She doubted it. He was just doing a good deed. For a grumpy git, he had his moments of kindness.

'Toasty, isn't it?' He reclaimed his seat and recrossed his legs. 'Maybe I'm suffering a middle age decline and I can finally appreciate log fires and comfy armchairs. All I need is a pair of slippers.'

'You're hardly middle-aged.' She took a sip of the wine and screwed up her nose. It wasn't a taste she'd ever acquired, but she needed it tonight.

'I'll be thirty-eight in May. That's definitely too old for life to begin and too young for it to end, so it must be the middle.'

'You don't even look that.' And even if he did, he suited it. He had a chiselled look and well-set features that came with maturity.

'Well, there's no escaping it whether I look it or not. Less than thirty months until I hit the big four-O.'

She smirked. 'Isn't that when life begins?'

'So they say. But what about all the stuff that went before?'

'The warm-up?'

He chuckled and took another sip. 'I like your thinking.'

'My mum had me at thirty-nine and eleven months. So, I guess a new life did begin for her.'

'Wow. And you're her first?'

'She tried before, but it never happened.'

'Then she hit the jackpot.'

'Did she?'

His eyes travelled down her face. 'I'd say. She couldn't get a nicer daughter, could she?'

Heat flooded her cheeks. And it was nothing to do with the fire, though hopefully he'd think it was. 'Thanks.' She took a bigger sip than she meant to and almost choked. 'Don't you normally reserve that charm for when the cameras are running?'

'I do. But it was worth saying and true.'

She took another glug of her drink, even though it burned her throat. His gaze bored through her, but she didn't rise. How could she? If she looked at him, she'd betray herself. How could she hide how much she fancied him? *Go to bed before you make a fool of yourself.* From the corner of her eye, she spied him downing his remaining wine.

She set her glass on the side table, rested her head to the side and stroked her ponytail over her shoulder. Her weary eyes closed for a moment and she smiled to herself. What a day.

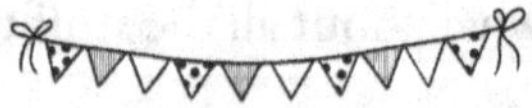

'Willow.'

A low voice was talking somewhere in the darkness. She tried to focus on the words, but they were muffled and distant. Her eyes struggled to adjust to the dim lighting.

'Willow,' the voice said again.

Something warm was on her shoulder. She sighed as a familiar woodsy fragrance pervaded her senses, reminding her of Marcus. The pressure on her shoulder intensified and she forced her eyes open, coming face to face with the man himself.

'What is it?' She tried to move into a better position but had seized up in the corner of the chair.

'Nothing,' he said gently. 'But it's getting late, and you'll crick your neck sleeping like that for too long.'

'I wasn't asleep.'

'Well, you've been sitting silently with your eyes closed for the last forty minutes then.'

'Forty minutes?'

'Yup.'

It was too late. Her neck was already cricked. Her back had seized up and her legs felt like useless jelly poles. 'Oh god.' She rested her forehead on the armrest and tried not to look at Marcus's gorgeous face – so close to her. *Please leave now.* So she could get started on the ungainly excursion upstairs… assuming she could move at all.

'Hey,' he said. 'Let me help you.'

'I don't need help.' How the lies flowed. It wasn't that she didn't need it. She didn't want it. Not from him.

Why did he have to see her like this at all?

'I know you don't *need* it, because I know what you're like. But take it because it's here. I didn't need your help to work the cameras. I didn't need it to ride the horses. But I took it because it made life easier and a lot more pleasant.'

Slowly, she turned her eyes to him. 'And how can you help me? What are you going to do? Carry me upstairs?'

'If you want.' He looked deadly serious. Could he actually do that? The fairy tale lover in her wanted him to do it just because. Never mind her damned legs, she just wanted to be carried upstairs by this hunk of Italian beef.

'I need to lock up before I go anywhere.'

'I can do that,' he said.

'But I should...'

'Hey. This has been a tough day. Let me. No one will think any the worse of you if I do it. I did it the other night when you were in the bungalow.'

'That was different.'

He shook his head. 'Mama used to say I was a real stubborn Taurus, but you... You're something else. But guess what? Mama was right. And I'm locking up.'

'Fine.' She let out a long sigh as Marcus left the room. Now alone, she tried to manipulate her limbs into a position where she might be able to stand on them. With her meds, she probably wouldn't have got into such a state, but her muscles were tense and her body exhausted. She'd barely shuffled forward on the seat when he returned.

'Ready, topolina?'

'You're not actually going to carry me, are you?'

'Only if you want me to.'

'All the way upstairs?'

He glanced around with a slight frown. 'Sure.'

She twisted her hair and pulled it tight under her chin. Were all her Christmas dreams about to come true? Cinders was going to the ball... Well, up the stairs in the arms of Prince Occasionally-Charming. 'Ok. If you can, it's probably the easiest way.'

'Come on then.' He moved closer and her heart walloped her eardrums.

She couldn't believe she was letting him do this. As if getting on the horse wasn't enough. He leaned over, slipped an arm beneath her legs and the other under her arm and around her back, then straightened up, taking her with him. She looped her wrist around his neck and it was the most glorious feeling in the world. They were eye to eye and he smiled at her.

'Just don't drop me.'

He stepped forward. 'Can't make any promises.'

She glared at him and he grinned, sending tingles through her body and making her alive with dancing butterflies. Could she draw him in and kiss him? He was close enough. Too close, but it gave her the warm fuzzies. Her breathing was rapid and uncontrolled. She hated the thought of needing help, but now she didn't want this moment to end. She wanted to live in his strong arms, be swept off her feet in his hold forever.

He shuffled her a little as they reached the door. 'Turn off the light,' he said.

She flicked the switch on the way past. He crossed the foyer and turned up the stairs, taking her with him like she weighed nothing.

'You're not even breaking a sweat,' she said as she brushed lightly against the evergreen foliage looped over the banister.

'You weigh less than my camera bag.'

She grinned. 'You just like showing off.'

'Don't be cheeky. You don't want me to drop you, remember?'

She cocked her head, so it touched his shoulder. She knew he wouldn't drop her. Being here felt safer than anywhere else in the world.

'Which room are you in?' he asked.

'The first one.' She needed it to be as close to the stairs as possible. 'Oh, shit.'

'What?'

'My crutch is downstairs.'

'Don't worry. I'll go back for it.' He ducked down still holding her and turned the handle. Any second now and Marcus Bowman would be in her bedroom. Her fantasies collided with reality. He turned around and nudged the door open with his back.

'There you go, safely delivered.' He gently set her down on the bed.

Would he sit beside her? A fraction of a second passed with the thought and him looming over her before he released her and headed for the door.

'I'll be back in a sec.'

Willow sat on the end of the bed, breathing slowly. Her heart split in two, one side wanting to bask in the joy of the moment, the other ready to weep that it was over. She didn't dare think what Marcus must make of her – the helpless weakling. The pain in her body urged her to lie down and rest but adrenaline was fighting it, keeping her alert and bombarding her with thoughts and wild ideas.

A light knock on the door interrupted her musings. 'I've got your crutch,' he said.

And there it was. Reality. The end of the fairy tale.

He nipped in and laid it beside her. 'Are you ok now?' Crouching, he rested his arm on the bed.

'You can sit there.' She patted the bed beside her. 'I don't bite.'

'I know, but... Ok.' He shrugged. The bed dipped as he shifted in beside her. His intoxicating scent filled her lungs and set off tingles all over her body. 'Is there anything else you want me to do before I go?'

Now was the moment a confident woman would pounce and tell him exactly what she wanted from him. 'No, thanks.'

He slid his arm around her shoulder. 'Thanks for this morning. I'm sorry about the shitshow this afternoon, but the riding was great.'

'Yeah. I enjoyed it.' Almost as much as she was enjoying this embrace.

'Sleep tight.' He squeezed her shoulder.

Their eyes met. Her heart stopped as she dropped her focus to his lips. If she just leaned in... They were so close. She could do it.

His lips swept past hers and he placed a chaste kiss on her cheek.

'See you in the morning,' he whispered, then got to his feet.

As the door closed, she raised her fingertips to her cheek and closed her eyes, savouring this bittersweet moment as long as she could.

Chapter Seventeen

Marcus

Yawning to himself, Marcus made notes on his iPad, checking the charts and sorting the forecast as he sat at the breakfast table. It looked like a changeable type of day with the possibility of snow. He was used to life in the city where it rarely snowed, so the chance of it arriving while he was cosily shacked up in the Highlands was quite exciting. Something he never thought he'd say – very little ever excited Marcus Bowman these days.

The likelihood of snow hitting this exact spot was still fifty-fifty, so he wouldn't get his hopes up too high.

Willow sidled in and approached his table. Her skin was pale and her eyes cool. If she was as tired as he was, he wouldn't be surprised. He didn't suffer from fatigue and his tiredness was his own fault – partly. Blaming his sleepless night on her would be unfair; how could she know anything about it? When she was tucked up snug and warm, he was wide awake, wired to the moon, whirring over the reasons she got so far under his skin and into his psyche. Even now, he didn't have the answer. He never had. Back in the studio, it had been the same. He'd obsessed over her to the point of forcing himself to ignore her. Only after he'd received the Valentine card had he allowed himself a flicker of hope but he'd never known if it was actually her who sent it or not.

'Can I get you anything for breakfast?' she asked.

No good morning? Nothing? Just professional Willow. Was she smarting from last night? It wasn't in her nature to accept help, and normally it wasn't in his to give it – not to just anyone. People he cared about were different. And Willow was someone he cared about.

'Same as before,' he said. 'But I don't mind getting something myself, or I can make something for both of us.'

'No, it's fine.'

'Willow.' He wanted to say something, but silence hung between them.

'Yes?'

'Um...' Since when had he been lost for words? 'I... No, sorry. It's nothing.'

'I can't help with your report this morning,' she said. 'I need to go to the chemist.' Her cheeks coloured. Was she embarrassed about needing medication?

'That's ok. I'll do it out the back in a sheltered spot where it can't blow over.'

Was she annoyed because he kissed her cheek last night? Maybe he shouldn't have, but it seemed so natural at the time; add a bedroom and dim lights and it set a scene for his senses to interpret before his brain kicked in properly. Whenever she was near, she did things like that to him. She always had and it made him act like a fool.

The guest family sat at a nearby table and Willow smiled as she served them, but it was muted and didn't quite reach her eyes. Marcus sent some messages to Laurenia and Toby while he waited for his food, trying to avoid making eye contact with the guest family. He didn't feel like making small talk.

'Thanks.' He sat back as Willow presented him with breakfast.

'You're welcome,' she said, turning quickly away.

With a sigh, he cut into a sausage. This kind of food was an indulgence for him. Normally coffee and a bowl of muesli was enough. Knowing Willow cooked it made him want to clear his plate.

When he headed out to do the report, she had her pink coat on and matching bobble hat pulled over her ears. Her long blonde hair flowed over her shoulders. She looked like a snow fairy.

'I'm heading off now,' she said. 'The other guests have gone, but if you're going out, just leave the door unlocked. I won't be long.'

'I'm not going anywhere. Just into the backyard to do the report.' He made to leave then turned back. 'I could drive you.'

'No thanks. You've got work to do and I can drive myself.'

'I know you can and that's not what I meant.'

'It's just... Well, people sometimes think I can't do stuff like that.'

'Yeah. But I'm not some people and I know you can.'

She gave him a brief smile and headed out. Marcus made his way to his car and collected the equipment. As he slammed the boot shut, he spotted Willow getting into a tiny white car.

He gathered his bags and headed for the back of the hotel. Doing this without Willow was deadly dull and irritating, but maybe she didn't want his interference. Had he offended her by offering?

When David asked him on air about Rocky Rainman and his attempted olive branch, his blood boiled, and he almost blew a fuse. One day, this smile was going to slip, but he kept it in place long enough to say he hoped it was the start of a less aggressive campaign. But privately he thought if he got his hands on this Rainman character, he was going to throttle him.

'Hi.'

He spun around midway through yanking out his earpiece. For a second, he expected to see Willow, but a tall woman in a bright orange hi-vis jacket peered back at him. His eyes widened and he stepped back. Her hair was blue and she had an aura of power around her.

'Er... Hello.'

'Do you work here?' she asked.

'No. I'm just visiting.'

She scanned over his equipment and frowned. 'I'm Cha Gilchrist from the Forestry Land Trust. There's some tree damage for an insurance claim that I'm here to assess. I don't suppose you know where I can find the owners?'

'They're away and the woman who's in charge in the interim has just nipped out. I don't think she'll be long. I was here when the tree came down, so I could show you where it is.'

'Yeah, that would help, thanks. I need to see it before I decide what to do. We might be able to cut it today if it's posing immediate danger.'

'It's not far.' He slung his bag over his shoulder and led the way down the path.

'Are you the weather presenter?' the woman asked.

'Yup. That's me.'

'I thought I recognised you. I love your show. Some of the places you go are awesome. Iceland looks amazing.'

'Yeah, it is.'

'Sorry, I bet you get people saying that all the time. Must be so irritating. It's like people asking me why I have blue hair.'

Marcus smirked. 'And why do you have blue hair?'

'Because I can.'

'Good answer.' He looked away, grinning. 'There's the tree.' He pointed to the sorrowful sight of it, leaning through the roof of the little bungalow. Thank god, Willow hadn't been in there. His heart thudded wildly at the horrific thought.

'Wow, ok.' She moved closer, her eyes roaming around. 'I hate dealing with insurance companies.' She let out a long breath and shook her head. 'They said this was a simple job, but it'll take hours to get this down safely and it's not something we can leave like that. I assume that's someone's home.'

'It is. She's living in the schoolhouse for now. An engineer went in to switch the power off and said the ceiling hadn't yet collapsed but it was cracked. If it falls in all her possessions will get damaged. The danger of that happening will increase if it snows.'

'If?' she arched an eyebrow. 'Not putting your neck on the line, huh?'

'Snow is notoriously hard to predict, especially precise times and locations.'

'Yeah, I hear you. I was kidding. My colleagues are in the van and they can get this down but you'll need someone else to fix the roof.'

'Yeah. I doubt that'll be a quick fix.'

'Probably not.' She thrust her hands into her pockets. 'I'll have to wait for the person in charge; there's a shedload of paperwork to get through before we do anything.' She looked around. 'This is a neat place. I heard it might be closing, which is a damn shame. A while ago, I did some outreach work here and it was great. I don't get how there's always money for pointless crap like eight-bedroom houses that no one can afford but no money for worthwhile things like this.'

'Would you like to do an interview about your feelings on the subject?'

'For TV?'

'Yes. I'm putting together a report to garner support. It might end up being a documentary. Just a few questions. You seem passionate about it.'

'Yeah, ok.' She checked her watch. 'We could do it now while I'm waiting for the manager.'

'Great. I'll set up the camera here with the schoolhouse in the background.'

She whipped her hair tie out and ran her free hand through thick blue waves, teasing out long strands as Marcus focused the lens on her. Unconventional hair colour aside, she was a striking looker and would look good on film.

'Right, I'll set it to run and we'll just talk. The editing team will clean it up later. Before I start I need your full name and official job title so I can introduce you.'

'Cha Gilchrist and I'm a project manager at Forestry Land Trust Scotland.'

'Great. Right.' Marcus adjusted his lapel and flexed his shoulders before hitting record on the pocket remote. 'I'm here with Cha Gilchrist,' he said, and they were off. She was a natural, smiling as she talked, explaining her role, then discussing her views on the schoolhouse and its place in the community.

She was just getting into her stride when Marcus spotted Willow exiting the back door of the schoolhouse and making her way down the path. Would she see they were recording?

Just in case she didn't, Marcus decided to wrap quickly. 'Thank you, Cha. It's been a pleasure talking to you this morning.'

Cha smiled and pulled her hair back into its ponytail. 'Was that ok?'

'Absolutely perfect. Thank you.'

Willow reached them. She stopped behind the camera, her brow furrowing and her eyes moving between Cha and Marcus.

'Hi,' he said.

'There's a man in a forestry van out front who says he's here to cut the tree,' Willow said to Cha. 'And you're checking it out.'

'I am,' Cha said.

'I just thought I'd do a quick interview,' Marcus added.

'Are you the manager?' Cha asked.

'No, but I'm looking after things just now.' Willow adjusted her glove.

'Great,' Cha said. 'We met before. You might not remember. It was at a ceilidh earlier in the year. Hayley introduced us.'

'Oh, yeah. I remember,' Willow said.

'Well, we need to talk about this tree,' Cha said with a smile. 'The insurance company made it out to be much less of a job than it was. I'll need you to sign some papers and go through an online form before we do anything.'

'Ok.' Willow's eyes darted to Marcus and something flashed in them. Was she jealous? His ego would take that. But then, he shouldn't be thinking like that.

'Are you ok?' he asked, lagging behind so Cha didn't overhear.

'Fine,' she said.

He stared at her, aware suddenly of how much taller than her he was. But she didn't cower away, she maintained eye-contact.

'Listen, Willow,' he said quietly, 'if my concern is unwanted, just tell me to back off. I meant no offence.'

'I'm not offended,' she muttered. 'I just have work to do.'

'Ok. I hear you. I'll let you get on.' He sped up, passing Cha on the path. 'Thanks for the interview,' he said. 'I'll get it to the editing team and they'll contact you about when it'll be aired.'

'Great, thanks,' she said.

He focused forward and threw a brief wave over his shoulder. He didn't want to bother Willow anymore just now. What was up with her? This was so weird. But maybe it was for the best. *My job's done here.* Finding Rocky Rainman hadn't happened. He would pack his bags and tomorrow he'd get the hell out of there. That was the plan anyway – but he'd never been very good at following his head where Willow was concerned.

CHAPTER EIGHTEEN

Willow

When the north winds blow, they bring the snow...

Why had she let pain get the better of her? Willow gripped her crutch fiercely as she did her best to storm up the path ahead of Cha, the blue-haired beauty. After the day she'd had yesterday and the sleepless night last night, she was worn out. Coming back to find Marcus interviewing her had been the last straw. *Did I overreact?* Of course she had. The way she'd spoken to him had been bad.

The sight of him smiling and chatting to Cha had set a fire raging in her tummy. Last night, she'd mistakenly thought she had a special connection with him, but she really was naïve when it came to men. Nothing in his mannerisms had suggested he was at all interested in Cha. Willow had done it again and leapt to a conclusion without giving him a chance. She had to apologise.

'Marcus Bowman seems like a nice guy,' Cha said. She may be in unflattering work clothes but she had an attractive face and easy confidence. 'Sometimes these celebrity types don't live up to their reputation.'

'Yeah.' What else could she say? Cha was right.

'It's so cool he's doing a local story like this. Hopefully it'll save this place.'

'Why was he interviewing you?' Willow said. 'What's your interest?'

'He's just gathering lots of local opinions. He was initially doing a report but he now wants to make a documentary about this place. Sounds like a great idea.'

Willow frowned as she opened the back door. He hadn't told her that. 'Didn't he ask you about Rocky Rainman?'

'No.' Cha unzipped her jacket. 'Do you want me to take these boots off in here?'

'If you don't mind.' Willow's brain was rewinding. Marcus hadn't asked about Rocky. He was actually trying to save the schoolhouse. Her tummy writhed like it was full of wriggling worms. She took a deep breath.

Once Cha had her clumpy boots off, Willow showed her into the main foyer. Marcus was now the only guest, so she wasn't exactly stretched. Her pain meds were kicking in and her muscles were slowly relaxing. Her mood was on the same ride. She kept her head down as she hit the wake-up switch on her laptop. A new message from Marion pinged in. She read it quickly.

MARION: Sorry I missed your call earlier. It's mad here. Barry had to go back in, as his wrist was still hurting. They've given him stronger medication and that's totally knocked him out. I just remembered we were supposed to go to Malcom McManus's community Christmas party at the Cross Keys this evening. I don't suppose you could go – even for a little while – and give him and Brenda their present? They're very pro the schoolhouse and have always been big supporters of ours. Hope all's well. Did the tree get sorted?

Where to begin with that message? First, she had to sort out the paperwork for the tree.

She scanned over the document, noting Cha's job title: project manager at Forestry Land Trust Scotland. *There you have it.* No wonder she had such a confident air. Willow would too if she could sign herself as something that sounded that important.

'Here's the form.' Cha swivelled an iPad to show her. Now that she'd lost the Orangina jacket, she looked tall and lithe. Willow remembered seeing her at the ceilidh in an incredible outfit that hardly anyone would have the nerve to wear, but she'd looked at perfect ease in it. 'We need to submit it online and I'll add some photographs.'

Time ticked on as Willow filled out the boxes. All the while, her tummy ached at how she'd spoken to Marcus. Half an hour later, with the paperwork filled out, Cha and her colleagues made their way to the tree. From the kitchen window, Willow pushed up on tiptoes and could just make out their bright jackets. The purr of chainsaws started up and she let out a sigh. All her possessions were in there, though thankfully she had most of the important stuff with her in her laptop bag. She didn't suppose she'd be allowed back in until building inspectors made sure it was safe. Annoying really, as she missed her anemometer. And she could do with her wheelchair just in case.

She replied to Marion as soon as she got back to the desk. Going to Malcolm's party was not something she wanted to do. She sighed. It wouldn't be too big a deal to drop by with a present, though she didn't really like him. Marion and Barry had known him for a long time and were very loyal, but Willow had heard so many stories about him and his wife. They were often involved in committees and community groups, only for things to go wrong. They'd even been charged with something before and Willow's gut feeling was that they were a bit shady. But she knew better than to say that to Marion, who would tut and insist it was just gossips and people who were jealous of Malcolm's community spirit.

At least she wouldn't be alone here with Marcus. He Everything was so awkward now. She should have refused his help last night. That was really why she felt so annoyed. It wasn't about him. It was her.

She buried her head in her hands for a moment, wishing Marion had said when she thought she'd be back.

Snow was in the air. She could feel it, almost smell it. A soft calm hovered over the schoolhouse. Come afternoon, the back door creaked open, followed by thumping on the mat. June from the village had arrived to clean the rooms the visiting family had vacated that morning. Thank goodness Willow didn't have to do that. Hoovering was really tricky.

'Bloody Baltic out there.' June clapped her hands together.

'Snow's coming,' Willow said.

'I better be done before it does. I hate driving in it.' June shuddered. 'My grandchildren will be happy though.'

'There's only one room to do, so it shouldn't take long.'

'Marion messaged me and said Marcus Bowman, the weatherman, is here. I wouldn't mind meeting him. He's a nice piece of eye-candy, that one. I could tickle him with my feather duster.'

Willow cast her a look. 'Please, don't.'

June chuckled, passing her desk on the way to the cleaning cupboard.

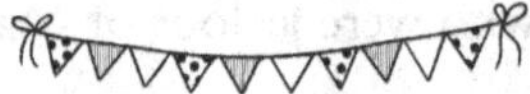

Willow slumped back in the seat with a sigh. The tree had been removed and the surgeons were off elsewhere. She hadn't seen Marcus since he'd gone out that morning. His car wasn't there either. Had he left and gone back to Glasgow? Maybe she should check his room. Just as she decided she'd have to, the sound of footsteps at the door clomped into her consciousness.

Marcus stormed in, bring a wave of chilled air.

'Hi.' Willow couldn't make her voice any louder and she wasn't sure he'd heard as he didn't look at her.

'Hi,' he muttered after a beat.

'Is everything ok?'

'Just bloody perfect.' He pulled out his phone. 'I have to pack.'

'Why?'

'Ginny wants me back tomorrow morning. I'll have to leave first thing.'

He's leaving. It's for the best. Willow ignored the stab in her heart. 'Oh right. Well, I'm sorry, but if you want food, you'll have to get something yourself. I'm going to Malcolm's Christmas party at the Cross Keys.'

'By yourself?'

Willow gave a little shrug. Did it betray how much she was freaking at the idea of going to something like that alone? She could just hand in the present and leave. If Hayley was going, she would stay, but Hayley wasn't a friend or a fan of Malcom. She was one of the best sources of Malcolm related gossip but that was it.

'Can I come too?'

'You?' Willow glared at him.

'Yeah. I need to talk to him about something he said in his interview. Also, I could catch some other villagers.'

What a relief it would be not to be alone... But would it be any better with him? She should keep her distance, not go to dinner with him. 'Well, I guess.'

'Great. I'll get changed.'

'Don't wear anything too fancy. I've only got stuff from the spare cupboard and I'll look like a frump next to you anyway.'

'Don't be silly.' He leaned his hands on the desk, his arms ramrod straight, and looked her in the eye. 'You look perfect, no matter what you wear, and don't let anyone tell you otherwise. Including yourself.' With that, he marched out. Willow stared after him. Wow. He really thought that?

Gorgeous aromas wafted around the dining room of the elegant riverside restaurant, the Cross Keys. Twinkling fairy lights adorned its low beams and a giant Christmas tree glowed next to the French doors. Beyond the window, though it was pitch black, a decked area was visible, lit up with light strings around the veranda.

Willow had held her breath almost the whole way there. She'd found a not too shabby dark green long dress with corresponding lace trim and thin straps in the spare cupboard. It looked a bit like a festival dress Marion had worn in the seventies but it did ok as an evening dress when paired with a white faux fur stole she'd also found. But Marcus looked ready for a photoshoot in his iron-grey shirt and open black blazer jacket. He towered above her, looking like an Armani model. As they strolled through the door, he placed his hand lightly on her back and she almost fainted.

'Interesting.' Marcus's eyes travelled over the poinsettia covered tables surrounded by diners. 'I didn't expect this many guests.'

'Malcolm knows a lot of people.'

He and his giant wife, Brenda, took up most of the room at the window table next to the Christmas tree. His low rumbling laugh and droning voice were clear over the rest of the chitchat.

'What's he got over them?' Marcus asked. 'Everyone looks like they're hanging on his words.'

'I don't know. Marion and Barry think he's great but I always think he looks a bit shifty.' He had a slightly unfocused left eye that gave her the impression he was watching something over her shoulder. She always wanted to turn around and check what he was really looking at while his voice lured her to look at him.

'Well, let's see where we're meant to sit.' Marcus increased the pressure on Willow's back and her skin burned beneath the lightweight fabric of the dress.

'I hope they don't think we're gatecrashing.'

Marcus stepped away from her and examined a seating arrangement on a sandwich board that looked suitable for a wedding. 'Table five,' he said, adjusting his cuffs.

'I didn't think you'd want to come out and be recognised.'

'Goes with the territory, I'm afraid.' He approached table five but before they reached it, Willow caught a glimpse of a hand going up at Malcolm's table. Brenda waved her over, looking her up and down.

'Oh god. I hope she doesn't throw us out. I better hand over the present and explain why we're here.'

Marcus drew closer and she couldn't deny his presence gave her strength. 'I'll come too.'

'You made it,' Brenda said. 'Marion messaged and said you were coming. I wasn't sure if you'd manage. Can you drive?'

'Yes. Of course I can.'

'Can't be easy for you,' Malcolm said in his deep, slow voice. 'What happened to you?'

Her teeth grated inside her mouth. 'Nothing. I was born like this.'

'Ah, poor girl,' he said.

'Aye, it's a crying shame,' Brenda said. 'You'd think in this day and age, they'd be able to do something to fix it.'

Willow handed her the bag, not meeting either of their gazes. 'Your present from Marion and Barry.' Her cheeks were hot. She hated ignoramuses like these two. It wasn't the first time she'd come across attitudes like theirs and it probably wouldn't be the last. She sighed. *Ground, swallow me up now.*

'She doesn't need fixing,' Marcus said and his voice was grave and commanding. 'That's an outdated attitude.'

'Ah hello, Marcus.' Malcolm smirked his crooked grin. 'Wasn't aware you were coming too, but nice to have someone so well kent at the party.'

'You certainly have a lot of guests.' Marcus glanced around. 'I thought everyone in the town would be tucked up waiting for the snow.'

Heat attacked the back of Willow's neck. Snow. She'd temporarily forgotten about that. She needed to post an update but with everything that had happened, she'd forgotten.

'Why not join us at this table?' Malcolm said. 'I'm sure we could make room.'

Seriously unlikely. He and his wife took up most of the table between them.

'I'll tell you some more about Rocky Rainman. I've been doing some snooping and I think I know who it is.'

Willow bet her bottom dollar he didn't have a clue, but it got Marcus's attention. He moved closer, frowning.

'Aye,' Malcolm continued. 'I noticed he hasn't said much about the snow today. He promised an update but it hasn't come yet.'

'I noticed that,' Marcus said.

'So, I suspect he's someone who works odd hours and can't always get to his phone, like a bus driver.'

'Oh yeah?' Marcus shook his head like he was unconvinced. 'He's just one sad individual as far as I'm concerned,' he added in a low voice, so Malcolm wouldn't hear.

'I'd like to get a seat,' Willow said. 'Excuse me.'

She slipped away from them and took her place at the table with a brief hello to the other guests already seated. Then she opened her phone. This was not as easy as doing it on her computer and her fingers scrabbled over the small screen, opening the weather charts and her social media accounts. 'Oh, my god,' she muttered. The winds had changed, and it looked like the snow could hit them at any second.

When the north winds blow, they bring the snow...

If you're enjoying a night out in Glenbriar, especially those of you at The Cross Keys, don't leave it too late to get home folks. This beast is moving in quickly and will bring havoc to the roads, possible school and business closures tomorrow!

And remember folks, be nice. Rocky doesn't hate Marcus Bowman and neither should you! Let's all play nicely.

Keep safe and snuggle in tight.

That's Rocky signing out for the night!

It was cheeky and risky, but she needed to update people and hopefully stop them being so horrible to Marcus. She hit send and off it went. Seconds later, Marcus joined her at the table and she put away her phone.

Inevitably, some people recognised him and started quizzing him as servers dished out food.

'I absolutely adore *Destination Forecast*. It's probably my favourite show on TV. Will there be another series?' a woman asked.

'Yes, I think so. It's been such a success it would be mad to axe it.' Marcus cut into his turkey.

Willow could hardly eat. They really should go in case the weather got bad... And it *would* get bad. Rocky Rainman said so.

'What brings you here?' another woman asked. 'Are we going to be on TV? Is Glenbriar going to be on *Destination Forecast?*'

'No, but you could be on TV, if you want to be interviewed. I'm doing a feature about The Old Schoolhouse and hoping we can keep it open.'

'Oh really? That's very interesting.'

Willow ate quietly, pushing the sprouts to one side. Marcus had a knack for conversation, though she recognised his fake TV manner. He was the master at chatting politely but giving nothing personal away.

She took a drink, and Malcolm's voice echoed loudly from his nearby table. 'Can't be easy for that poor lass. I thought she'd been in an accident or something. Crying shame, so it is.'

Even his whisper was louder than a foghorn. Did he think it was ok to talk about her like that when she was right here? Her skin burned, as did her chest.

Marcus cleared his throat and raised his voice as he carried on his conversation. Willow appreciated his attempt to drown out Malcolm but it didn't take away the fact he'd said it in the first place, and who knew what else he was saying.

'So is this young lady your d—'

'She works at the schoolhouse,' Marcus cut off the questioning woman. Willow suspected she was going to ask if she was Marcus's date... but had he panicked, thinking she was going to say daughter? He wasn't *that* much older than her. And seriously, with that body, he didn't look old at all.

'Ah, but you're here together. How nice. You must know Marion and Barry.'

'I'm here in their place,' Willow said. 'Because Barry broke his wrist.'

'Yes, I heard that. Such a shame and so close to Christmas.'

Willow caught Marcus's eye, and she flicked him a brief smile; he returned it with a slight quirk of his lips.

'Here, look at this.' One of the men at the table held up his phone. His voice was so carrying that people from other tables looked over too. 'Finally, there's a post here from Rocky Rainman. Snow's coming, and he even gives us a mention.'

'What?' Marcus frowned at the man.

'Yeah. He says anyone out and about in Glenbriar should get home straight away. Snow's here.'

Willow froze, not sure where to look or how to arrange her face. Was this funny or terrifying?

'And he says we're all to like you,' the man said to Marcus. 'Aww, that's cute.'

Another man near the window jumped up and peered out. 'He's right as always. It's coming down like crazy. Would you look at that? Rocky's a genius just like me.'

'Shut it, Robert.'

'Who you telling to shut it? For all you know, I might be Rocky Rainman.'

Marcus glared at him, then said to Willow, 'I need to find out if it's him. It's definitely someone here and the game's up.'

CHAPTER NINETEEN

Marcus

Someone in this overcrowded hotel bar was Rocky Rainman. Was it Robert, the man at the window making a scene? Marcus's eyes travelled from him over the band of locals sitting around. Some of them were getting up from tables in the dining area and others had moved to comfy seats by the fire and were looking around to see what all the shouting and laughing was about. Could it be a conspiracy Marcus had landed bang in the middle of? One of these close-knit communities where everyone knew everything, and they all played the newcomers?

That was farfetched and, seeing them like this, they looked normal to the point of dull. Malcolm had a stupidly loud voice though, and everyone would have heard him talking to Marcus. Whoever was the Rainman must have realised he was there and done this to taunt him.

'Well, if Rainman said we should shift, then we should,' a man near to Marcus said.

'Do you agree with his predictions, Marcus?' Malcolm asked, wandering over to stand by their table.

'Well, anyone who looks out the window can see for themselves it's snowing.' Marcus knocked back a swig of coffee and caught Willow's eye. She frowned. If only she would smile. Just one last smile because tomorrow he was leaving, assuming the snow wasn't too heavy. And it looked heavy... and thick. Why hadn't he had the nerve to call it? He didn't want to leave Willow so soon but Ginny had given him his marching orders.

Willow looked strange. Was she ok? She'd hardly spoken all evening. Her face back at the schoolhouse had told him how nervous she was about coming out alone and the protective side of him had roared into action again. Maybe that was more interference she didn't really want.

'We should go,' she said.

'I'd like to talk to that Robert person.' Marcus looked around.

'He's gone outside,' Willow said. 'Him and his pals left just a second ago.

'Seriously?'

'Please, can we go?'

'Yeah, course.' Marcus scanned the room again before saying goodbye to Malcolm and heading for the car park.

Marcus hovered as Willow made her way down the stairs. He didn't want to fuss but unbidden visions of her slipping and falling kept assailing his mind. He could hear people still laughing and talking in the darkness. It sounded like some of them were fooling around in the snow. 'I wonder where Robert went.' Marcus opened the car door and held it for Willow.

'No idea.' Willow leaned back in the headrest as he started the engine and pulled off.

'Do you think it's him? Or Malcolm pulling a double bluff? You know these people better than me.'

'I don't think it's either of them; they're not smart enough.'

He clenched the steering wheel as he wound around the twisty road, peering forward. The surface had a layer of white covering it. 'You think Rocky's smart?'

'Smarter than you anyway.'

'Pardon?'

She chuckled and it melted the frosty sensation that had gripped his heart. 'That's a bit rude.' He tapped the wheel, feigning annoyance.

'You just can't take it that someone might be better than you.'

'Seriously?' Though she was right of course.

'Oh yes.'

'Yeah, well. I always had you pegged for a Rocky lover.'

'You know what?' Willow said.

'What?'

'I bet I know something else you can't win at.'

'What's that?' He tapped the wheel.

'Snowballs.'

'Pardon?' He turned into the car park at the schoolhouse.

'A snowball fight.'

'You want to take me on in a snowball fight?'

'Sure, I'll take you on right now.'

'Shouldn't we wait until dawn for the showdown? Or is it the snowdown?'

'Chicken,' she said.

'Me?'

'Yup... Come on... Out back now.'

'Seriously?'

'Let's fight it out, woman on man.'

Marcus raised his eyebrow. Now she was talking, but fighting wasn't what he wanted to do with her. Her face was set however with an expression hovering between a grin, and a determined *I dare you* look. 'Fine, now it is. But very soon you're going to wish you'd never been born.'

'And you'll be ringing an ambulance face down in the slush.' She flung open the car door and stormed towards the schoolhouse. Even with the crutch in tow, she clearly meant business. Marcus watched with his heart still in his mouth, picturing her coming a cropper. He had to admire her spirit. And come to think on it, he hadn't had a snowball fight in years.

He followed her to the door, fizzing as he replayed Rocky's post in his mind. Why the sudden rush of love? Was Rocky going soft by asking his followers to play nicely and be kind to Marcus? Marcus had been around long enough to not believe a word of it. Whatever Rocky's new game was, Marcus wasn't going away that easily. He glanced up as the door swung open again and Willow burst out. She'd thrown her pastel pink jacket over the long green dress and was putting on the matching bobble hat, thick scarf and gloves. Her feet were encased in snow boots which made the whole outfit look hilarious. Who had a snowball fight in an evening dress? *Willow Roxburgh, that's who.*

Their eyes connected. A psychological battle ensued. Who would look away first?

'Wouldn't you rather stay inside and keep warm?' he suggested.

She made chicken noises. 'Knew it. You just can't take anyone being better at anything than you, can you?'

That did the trick. Marcus looked away.

'Let's be having you then,' she said. 'Or would you rather surrender and go inside? If you do, we'll call that your loss.'

Ha. If she wanted him to surrender, she could have him. All of him on a plate. Right now. Screw the snowballs, though he'd rather screw her. His groin twitched at the thought. He needed to shove his head in a pile of snow and cool off.

'I'll get my coat.'

'I'm surprised you're going to risk getting it wet.'

'Oh, I'm full of surprises,' he said, leaning in as he passed her. 'As you're about to find out.'

She rewarded him with an obvious once-over. 'Hurry up then.'

The back door was ajar when he got back down. For a weather presenter, Marcus really didn't have an appropriate wardrobe. He had on his North Face jacket, the one he'd worn riding, but no hat or scarf and his leather gloves were too good for messing about in the snow.

He pulled open the door, stepped outside and *smack*! A snowball slapped his right shoulder. Somewhere in the exquisite darkness, Willow laughed. Fat snowflakes fell around, deadening the sound and giving a lustrous quality to the landscape.

'Oh, come on.' He brushed off the flakes from his coat. 'I'm not even outside yet.'

Whack. Another one landed on his neck. Icy drips got inside his collar. 'Oi. Quit that. Let me out first.' He shook, trying to dislodge a lump of snow. Another one hit his upper arm. This really was war.

'Ok. You asked for it.' He grabbed a handful from the ground and had barely straightened up when a snowball slammed into his ankle. Where the hell was she? She'd stopped laughing. 'Come out, come out, wherever you are.'

He jumped back just in time before another one hit. This time, he saw it had originated from a clump of trees just behind the wheely bins. She was scooping a wad of snow from the tops. Clever girl, but he had her now. He tossed his snowball in her direction but she casually moved aside. He grabbed some more and approached her position but she was pelting them thick and fast.

'Bloody hell, Willow.'

She giggled. 'Not so cocky now, are you?'

'I am not cocky.'

'Oh yes, you are.'

'Oh, no I'm not.' How had this turned into a pantomime?

'Everyone knows you are. It's your number one personality trait.'

'No, it bloody isn't.'

'Is too.' She lobbed another snowball at him.

He batted it away and marched straight for her. 'You know what?'

'What?' She gazed up at him, her eyes twinkling in the light emitting from the lamp near the back door.

'If you're going to play dirty, so am I.'

She backed towards the wall. He shadowed her until he was right beside her.

'How would you like a dunk in the snow?'

'Don't even think about it. This is a snowball fight. Dunking is cheating.'

'Oh yeah? I think this has passed being just a snowball fight.'

'Only because you're losing.'

He looked away and ran his hand down his face. She had a point. He backed off. She had spirit but he was a lot bigger than her and maybe cornering her wasn't fair.

'Hey.' She grabbed his hand.

'What?'

She let go, but her eyes didn't leave him. He held his breath. Was she thinking what he was thinking? Because if she was, he wanted exactly the same thing. He wanted to lean in, take her beautiful face in his raw hands, and kiss her until they melted the snow with the fire in their souls.

'Let's call a truce,' she said.

'I concede. You won.'

'What's my prize?'

'I thought you'd make me do a forfeit.'

'Ok. Take off your shirt.'

'Are you joking? Out here, in the snow?'

She grinned and raised her eyebrow.

'Oh, I see. My forfeit is also your prize,' he said.

'Seriously? You think that's what I want?'

'Isn't it?'

Her mouth dropped open. 'Well... no.'

'No?'

'No.'

'Fine. Shall I start?'

'Doing what?'

'Taking my clothes off.' God knew he wanted to. He wanted to bare himself and have her do the same. Surely when their naked skin touched, the world would combust.

'No.'

'Ok, fine. Are you still grumpy with me?'

'Maybe.'

'What did I do wrong?' he asked.

She gave a little shrug.

'Tell me and I'll try to make it right. What can I do to make it better?'

She teased a strand of hair around her gloved finger. 'Kiss me.'

'What?' Soft snowflakes tickled his face. They were on Willow's hat and covering the long hair trailing over her shoulders. She'd finally batted the ball out there, and it was sitting up, waiting for him to grab it. 'That doesn't sound like a forfeit,' he said. 'That sounds more like a prize.'

'For who?' Her eyes didn't leave his except to glance at his lips.

'Me.' He dipped down and cupped her warm cheek in his hand. 'Hopefully both of us.'

'You're freezing,' she whispered. But she was the one shivering.

'And you're beautiful.' He leaned in. His eyelids closed as he sealed his lips over hers. The contact was electrifying, but delicate. An impossible mix that was all Willow. He was burning enough to move in, get her closer, taste more of her sweet mouth, but she was in no rush. If anything, she was uncertain, hovering her lips just out of reach as he bent to capture them again. Had she had enough? Or maybe she hated it. *Fuck.* Normally, the women he was with were all over him, and it was obvious what they wanted. He pulled back and straightened up. 'Not good enough for you, topolina?'

The way she looked at him sent a shiver down his spine – easy to pass off in this weather.

She was almost shaking. Was it just from the cold?

'We should go in. It's getting cold,' she said.

'It's been minus two since we came out.'

She was already on her way to the door.

'Willow. Is everything Ok?'

'Fine.'

'Are you sure?'

She didn't look back. With a few strides, he caught her.

'Please, talk to me. Have I done something wrong?' Christ, she'd asked him to kiss her. She wasn't going to hold it against him now, surely? Maybe she wished she hadn't, and it would always be a moment she regretted in life. He didn't. Not yet.

She stepped inside, and her whole body shuddered. 'I just need to warm up.'

He cocked his head. That wasn't it, not really. Something else was up. Her eyes told him. 'Do you hate me for doing that? Should I have said no and walked off?'

She shook her head and raised her eyes to the ceiling as if searching for divine intervention. 'I don't hate you. I never hated you.' She started moving again towards the door to the common room, unwinding her scarf as she went. Drips spattered on the carpet as the snow clinging to them started to melt. 'I just can't...' Her voice was quiet, and she was facing away like she didn't really want him to hear – or maybe she did, and it had taken all her courage to say it.

'Can't what? Look, I've been around a bit. I understand sometimes a kiss is just a kiss. I don't have any expectations, if that's what you're worried about.'

And it was true. What he did have was a hell of a lot of lust pounding round him, crying out for her. The Neanderthal in him wanted to pick her up and carry her back to his cave, but he'd evolved into a man who could control himself and show her the respect she deserved.

'But I do,' she said.

'And I don't fulfil them?'

'Of course you do.' She spun around and red flashed in her eyes. 'Why else would I have asked you to kiss me? I've fancied you forever. Back in the office and since you walked in the door a few days ago. Maybe it's not expectations I have, just crazy fantasies.'

What a sideswipe. Jesus Christ. *She fancies me.* He'd fancied the pants off her as long as he'd known her. Even when he tried so hard to deny it and when he couldn't explain it.

'Willow, I—'

'Please.' She pulled off her damp hat and shook her long mane. 'It's fine. I know nothing can happen and that's fine because I don't want it to.'

'You don't?'

'Not everyone wants a one-night stand or a fling. Just because I fancy you doesn't mean I need to do anything about it.'

'Ok.' He held up his hands. 'I hear you. Loud and clear. You're absolutely right.' She had a point. Two. Both really good ones.

'And really... Well, look at yourself.'

He scanned downwards at his now soaking jacket. 'Yeah. I'm a mess.'

'Shut up. You're what, six foot ten?'

'Five.'

'Close enough. You could give Henry Cavill a run for his money with your muscles and you're... well, you're you.'

'And? I'm clearly missing the point here.'

'Stop pretending. You know what I mean. I'm me. I can barely stand up straight. You've probably had hundreds of girlfriends. I've had two boyfriends in my whole life and they weren't exactly much to write home about. One was a high school prom date and the other was, well, a disaster.'

'I haven't had hundreds of girlfriends. That's a bit insulting.'

'Sorry.'

'So, what are you saying? Somehow we're not compatible? Like I'm from Krypton and you're a Vulcan?'

She rolled her eyes then shrugged. 'Actually, that's not far off. Now, please. Let's stop.'

'Ok. Fine. Have it your way.'

She shuffled out of her jacket and Marcus stared into the common room where the fire was dead and everything looked cold. Even the Christmas tree lights had stopped flashing and were gradually dimming, then reappearing in slow motion. Something had gone wrong here. What did she think? That he had a problem with her disability? She might have body issues and fears, but they were her hang-ups, not his.

He glanced around, but she'd already gone to hang up her jacket. Should he wait and say something? Or just go to bed? He put his foot on the bottom step. What was the point of saying anything else? She had made herself very clear.

CHAPTER TWENTY

Willow

Willow hung her coat on one of the old school pegs and rested her forehead on her cold, damp hand. She wanted to cry. Her chance had been right there and she'd shot it in the head. Marcus had kissed her. Actually, properly kissed her and she barely responded. Shock and terror had seized her.

What kind of an idiot am I? How will I ever find anyone if I never try? But not him. She couldn't bear it if everything went tits up and she did something humiliating. All it would take was her leg to seize up or for a muscle to spasm right in the middle of a heated encounter. And what would he think of her then? She needed to practise with someone she didn't care about... Or was that worse?

'Arghh,' she growled. It was so confusing.

Was he still in the foyer? Only one way to find out. Holding her breath, she teased open the door and peered out. He was gone. It was safe. Now, she needed to get upstairs and into bed without her fairy-tale prince this time. She locked the front door and checked all the lights were out, then shut the door.

'Willow.'

'Holy shit.' She jumped a mile and her hand clamped to her chest. 'You gave me a heart attack. I thought you'd gone up.'

He leaned on the wall at the bottom of the stairs and rolled his lips together. 'I did. But I have something to say to you.'

'What?'

'You said we weren't compatible because I've got muscles and you can't stand up straight, but that doesn't make sense. We've both got muscles. Yours just don't work the same way as mine.'

'Right. So, you came back down to give me a biology lesson and tell me what's wrong with me.'

'No. Why do you always assume you know what I'm going to say? You assumed I was talking about you in Ginny's office and you were wrong. Give me a chance, will you?'

She bit down on her lower lip. He was right. She had such a bad habit of doing that but her heart trembled at what he was going to say.

'I want to tell you about... my feelings. You said you've fancied me for years. Well, newsflash, I like you too. I always did and tried to deny it, but it was there. You used to distract me just by existing, so I was grouchy and did my best not to talk to you or even look at you.'

'Oh yeah?' She folded her arms and leaned her elbow on her crutch.

'Yeah. Totally. Then, well, I started to enjoy you being about. I liked it when you sat near me and we did the charts together.'

'Is this you trying to get into my pants?'

He looked away with a smirk. 'Can't blame a guy for trying, huh?'

'Seriously?'

'No, Willow. It's all true. I get where you're coming from. You think I'll be put off by the fact you have cerebral palsy.'

Wow. That was direct, but true. Finally, someone had the balls just to say it.

'But even if I tell you it doesn't bother me,' he continued, 'you won't believe me. You'll just think it's me trying to get in your pants again.'

Willow covered her face. *Laugh or cry here?* It was a toss up. This was awful. She didn't know where to look, so she kept her eyes covered.

His warm fingers slid around her wrists, gently prising them apart. 'But for the record, it really doesn't bother me.' He gazed into her eyes. His deep irises twinkled with amber flecks like a rich malt whisky. 'You should have more faith in yourself. You don't let anything get in the way of your job, so don't let it mess with your private life. Believe me, I can tell you from an expert standpoint, there are a lot of guys who would find you attractive.'

'Even if that's true, it doesn't change anything.' She blinked under his powerful scrutiny. 'You don't know what it's like. What it was like... When I tried... to be with someone before.'

'You're right, I don't. You can tell me if you want or leave it. I don't need to know, but I'm ready to hear it if you *want* to tell me.

Your happiness is important to me and if I can bring it about even for a short time, then say the word. And if that means listening to you, I will. If it means leaving you alone, I'll do that.'

No. That was the last thing she wanted. If he left her alone, she'd never forgive herself for letting this opportunity pass her by. He was right here – a guy she really liked and trusted. Would it be so bad? 'Maybe one more kiss.' Her breath caught.

'Just one?' he said. 'Your wish is my command.'

She stared into his deep black pupils; her whole body had frozen but she was shaking inside. He pressed his lips on hers and she closed her eyes. This time, his arms coiled around her, tugging her close, and she melted with a moan. 'Oh Jesus.'

'Marcus will do,' he whispered. 'Want another one?'

She smiled her assent and he kissed her again. Her fingertips tingled with an eagerness to touch him, but she wasn't sure exactly where to start.

'It's ok,' he breathed in her ear.

'What if I do something... wrong?'

'Nothing you do will be wrong. It's all a learning curve. We're just getting to know each other.'

With a deep breath, she slid her hands around his waist. He nudged into her, kissing her deeper. Her tongue touched his, and the electric shock stunned her.

'You really are wonderful.' He stroked his thumb across her cheek. Her limbs were gooey and she was only upright because he was holding her. He'd drugged her with his kiss and she was under his spell. 'But you've had your kiss. And that was all you wanted.'

'I don't want to stop.' The words tumbled out before she changed her mind. 'I want you.'

He shook his head. 'Willow, are you sure? I'm only here until tomorrow. I can only be a one-night stand. You said you didn't want that.'

'I've changed my mind. You were right. You said I need to have faith. I'll never do anything if I don't try. And I want to try with you because I trust you.'

The last time she had sex with anyone was also the first time, and it was dreadful. Maybe she was setting too much store on Marcus, but she believed in his kisses and the way he was holding her. She believed this would be good, or at least better. And if he was going straight away, maybe that was best. They wouldn't have to digest her performance slowly.

'Only if you really want to,' he said.

'Is Prince Charming going to carry me to bed?'

'I thought you didn't like me doing that.'

'Not because I can't manage it. I want you to sweep me off my feet.'

'As you wish.' In a swift movement, he scooped her up and spun her. How surreal and completely ridiculous. It was like being in a cheesy movie. The lights from the Christmas tree in the corridor twinkled behind them. She giggled so hard it hurt her side.

'Marcus, this is mad.'

'Maybe so.'

She wrapped her arms around his neck and smiled. He returned it, then at the same moment, they leaned in and sealed their lips together. The happy bubble inside her soared like mercury, pushing up the temperature and her confidence. She grabbed his cheek and held it as their mouths played together. His jaw moved under her fingertips as he worked on her lips. Just kissing like this started little fires all over her.

He pulled back and marched to the stairs. 'Casa mia o casa tua?'

'What does that mean?'

'My place or yours?'

'Very funny.'

'Ok. Il tuo letto o il mio?'

'What?'

'Your bed or mine? Or would you like to try every bed in the house?'

She rested her forehead on his warm neck. 'If you have that kind of staying power, you really are Superman, but I think I'll be asleep long before that.'

'You think I'll bore you?'

'Let's find out.'

'My room,' he said.

She went with it. If she thought too hard, nerves would get the better of her and she wouldn't do anything. Her heart was singing being this close to him, knowing he wanted her. At least the room would be dark and he wouldn't see her scars.

He skilfully opened the door, still holding her as though he did this kind of thing every day, and knocked the light switch with his elbow.

'Topolina.' He laid her on the bed.

'What is that?' She sank into the soft duvet as he flicked on the bedside lamp.

He winked and returned to the door to put off the main light. When he faced her, he held her gaze and slowly unbuttoned his shirt from the top down. Her eyes popped and her pulse rocketed off the scale. Her skin burned. She could be drooling but she couldn't look away. Her body was alive with need.

He tugged off his shirt. A topless Marcus Bowman stood before her. He was so hot, all chiselled abs and a six-pack like something off TV. Which was exactly what he was, after all. This was the hottie from *Destination Forecast*. She'd watched his topless moments on YouTube more than she cared to confess. Here he was in the flesh. She could hardly breathe. No way did this guy want her.

'Forfeit complete,' he said.

'It doesn't count if you're inside.' Her voice was low and raspy and nothing like she was used to.

'You want to go back out?'

'No.'

'Let's make it count then.'

He sat on the bed facing her and her heart hammered in her eardrums. Her breath came in quick snatches as he leaned towards her. One hand skimmed across her shoulder, sliding down the straps of the green dress, then detouring over her breast. She inhaled sharply. He shifted closer and kissed her again.

'There's no one quite like you,' he whispered onto her lips. 'Beautiful. Inside and out.'

'You're the one with the body of a god.'

'It's all yours. You can do whatever you want with it.' He lay down beside her, his chest right there, ready to touch. His hand snaked up, cupping her cheek and drawing her towards him. All her fantasies were about to come true. Where should she begin?

In the dim light of the bedside lamp, Willow saw her own body flushed and covered in a fine layer of sweat. It was really her. She couldn't speak. If she did, she knew some incoherent drivel would come out. She was laid bare, a pillow beneath her hips and a hot wall of muscle between her legs. This Roman god was joined exquisitely to her, making her his goddess as he moved powerfully and rhythmically. She'd already come undone to his fingers and his lips. Now he was going to do it again. Her body shook at the immense power he imbued in her. No muscle relaxants had ever been half as good as this. She let go, closing her eyes. Hot, strong arms wrapped around her, bringing her flush against him.

'Marcus.' His name left her lips in a whimper as stars burst inside her.

'Willow.' He groaned, holding her close as he quickened his pace, rasping in her ear until his heavenly body was reduced from a slab of hot stone to jelly. Willow stroked his back, adoring the closeness and joy of the moment. She was still trembling with pleasure at the wild new sensations she'd experienced. He held her tight, keeping his weight on his elbows but giving enough for her to enjoy the immense heat of him. He breathed fitfully, letting out a slow moan.

His warm hands splayed on her back. She'd just had sex with the hottest guy on the planet, and it was... Off. The. Scale. No wonder the last time was so bad. It was nothing to do with her. The guy was a useless tosser. Marcus might not have had hundreds of girlfriends as she rudely suggested earlier, but he must have had enough to have honed his skills somewhere. Because he was good. Really good. They were still on top of the covers, and the bedside lamp was on. She was living dangerously, but seeing Marcus was part of the experience. He was gorgeous. Had they really done what they'd just done? Was this a dream? Could she please erase the memory of her first time and pretend this was it?

Her senses started ambling back into the real world. She was a bit stiff and still wobbly, but she loved how she was tingling and content. An accomplished feeling like the one she got after riding

– a really stupid or very apt comparison – flooded her system. She'd done it. For real. And it had blown her mind.

'Are you cold?' Marcus's warm palm circled her shoulder and he rolled off her.

'I am now.'

Was this where the dream ended and he kicked her back into her own room?

'Do you want to stay here?' He curled his fingers around the hair behind her ear and gently stroked it down her body and past her waist. His hands strayed further and he cupped her bottom. 'Or shall I port you back to your own room?'

'Can I stay? Or would you prefer me gone?'

'I want you right here, topolina.'

'Then I'll stay but tell me what topolina means.'

'Make me.'

'Oh, stop your nonsense.'

He laughed with a low rumble. 'If you still want me in the morning, I have some more wicked things I'd like to do with you.'

'Should I be scared?'

'I hope not.'

He got out of the bed to dispose of his condom and Willow shuffled under the covers. Cold air replaced his warm arms, but not for long. He flipped back his side of the duvet and climbed in. It was cool between the sheets but as soon as the human hottie returned, warmth seeped into every vein and she was back in seventh heaven. He coiled her in his arms and placed a kiss on her forehead.

'Did you always want to be a weather presenter?' she asked.

'No. When I left school, I wasn't sure what I wanted to do.'

'So, how did you get into it?'

'How come pillow talk got us here so quickly?'

'It's better than talking about your exes, isn't it?'

'Almost one and the same.'

'What do you mean?'

'Because my TV career started with an ex. The first of a long line of fake women. I was her protégé and her bit on the side, but it backfired. She thought I'd be a nice little earner for her and I'd stick around once she got me into TV and I'd pay for fancy holidays for us. She refused to leave her husband and told him she was away with friends, not with me. I was nothing but a plaything but I wised up and left. She couldn't take my job from me. The rest of my life has been on a par with that. So have my exes. People out for themselves, willing to make up any stories along the way to keep me sweet, until I stopped trusting any of them.'

'What about your ex-wife?'

'She didn't like the media interest and that started the decline. When my family came to stay, it was the last straw. She always said it wasn't about the money but that was a lie. After she left, she took me to the cleaners.'

Willow cringed inside, remembering her own lie. Now was not the time to even consider the existence of Rocky Rainman.

'Let's talk about something else,' he said.

'You didn't fake your qualifications though, did you? To get the job in the first place?'

'No. I have a degree in mathematics. That's all I needed to get into the Met Office training programme. But I had other talents that fast-tracked me up the ladder.'

'I noticed.'

'Exactly,' he said. 'I got to the top very quickly.'

'You shagged your way up?' She couldn't hide her shock but she couldn't move either, so her accompanying stare of disapproval was lost.

'Pretty much.'

'Wow. Ok.'

'I'm not proud of it. Not at all. I look back at my younger self with nothing but disgust. I wasn't brought up to behave like that. My mama would have a fit if she knew. Thank god, she never will.'

'Well, I'm sure she was proud of what you became. You made good.'

'Did I? Sometimes I'm not sure. I don't enjoy it as much as I should.'

'The early mornings, you mean?'

'Partly them. I don't know. It's gone sterile.'

'I don't know what you mean.'

'It's like everything is set up to clinical standards and I turn up, smile and say my piece. The weather changes every day but my job doesn't.'

'I thought you liked it like that. Everything lined up neatly, like your pens.'

'Hmm. Very funny. Like the ones you used to knock off or nick.'

'I didn't. Well, maybe I knocked them over once or twice… And possibly borrowed one occasionally.'

'Uh-huh. I knew it was you.'

A little giggle escaped her. 'So, why doesn't that work for you anymore?'

'Not sure. Maybe I just need a change.'

'To do more TV, like *Destination Forecast*?'

'Possibly.' He kissed her forehead again and she closed her eyes, loving everything about this moment. The contact of his skin on hers was the most calming and comforting feeling she could imagine. Her whole body was more relaxed than it had been after any therapy sessions and her mind was loose and free, with no irritating thoughts poking in to spoil things. 'We should sleep,' he whispered. 'Night-night, topolina.'

'Night, Marcus, and thank you.'

'What for?'

'Helping me find faith. And giving me the night of my life.'

His chest twitched as he breathed a short laugh. 'Mutual, I assure you. That was as hot as hell, topolina. And I hope you never doubt your powers of seduction ever again. You're perfect. Absolutely perfect.'

Chapter Twenty-One

Marcus

Willow's head rested on Marcus's chest, her long hair all over the place. Her shoulders rose and fell slowly as she slept like Sleeping Beauty. Marcus's eyes had accustomed to the darkness and according to his phone, it was six fifteen. He stroked Willow's hair from her face. It got everywhere, but something about it was just so her and he wouldn't want her to change it for the world.

He prided himself on being a man of routines and good habits. Mostly. Sometimes they verged on OCD. Everything had got stale and calculated. If Toby left and Laurenia moved, he'd be alone for the first time in a long time. The chaos of family life would be gone and he could organise his personal life in exactly the way he did with his professional life. Only he wasn't sure he wanted to. He'd got used to the spontaneity... And the love. Coming home to an empty house would be cold.

Pressing a kiss to Willow's warm forehead, he sighed. Yes, even Marcus Bowman craved love sometimes. The waxwork with the impeccable image and cool heart needed human connection to feel whole just as much as the next person.

Willow. He ran his fingertips gently across her shoulder. His mind rewound to last night. They'd made a connection alright. A beautiful one. This was something... someone he wanted to cling to and never let go.

He should be up, getting ready to leave, but no. However long he could make this moment go on, he would. If she woke up, he wanted to make love to her all over again. This was what she did to him. He wanted to call it love and keep her close. He drew her up against him. His body and soul were hot for her and craved satisfaction. *How can I leave her?* But he must. His life wasn't here.

'I can't move,' she murmured.

'You're awake.'

'Kind of.'

'Are you stuck?'

'Only because I don't want to move.'

'Me neither. Well, I do, but not far.'

She slid her head up to look at him and he leaned in for a kiss, gliding his hands over her naked back.

'Isn't morning kissing taboo?' she said.

'I'll risk it if you will.'

'Definitely.' She rolled over and, with a little push from him, straddled him.

He didn't need any encouragement. He was ready to play. If he accepted this as a game, he wouldn't get hurt. She could use him as a toy. And really, he was so used to that role it shouldn't bother him. He'd had women use him for their own pleasure for years. If he'd accepted it in the beginning, he could have saved himself countless painful breakups. But something was different this time.

A quick bathroom break was called for but when they resumed their position in the bed, Marcus had forgotten everything he'd been thinking before. All he could focus on was the naked beauty on top of him, leaning over so her long locks curtained his face, blocking the outside world and locking them in a tunnel of passionate kisses.

He reached up and played with her cute little breasts. They perked up with the attention and she arched back. He followed her lead, making sure he did nothing too suddenly or moved her in a way that might hurt her. They didn't need much to warm them up. He assumed she, like him, had been dreaming about it for several hours; their dream-selves had done the foreplay for them. She was so hot for him, watching with hungry eyes as he grabbed a condom from his wash bag on the beside cabinet.

He loved touching her and making her moan. Her smile was so wide as she bounced on top of him he couldn't help but grin back. This was joyful. Quicker than last night; fun as well as mind blowing. He held her hips, massaging them in sync with his. Their body friction had Willow squealing and shaking. She was beautiful anyway, but when she let go, she was perfect. Her skin flushed, her small but perfectly shaped breasts distended and her neck arched back as she panted. It was enough to push him towards the edge. He slid his hands around her waist and her hips answered his thrusts. Another smile spread across her face and it tipped him into oblivion.

She flopped onto him, laughing. He hoped she was laughing anyway, not crying.

'Are you ok?' His voice was hoarse and his breathing ragged. He was still raw and sensitive. Her breath tickled him.

'Never better. You?'

'Same.' He let out a sigh into the crook of her neck, turning it into a kiss, and she nuzzled him.

An angry buzzing blared from nearby.

'Shit.' He stretched one arm towards the bedside table and fumbled for his phone. 'It's Ginny. Christ.'

'Are you supposed to be on air?' Willow pushed up and stared.

'Not today. No, but I was supposed to have left. Damn it.' He swiped up and pressed the phone to his ear. 'Hello.'

'Where are you?'

'Where I should be.'

'Really?'

He tried not to look at Willow's horrified expression. 'We've got some Wi-Fi issues.'

'What's that got to do with anything?'

'Er... Nothing.'

'Are you on your way back?'

'Just leaving shortly.'

'Well, if you're still there, you can do the morning forecast before you leave.'

'What?'

'Half an hour. Be ready. Sadie still isn't back and it's a bloody nightmare. Also, we have a studio meeting later and I need you there. Your little holiday is over as soon as the forecast is done, understood?'

'Holiday?'

'If you need a break, take some annual leave the next time.'

'You're the one who sent me. I didn't ask—' He glared at the now blank screen. 'Bitch ended the call.'

'Oh, Marcus, I'm sorry. I hope I haven't got you into trouble.' Willow chewed on the end of her nail, looking so damn cute he wanted to have her all over again.

'It takes two to tango. You haven't got me into trouble. I'm capable of doing that myself. I better take a quick shower.'

It was very quick. He shoved on trousers, a shirt and his coat over the top. No one could see what he was wearing under it anyway.

'I should help you,' Willow said.

'No, it's fine. You take your time.'

Outside was a white out but the snow wasn't deep enough to shut the road. Thank god. That would push Ginny over the edge if he got snowed in. At least one car had passed through, leaving muddy tyre tracks. His forecast was the most unprepared pile of shit ever. When he should have been reading charts, he was in bed, having the time of his life. He hadn't been this irresponsible since he was in his early twenties. Was he forcing Willow down the same path? Christ, she was only twenty-six. What was he playing at? She was eleven years younger than him.

David was presenting again that morning and Marcus swore to god he would scream if he mentioned Rocky Rainman.

'So, not the snow we were hoping for?' David said.

'It's unlikely at lower levels.' As Marcus spoke, renewed flakes drifted around, landing on the lapels of his coat and his shoulders.

'But you seem to be getting it in the highlands.'

'Yes. There will be a few flurries today.' His chest compressed as he waffled. He hadn't seen an update since the previous day and was going on instinct and very little else. Ginny wanted him back and that meant he would have to leave straight away. He didn't have any excuse to stay. Except Willow. And that wasn't an excuse Ginny would accept. Nor should he.

Willow was at the desk in the office when he returned. She looked all clean and shiny, her long hair brushed and only the slight flush in her cheeks gave away anything different about her.

'Hi.' She minimised a screen and he frowned. His mind was so screwed he'd thought for a second it was a weather map she had up.

'Hi.' He ruffled the wet snow from his head. 'I should get properly dressed. I need to leave.' He raised his eyes to hers.

'I know.' She looked back at her screen, twirling her hair around her finger in that endearing way of hers.

'Yeah. Sorry. Talk about bad timing, huh?'

'Have you seen the weather?'

'Have you forgotten who I am and what I do?'

'No.' She eyed him over, setting his insides on fire again. 'I think you're crazy to leave just now. It's an accident waiting to happen.'

He cocked his head. Bloody hell, she really cared about him. It melted his heart so much. Very few people would care enough to want to stop him from driving in bad weather. Just Laurenia really.

'I promise I'll take care,' he said.

Willow shook her head. 'It's mad.'

He ducked down to pet Marshmallow and glanced back at Willow. 'I'm sorry, Willow. We both knew it was going to happen, but—'

'You really shouldn't drive anywhere in this weather.'

'I have no choice. It's not just Ginny. I have to get back to Laurenia, my sister. I promised her I wouldn't be away long. She deserves better than always being left caring for Toby while I jet off here and there.'

'Oh, yes. Of course.'

Yes, there it was. Once he was back with his family, the dating opportunities would fade away. Toby would at some point leave Marcus's care but until then, this was the reality of his life. His ex-wife couldn't cope with the influx of his family in her home and her leaving after that sat there like a warning beacon.

After packing up all his equipment and checking he had everything, he was almost ready to face leaving Willow. For now. Maybe he could arrange to come back soon. If Laurenia was still dead set on moving up here, maybe he could come too. If he gave up on worrying about Rocky Rainman, he could quit the forecasting and focus on presenter jobs, then he wouldn't be tied to the studio the same way. He could figure something out for Toby. All this assuming Willow wanted him and the whole package he came with.

The curtains in the bedroom were still closed and he threw them back. 'Holy shit.'

Thick snow was falling again, and fat, furious flakes obscured everything. The tracks that were on the road this morning were covered and a thick layer of new snow had already built up. Willow was right. This looked treacherous and a lot worse than he'd forecast. No. No. No. Trouble was coming for him. Unless a snowplough came down this road, and soon, he was going nowhere and Ginny would blow like Vesuvius.

He grabbed his phone and scrolled straight to Rocky Rainman's feed.

As the snow beast travels down the way, listen carefully to what I say, widespread disruption for most of the day...

Heavy snow moves south, so expect disruption to transport links and school closures across Scotland.

Rocky recommends staying at home and keeping warm if you can! Take care, folks.

No way. Just no way. *How did I not see this snow coming?*

Chapter Twenty-Two

Willow

As the snow beast travels down the way, listen carefully to what I say, widespread disruption for most of the day...

Snow swirled thick and fast, just as Rocky Rainman had predicted. And Marcus hadn't. He'd been distracted – by Willow. She'd tried to tell him but he was having none of it. She opened the front doors and looked out. If he tried to get out in this, he would get stuck before he reached the village. They weren't on a bus route, so it could take twenty-four hours for the snow plough to come by, depending on how bad it was elsewhere – and it was bad everywhere.

Her body often felt like it had been dragged through a mangle, but today's muscle spasms and twinges kept happening in different places, reminding her of Marcus and their time together.

Her heart was the achiest part. She never deluded herself that he'd stick around or anything more could come from this, but knowing he'd be away soon was like a glacier in her chest. She'd be here alone, not knowing if he was alive or dead. And she wanted him in her arms, with her, nowhere else.

'Hey,' Marcus said. His hand landed on her shoulder. 'This is... More snow than I expected.'

'I called it.'

'You did. And who else do you think called it?'

'Rocky Rainman?'

'Yup. And now I'm the second Michael Fish. I—' His phone buzzed and he slapped it to his ear, rubbing at his forehead.

Willow dipped her chin to her chest and nibbled on her lower lip. Poor Marcus. She knew it wasn't her fault he didn't do his forecast properly but she couldn't help feeling responsible. Last night – and this morning – had been amazing but he could have been preparing a forecast, though he hadn't known Sadie would be off again.

If she crossed the line in her brain and allowed herself to imagine anything further with Marcus, it made her sick, because she knew she couldn't have it. She mustn't be greedy and she wasn't silly enough to think one night would lead to anything more, especially when Rocky Rainman still loomed between them. Judging from his current mood, now wasn't a good time to confess. Maybe that day would never come... If this was to be goodbye.

'Look, I told you,' he said into the phone. 'We had Wi-Fi trouble.' He pulled a face at Willow. 'I couldn't make a proper forecast as I couldn't access the charts. Snow flurries is what I said. I just didn't think they'd be this heavy.'

'You also said no snow at lower levels but we have it here too!' Ginny's voice was so loud Willow could hear it clear as a whistle.

'I said it was unlikely, not impossible.' He held the phone away from his ear as she ranted. 'I don't think I'll get back until at least tomorrow. I'm not leaving here until the snow plough clears the road, it's too risky.'

'You're a forecaster, Marcus!' she screeched. 'And somehow you managed to get yourself snowed in in a snowstorm you didn't predict.'

'That about sums it up.' He closed his eyes and blew out a breath as he returned the phone to his pocket. 'That's me cocked up big time.'

'But on the plus side, you're not leaving.' Willow couldn't keep the cheer from her voice.

'I am. Just not today.'

'Yeah, of course... I know that. I meant you don't have to drive in the snow, so I won't worry.'

'Why would you worry about me?'

'Because I...' She shrugged. 'Quite like you.'

'Not just my body.' He raised his eyebrows.

'An added benefit. I always liked you. You know that... I sent you a Valentine card, remember?'

'Ah, so it was you. That was very cute and well written.' He nodded. 'But then you told me you had a boyfriend and it wasn't you.'

'I was embarrassed.'

'I always hoped the card was from you, but I believed you had a boyfriend so I discounted you.'

'Really?'

'Yes.'

'Well, I didn't. I mooned after you. Or I did until I thought you'd been rude about me.'

He took her hands in his. 'I like you too, Willow. Very much.'

'Why have we gone all sappy?'

'Dunno.' He shrugged. 'I just need something to cheer me up.'

'I could make hot chocolate and put on some music. Or we could watch a film. Do you like *It's A Wonderful Life*?'

'I'm not sure I've ever seen it.'

'What? It's a classic. How can you have missed it?'

He held out his hands. 'No idea. So, you want to sing, dance, watch movies and drink at ten thirty?'

'Why not? Apart from the fact I'm supposed to be working? But who cares? I'm just happy you're not leaving and I won't be here alone. I'm sure Marion wouldn't mind if I took a break. I've done loads of extra stuff the last few days.'

'You certainly have. So, let's do it.'

She gazed into his eyes for a moment, lost in their depths, and warmth seeped through her body. Pushing on to her tiptoes and slipping her hand around his jaw, she pulled him towards her and kissed him. His fragrance surrounded her and she drank in his minty fresh taste. No holding back now. She didn't need to worry about him not liking her or feeling awkward about her body. She knew he was into her. He'd treated her like a goddess in the bedroom, not a porcelain ornament that might break or a rag doll to throw. He was the perfect gentleman. A lover. An equal. He wasn't afraid to ask her how different things felt or let her guide him. If she needed time or her muscles locked, he was kind and soothed her with words and kisses. He was gentle but firm enough to make everything feel good without hurting her and he gave her time to relax and didn't rush her. Just like these kisses. They were so soft and yet so deep. She wanted all of him and she chased his mouth with hers.

'If I didn't know better,' he rasped, 'I'd think you were a weather sprite who arranged this just to keep me here.'

'If I was, then I would have. I guess you'll never know.' With a little prod, she left him and went to fix up the hot chocolates. As the milk boiled, she messaged Marion and told her about the weather situation and that she'd delivered Malcolm and Brenda's Christmas present to the party.

In the lounge, Marcus was kneeling by the wood-burning stove, chucking logs in it. 'I've grown to love this fire.' He rubbed his hands in front of it.

'I never had one until I came here,' Willow said. 'My mum was scared I'd fall into one.'

Marcus smirked. 'Oh, Willow.'

She laid the cups on a side table then sat down. Her smile must have made her look like a right goof but every time she saw him, she couldn't help it. Little memories of the night before kept creeping in and adding to the light sensation in her head. Marcus held out his hand and she took it. With a little wincing, she joined him on the floor.

The fire blazed, kicking out a glorious heat as they sat on the rug with their hot chocolates, side by side, leaning on the chairs. Marcus sipped his drink and laid his hand on Willow's thigh, gently kneading it. It was intimate and possessive.

'If I had to choose one person to be snowed in with,' he said, 'it would be you every time.'

'What?'

'Why not? I don't remember feeling this happy and relaxed for a long time.'

He leaned over and kissed her. Soon, their tongues were dancing and she shuffled round and straddled him. Her hips had been known to lock in awkward positions, but if they did, she wouldn't have to worry. Marcus hadn't been bothered that morning and the same was true for now. It could have turned into the world's longest kiss. Just her making up for lost time. She was twenty-six and had hardly kissed anyone. Now, she didn't want to kiss anyone else ever again. Would any other lips taste this good? He anchored his hands around her waist, drawing her closer. She rubbed up against him and it was exquisite.

'We should take this upstairs,' he said.

'Let's not.'

'Ok. Then we better stop.' He pulled his head back and leaned it on the chair behind, breathing rapidly. 'Get that film on, play music or whatever. You're going to have to distract me somehow.'

'I mean, let's do it here.'

His eyebrows lifted in tandem. 'In the common room?'

'It's not like anyone can get here, is it? I think we'll be quite safe.'

A grin spread across his face. She'd never hidden how much she loved the look of him but now it was more. So much more. When he smiled, he lit her world.

'Ok. But I need to go upstairs and get something. I'm not exactly prepared for this.'

Her turn to grin. She clambered off him and he jumped to his feet. Her eyes ran over his body and she smiled at what she saw.

'Don't be too long.'

She lolled back and waited. Who would have forecast the week turning out like this? Marcus had flipped her world on its head. Her body was tingling and shaking, desperate for a repeat of hitherto unknown pleasures. He'd opened a door for her last night and she had stepped through it with him into a new place, an exciting place, and she was eager to explore further. How unfortunate they only had a few days, maybe only hours.

He was back. Willow rolled her head to watch him approach, her mind already undressing him. He sat beside her and ran his hands down her cheeks, then pushed her hair over her shoulders and kissed her neck.

'You're a woman of beauty.' He pushed her neckline to the edge of her shoulder, placing more kisses on the exposed skin. 'I want to know every inch of you. You're my goddess, topolina. You deserve to be worshipped.'

She tossed back her head as he worked his way over her body, removing clothes when needed. She indulged in every sensation. He had magic hands and a genius tongue. A decent girl like her should have felt shy at being laid bare at midday in broad daylight in a public room. But she couldn't think straight enough to even remember her own name. She was coming undone. Spasms of ecstasy tore through her, leaving a trail of lights brighter than the sparkling Christmas tree and its glinting baubles. She moaned like she'd lost her mind, her nails digging into the threadbare rug.

'Oh, Marcus.'

'Yes, Willow.' He took her in his arms, rocking her, stroking her hair and kissing her forehead. She was the most special person in the universe right now.

The fire was pumping out almost as much heat as Marcus. He was scorching between the sheets... And on top of them... And on the fireside sofa where they'd ended up. His sculpted and perfectly tanned body was a feast for her eyes as he thrust between her hips. She lounged back, enjoying the view and the incredible sensations in her body. The sight of him losing control sent shocks of delight coursing through her. Marcus Bowman and little Willow. He was covered in beads of sweat. Her heart raced like mad. *I did that to him.*

They cuddled up close and she curled into him as he got his breath back.

'I don't recall ever having done this in such a daring place before,' he said.

'Yeah. I suppose someone could have hiked from the village and be looking in the window.'

'Don't joke. The last thing I need is for people to find out what Marcus Bowman actually gets up to when he's supposed to be weather forecasting.'

A giggle escaped her lips. They were swollen from all the kissing.

'What are you doing for Christmas?' he asked.

'I'd like my parents to come here but one look at this weather and they won't leave their house again until April.'

He chuckled.

'You can laugh but it's not far from the truth. Neither of them are confident drivers in the snow. It's a shame because I miss them and I think they'd love Christmas up here. I guess I'll go back to Glasgow and see them.'

Marcus stroked her hair off her face with a slight frown. 'You seem so independent. I didn't think you would miss them.'

He thought that? *Job done.* 'Of course I do. They've always been good to me. I just needed breathing space. That's why I moved away. Sometimes their help was stifling, you know. But other times... Well, I just feel lonely.'

'But you're not normally here on your own, are you?' He carried on toying with her hair, twisting it over her shoulder, making her tingle again.

'No. And I have Hayley, my cousin, she's great. And my other cousin, Finlay, Hayley's brother, and my aunty Lisa. It's just not quite the same as my parents though.'

'No, I suppose it isn't.' He sighed, pushing more strands off her forehead and tucking them behind her ear. 'I miss my mama too. It never goes away completely. The loss. You learn to live with it but some days...' He shrugged. 'Things come up and I think, oh, mama will love that, and then I remember she's not here to tell.'

Willow bit back a lump in her throat. 'Oh, Marcus. That's sad.'

'It's also life unfortunately. But I have a hunch your parents will make it here for Christmas. In fact, I, Marcus Bowman, meteorologist and formerly Scotland's favourite weather presenter, shall stick out my neck and say the likelihood of a white Christmas is very slim.'

'I'll let them know. My mum definitely thinks you're number one.'

He shook his head but looked unable to keep the smile off his face.

'What about you?' she asked. 'Where will you have Christmas?'

'At home with Toby and my sister. I promised her I'd be back. Her husband works on the rigs and he won't be home until the twenty-eighth.'

'Oh, that can't be easy.'

'It isn't.' Marcus sighed. 'She wants to move back to Glenbriar – it's where we grew up – but we need to find accommodation for Toby. It would be ideal if we could keep this place open and get him here, but I'm not sure how that would work. He wasn't for staying the last time we tried.'

'Maybe if you weren't so far away.' A brief glimmer of hope sparked in her chest.

'Maybe. We'll see. I can only leave Glasgow if I leave forecasting and, well... I'm not ready to do that just yet. I definitely don't want to give up broadcasting entirely. It's all I've ever done and I don't want to start something new this late on.'

'The way you talk sometimes is daft, like you're ancient or something.'

'I am compared to you.'

'Shut up. That's ridiculous. Look at yourself. You're in incredible condition. I've never met anyone my age who looks as good as you.'

He rubbed his nose along her forehead. 'You don't half know how to boost a guy's ego.'

After they'd lain together for an indecent length of time, Willow remembered she was getting paid to be there. 'I should do some work.'

'Me too,' Marcus said. 'I could clear some snow from the drive just in case the plough comes through.'

'Ok. There's a shovel out back.'

It was a wrench leaving the warmth of the fireside. Willow sat on the windowsill and watched Marcus heading into the carpark. She pulled out her phone. She needed to talk to Marion just in case she decided to attempt a journey in this.

'Hello, hello.' Marion answered on the second ring. 'How are you? What a nightmare you're having.'

'No, I'm fine.' And she really was. She hadn't felt this good in a long time despite all the bizarre things that had happened that week. 'How's Barry?'

'He seems a lot better and we were going to try to get back but have you seen the weather?'

'Yes. We're snowed in too, so I wouldn't travel just now. Maybe later if the ploughs go through, but if you've got somewhere nice to stay tonight, then do. It's Saturday tomorrow and we have no guests, so there isn't a lot to do.'

'Is Marcus Bowman still there? I'm so gutted to have missed him.'

'He's here, but he's hoping to leave later if the roads are cleared.' She prayed Rocky's forecast was accurate and that Marcus would have to stay – for at least one more night.

'And has he got anything for his report?'

'I think so.' He still hadn't officially told her if he was going to make the report into a documentary and with everything else, she'd forgotten to ask him.

'Well, I'm praying it works. If we don't get some more residents on the books, we won't be able to open again after Christmas.'

Willow sucked on her lip. Everything really did depend on Marcus and his reports being a success, but would it generate enough interest and publicity?

She ended the call and laid down her phone, watching him tossing a shovelful of snow into the wall. If only he would stay but she knew he wouldn't. His career was too important to him. This little fling had been fun but now she needed to end it and draw a line under it. But how? She had no experience in this kind of thing.

She checked the time. Would Hayley be up? She probably couldn't get to work either and if she did, would her clients? Maybe she'd have time to chat.

Willow sent her a quick message.

WILLOW: Hi, can you chat?

A few seconds later, the phone buzzed and Hayley's name flashed on the screen.

'I certainly can,' Hayley chirped. 'It's snowing!'

Willow laughed at the cheer in her voice. 'I had noticed.'

'It looks amazing but I've had to cancel all my clients today. Nobody can get anywhere safely. I'll probably lose money but hey-ho, I can build a snowman instead.'

'Send me photos later.'

'I will. So, what do you want to chat about? Is everything ok?'

'Kind of.'

'Oh dear.' Hayley's voice dropped. 'That doesn't sound too good.'

'I need to talk to someone... confess something.'

'Oh my god, what? What have you done? You don't have another secret identity, do you?'

'No. I don't. Do you remember I used to work with Marcus Bowman?'

'That scumbag. How could I forget?'

'Yeah, him. Well... I discovered it wasn't me he was talking about when he said that stuff. In fact, I discovered that he always liked me. And I... well, I think you guessed that I liked him.'

'What? What? What? Wait, just what?'

Willow imagined Hayley's wide brown eyes goggling in disbelief.

'How did you discover all this? Has he contacted you?'

'He's here, staying at the schoolhouse. He's doing a feature on it, so hopefully we get enough publicity to stay open.'

'Oh my good god. I cannot believe my ears.'

'But that's not all. He also wants to find Rocky Rainman and expose him.'

'And does he know it's you?'

'Nope.'

'Does he suspect?'

'I don't think so. But it's way worse than all of that.'

'It is?' Hayley had a lovely, kind voice, but Willow couldn't miss the edge of panic.

'The crush I used to have hasn't gone away and he kind of has it too.'

'Oh my god. Are you...? Have you and him been testing all the rooms?'

'Not quite.' Heat flooded Willow's cheeks. Thank god Hayley couldn't see her.

'Bloody hell, Willow. It's the quiet ones you have to watch after all.'

'I'm so scared. I don't know what to do.'

'About what? Have you and him actually done it? Or you mean you're scared to do it with him? I would be... He's a freaking TV presenter, after all.'

'We did it.'

'Holy baby Jesus. So... What are you scared of?'

'About seeing him again. What will I do when he leaves? I don't think I can stand it. I've never had a fling. And I'm not stupid enough to think we could have an actual relationship.'

'Why couldn't you?'

'Oh, come on, Hayley, be real. Ditto what you just said about him being a TV god. His life isn't in a small town like this. He has a career and a family.'

'Aw, sweet Willow, my beauty. If you like him that much, you need to talk to him. It's the only way. You might find a way around it.'

'That's just so hard... I mean what will I say?'

'Just ask him how he feels about seeing you again. Don't assume you know what he'll say. Ask him if he'd like to meet up again soon. Tell him you enjoyed his company. And don't go thinking he's doing you a favour. You're just as important as him and if he really cares about you, he'll find a way to work you into his life with his career and his family.'

'Ok.' Willow took a deep breath. Hayley spoke sense but putting it into action was something else. She had to find the words.

'But, Willow,' Hayley added. 'Are you going to tell him about Rocky Rainman?'

That was the million-dollar question and she really didn't know the answer.

Chapter Twenty-Three

Marcus

Marcus's back ached as he tossed another shovelful of snow onto a pile beside the wall. He was used to working out, but this action was repetitive and spine crushing. He discarded his jacket, ready to face the blizzard in a sweater. Better ways to work up a sweat must exist. All the versions his imagination threw at him involved Willow. Willow. Beautiful Willow.

'God, I love her,' he muttered to himself.

The fresh air had cleared his brain enough to see the truth. He loved Willow. Back in the office, he'd liked her smile and her good nature. She was a smart girl, who liked sudoku and picked up things quickly. When he'd given her jobs to do, he'd never had to worry about her not getting what he meant; he hadn't had to explain things so often he'd have been quicker doing it himself.

He could be the most authentic version of himself with her. No need to hide or pretend. He could talk about himself and his family without being judged or saying what people wanted to hear. *But where the hell does that leave me?* Would Willow want a life in the spotlight? He was so much older than her and she'd admitted to having little experience of relationships. This was maybe just a practice for her – a *find a guy who knows what he's doing and make use of him* kind of thing.

And there was his family. His ex-wife hadn't taken to being thrust into living with them, but it was different now; those days were coming to an end. He launched another batch of snow with a grunt. His ex had been upset that he paid so much attention to his family. But he had to. He'd never abandon his family the way his father had. He owed it to his mama. She'd given her all – her life – to make sure they grew up happy. He wouldn't let that be in vain.

His phone buzzed in his back pocket, interrupting his thoughts. *Bet it's Ginny with another bollocking.* If it was, he could tell her he was punishing himself with manual labour.

'Oh no.' He groaned. It was a DM call from Malcom Mc-Manus. Why had he given him a way to contact him? What the hell did he want? 'Hello.'

'Hello, Marcus. How are you?'

'Fine. What can I do for you?'

'I've just had a very interesting call.' Malcolm's voice droned like a low rumbling generator.

'Which is?'

'Did you hear Robert Mackie confessing to being Rocky Rainman yesterday?'

'I did.' A fact he'd almost forgotten after his night with Willow.

'Apparently he's out on the main road in Glenbriar building snowmen with his kids and telling people he's Rocky and the snowmen are statues in his honour. I think you might want to investigate him.'

'Yeah. I should, shouldn't I?'

'I can give you his address if you want to visit him. The name Robert sounds a bit like Rocky, I suppose.'

'Listen, I'm snowed in. Don't you have a phone number or anything?'

'No, I don't think so. But he's at the top end of Glenbriar, one of the last houses, so you could walk it from the schoolhouse.'

Marcus squinted down the road at the thick wads of snow covering it. 'How far is it?'

'It takes about half an hour on foot. And you can go down the road today as there won't be any cars. There's a path through the woods too but that might be worse in this weather.'

'Right. I'll try the road if you give me the details.'

A half-hour walk wouldn't do any harm, especially if he could finally unmask Rocky Rainman, even though it sounded like he had unmasked himself.

Chucking the shovel up beside the door, he nipped into the foyer and kicked off his boots. Willow wasn't about. Where had she got to? He checked around the foyer, the common room and the kitchen.

Back in the office, he grabbed a notepad from her desk and scribbled on it.

Willow

Don't know where you are but I just had a call saying that Robert Mackie is pretty much a dead cert for Rocky Rainman and I should investigate him. I'm just going to nip down the road to Glenbriar and check him out. I should be ok on foot.

See you in a bit. Won't be long. I'll be back before you can say Rocky Rainman is a pain, man!

Marcus

xx

That should do it. Marcus pulled his jacket on. He had another quick check he hadn't missed Willow in the common room but she wasn't there. If he got Rocky, Ginny might allow him to leave the doghouse. She'd love to have the big reveal on air. Also, if Rocky Rainman lived within walking distance of the schoolhouse, that might help the cause. He had thousands of followers. Surely that would count for something.

Battling against the snow was hard work and, on the ground, it was above his ankles and seeped uncomfortably into his boots. Being back in the hotel with Willow would have been much cosier than this. Hopefully she was ok. His mind clouded with doubt. Where was she?

Maybe he should turn around. But he'd been going for fifteen minutes. That was halfway, right? On a normal day. Malcolm hadn't been talking about a day like today when he said half an hour, had he? Not when it was taking about a minute for each step. Marcus unstuck his feet and knocked compacted snow off his soles every few inches.

This was getting more and more dangerous with every step he took.

Chapter Twenty-Four

Willow

The wind's still blowing.
It's still snowing. Will it
ever stop? Be safe, not bold.
Stay out of the cold...

Will this snow ever stop? Rocky Rainman knew it wasn't going to clear for another few hours at least. The council website said gritters and ploughs were working in the area. But they couldn't guarantee the road past the schoolhouse being cleared today as they were prioritising main routes. Willow looked out the upstairs window and shook her head.

She'd spent some time tidying the cupboard with the spare clothes in it and got a little carried away. The sound of Marcus shovelling snow had stopped. In fact, she had heard it for a while. She'd thought she'd heard him come in a little while ago but he hadn't come up. Maybe he was in the common room. She made her way downstairs. Through the little sliding window into the office, she spotted Marshmallow sleeping on the swivel chair. The door was shut and she'd obviously been shut in. Willow opened the door.

'Want to come into the common room? It's warmer.'

Her eyes landed on a note on the desk. She picked it up and read. 'Oh no.' Her heart pounded and blood rang in her ears, making her sweat.

Marcus had gone out in that. People occasionally walked to the village from here when the weather was nice but in this blizzard, it was insane. And what would he find? Some faker who was kidding on he was Rocky Rainman for five minutes on TV? Would Marcus believe it?

Willow got to her feet and fanned her face. It might be cold outside but she was burning up. How would she forgive herself if anything happened to him? He didn't need to leave the schoolhouse to find Rocky Rainman. *I'm right here.*

'Oh god.' She clutched her cheeks. What could she do to get him to come back right now? Message him? Her fingers were all over the place as she pulled out her phone. His contact number was on the check-in form. She clicked through folders to find it, then typed wrong numbers several times. 'Seriously?' She was all fingers and thumbs.

Finally, she got the right one and held the phone to her ear, willing him to pick it up. Voicemail. Bugger. The schoolhouse got decent reception but further down the road it wasn't so good.

He must be out of reach. Or he might have fallen in a drift and be dying of hypothermia.

'Oh, help,' she said. She needed to go after him. Walking to the village even on a good day was a massive ask. In this weather, it was going to be damn near impossible. But she couldn't stay here doing nothing.

How could she bear it?

With her ears pricked for any sound, she pulled on her coat and wrapped her scarf around her neck.

A clock ticked in the entrance hall and Marshmallow licked her paw, but everything else was silent. The Christmas tree flashed warmly, not like the warning she was expecting. Where were all the people telling her to be careful? She probably shouldn't be doing this but sitting waiting was agony.

Outside, the carpet of snow deadened any noise and the schoolhouse looked like a Christmas card. She could just go to the gate and shout. Maybe he would hear her. Hopefully she wouldn't cause an avalanche in the process.

The path Marcus cleared earlier was already covered in a fresh fall, but it was easy enough to get to the gate. The main road, not so much. Willow pushed her crutch into the snow, and it sank at least four inches. Her foot followed. This would be tough going. One wrong move and she would be the one face down in the snow.

It was literally one step at a time. She was almost climbing the snow, then sinking into it and dragging herself out again. Her hips tensed, and shooting pains travelled the length of her legs.

'Marcus!' she yelled.

She stopped to catch her breath. The schoolhouse was just there. She'd barely gone fifty metres, but it felt like she had done a marathon.

Where are you? If only she could fly. She needed to find him and bring him back. If she went into the house now, she'd sit and panic, but she wasn't going anywhere in this. She had to go back. Going any further was just stupid and Marcus was nowhere in sight. One step back and her foot sank deeper. Her boots had excellent grips and supported her ankles, keeping her feet in the right position – almost. Her left one would never be straight. As a child, she was often on tiptoes and had to do all kinds of exercises to flatten her arches. She'd had operations that kept her off school for weeks. Her right leg was slightly better. No one knew if that was down to the operations or the way it would have been anyway.

The blizzard was so strong she could barely see a few metres in front of her face.

She dragged her right foot from its snow pit and took another step, but her left foot didn't follow. It caught and she slammed to the ground. Her crutch flew out of her hand. 'Ow,' she cried. The surrounding snow was soft but so cold and thick. Her legs hurt. She fumbled around, trying to find a way to push herself up, and icy droplets seeped in between the edge of her gloves and her cuff, chilling her wrists. *Please, let me be back now, in the schoolhouse with Marcus.* If only he hadn't gone out.

She grabbed her crutch and, with a tremendous effort, clawed herself to her feet. Her muscles were numb and cold, her legs so tense she could hardly take another step.

Keep going. Get back. She said the words over and over inside her head. *Keep going.* But every step was getting more and more painful and the Schoolhouse didn't seem to be getting any closer. She couldn't do it. A row of Caledonian pines stood along the fence with branches heaving under the weight of snowfall. If that dropped into her path, it would be a snow wall she'd never get over.

The distance between her and safety now looked so far. *How can I do this?* She wanted to sit down and cry, but she had to get back. When did she become so reckless? Her parents had been right to keep her wrapped in cotton wool all her life if this was the stupid choice she made when left on her own. Why did she ever think coming out was a good idea? All she knew was that the idea of sitting doing nothing seemed even worse.

The last time she did something this idiotic was when she walked out of her job and never went back. Then she'd moved a hundred miles away from her family and the norm. Since then, other than keeping her Rocky Rainman persona a secret, she hadn't put a foot wrong. Marcus had been back in her life for five days and suddenly she was behaving like a fool again, only this time it was because she couldn't bear the thought of something happening to him.

She'd fallen for him again, just as she had before. That's why she'd been so hurt when she thought he hated her. That's why she wanted him back safe in her arms. 'I love him. So much.' The words came out aloud through a mist of icy tears. But it was all impossible and utterly hopeless. Marcus may have given her the best night of her life, but he wasn't staying here. What would he stay for? Did they have anything in common? Apart from liking horses, and sudoku... and weather.

Oh god.

The weather and Rocky Rainman. That foolish invention was going to be the death of her.

CHAPTER TWENTY-FIVE

Marcus

Marcus couldn't see his hand in front of his face. He didn't have a clue if he was anywhere near the town or not. His phone had no reception and since he'd gone out of range of the schoolhouse, the Wi-Fi and 4G were non-existent too. This was insane.

Willow was right. He should have stayed put. What was the point going any further? His equipment bag was waterproof but there was so much snow on it, it was bound to have seeped in. Wouldn't it be just the thing if he got there and all the equipment was ruined?

Time to turn back.

So much for a half-hour walk. He must have been away for an hour. Poor Willow. The first person outside of his family who'd cared about him for a very long time and he'd left her alone with only a note saying where he'd gone. Hopefully she wasn't freaking out.

Being back with her would make all this seem pointless. She was right from the start. What the hell was he bothering with this person for anyway? He didn't need to find anyone. What he needed was a new direction. It was his job and his life getting him down. Rocky Rainman was a good excuse to get out of the office for a week, but that was it. Marcus needed to remove himself permanently from it. Finally, out here in a crushing snowstorm, he saw it clearly. He could hand in his notice straight away. The money from *Destination Forecast* would be enough for the near future and if he could get more jobs like that throughout the year, everything would be fine. Screw Rocky Rainman. If Marcus wasn't a weather presenter anymore, it didn't matter one way or another who Rocky Rainman was or what he did. If Rocky gloated, so what? Marcus had bigger and better things to do.

If Ginny gave him the go ahead to make his report into a documentary, it might be the opening for more shows like that. Opportunities lurked everywhere if he was brave enough to snatch them. And he was ready. After his balls up with the latest forecast, Ginny would probably be delighted to see him go.

He started the long trudge back. If it was hard getting this far, it had got a whole lot worse in the last ten minutes. He had long legs but it was like climbing fences. Snow battered his face and he pulled his hood together so there was barely a slit to see out.

It must look like a slapstick comedy as he blundered forward, but it wasn't funny. It was a fight against the wind, the compacted snow on the ground and the bitter cold. All he could think about was getting back to Willow. Willow. The light at the end of the tunnel.

He squinted forward. The Schoolhouse was just visible but hazy, through the swirling flakes. Was that someone on the road just at the gates? A swooping gust lifted the snow from the fence posts, whipping it into his eyes and obscuring the view for a moment. He screwed up his face. It was someone. Who the hell was out on a day like this? Where had they come from and where were they going?

His heart sank to the soles of his snow-covered boots. Was it Willow? Why the hell was she out?

'Willow!' he yelled, but the wind carried his voice away. She was stooped over, barely moving. A surge of adrenaline pushed him forward. Stumbling, he got within shouting distance. 'Willow!'

This time, she turned. He staggered on, clambering through the snow, until he reached her.

'Willow.' He grabbed her and pulled her into him. 'Why the hell are you out here?'

'I wanted you to come back.' Her voice was weak, almost a whimper, or maybe she was crying.

'I'm back now. I didn't get far. Come on. Let's go home... I mean to the schoolhouse.' His teeth chattered, making him talk gibberish.

'Ok. But Rocky Rainman.'

'Screw him. I don't care. I only care about you.' He put his arm around her and helped her along. His hood blew down and his face took a walloping.

'It is me,' she said.

'Yes. You. Exactly. It's you that I care about. I really do. If I'd realised you cared this much when we were in the newsroom, I would have… Well, I don't know what I'd have done exactly, but I'd have been a lot nicer. You were gentle and sweet. I always liked you. You brightened my days, and you were the only person in the office I liked speaking to and could trust.'

'No, Marcus.'

'I know. It's stupid. I'm sorry I'm so anti-social. But when I'm with you, it's different. You and I are good together and I'd like to find a way to see you again.' He talked for the sake of talking and to keep them going, but it was true. 'I'm not sure how it would work.'

'It can't,' she said, her voice faint.

'Let's get back, then we can talk properly.'

He should be quiet. Out here, his words were lost on the wind, and maybe she didn't want to see him again. It was possible that in the last twenty-four hours, she'd got exactly what she wanted from him. Having sex with him was one thing, dating another. He needed to park the ideas and get them back. He could carry her the rest of the way, but he didn't feel steady enough to do it. If he fell carrying her, it'd be a lot worse.

'We're nearly there. Are you ok?' Stupid question. She was so bowed and stooped she looked ready to keel.

'I fell.' She looked away, like she was trying to hold back tears. 'And now I'm so cold. I can't do it.'

'Come on. You can. Please.'

'I should never have gone out.'

'Neither should I. I should have stayed with you.' That's what he needed to do. Not just today but always. Stay with Willow. 'We're so close. The schoolhouse is just there. Come on. I would carry you but I might slip and fall. I can guide you though. Here.'

He took her weight – it was nothing – and led her forward. She looked like she was on autopilot, her eyes glazed as he helped her over a ridge.

Finally, they were back. The snow was easing a little and the whole place looked like a beautiful Christmas scene. He couldn't stop and look. Willow needed to be inside.

Her hand shook violently as she searched her pocket for the key. Her skin was red raw. She pulled out the key and it fell into the snow.

'Noooo,' she groaned.

'It's ok.' Marcus picked it up and unlocked the door. A wall of heat greeted them and he closed the door on the blizzard. 'We made it.' He took her rosy cheeks in his hands. 'Willow. I feel so much for you. You're about the only person in the world who would have come out after me. It was dreadful of me to put you in that position.'

'I need to warm up.'

'Let's get the wet stuff off and I'll fix up the fire.'

She let out a long sigh. 'I'm sorry.'

'Hold on to me and you'll be ok. We'll both be ok.'

CHAPTER TWENTY-SIX

Willow

Cold and pain were causing brain fog, but not so much Willow wasn't fully aware of what Marcus had just said. Together they'd be ok. She needed to lie down for oh so many reasons. Did that mean he wanted to be with her? Did he know she'd been in love with him for years? Only now, she was realising a broken heart had brought her here. And maybe another waited just around the corner.

'Marcus... I...' How could she tell him she felt the same without admitting she was also his most hated enemy? All her energy drained into her body, keeping her upright, and she couldn't face the backlash a confession would bring.

'It's ok, you don't have to say anything. Let's get you into a seat.'

'I need to lie down and warm up.'

He helped her out of her soaked jacket, and her legs buckled.

'Can I carry you upstairs?'

'You must think I'm ridiculous.' She felt it. What would she have done if he hadn't been there? *You wouldn't have been out walking in the snow for a start.*

'I don't think you're anything of the sort. I think you're kind and compassionate. Who else would have cared where I was? I'm just sorry you had to. I shouldn't have left.' His eyes connected with her, asking the question again without words.

'Yes.'

He lifted her and the relief in her legs and ankles was immediate. Pain still throbbed but the pressure eased. Willow closed her eyes and rested on his shoulder. He'd taken off his jacket and her cheek pressed against the cool knit of his sweater. She didn't open her eyes until he placed her on the bed. His bed. She didn't object to him helping her undress. Last night, this was much more erotically charged. Now, it was different. His hands were cold as they pulled off her top. She was shivering in her underwear. He ran his fingertips over the goose bumps on her upper arm.

'Lie down.' He gently pulled back the cover.

Willow shuffled under and he placed the duvet over her.

'There's a hot water bottle in the cupboard,' she said. 'But you'll have to fill it downstairs in the kitchen.'

'That's fine. I'll do it.' He leaned over and kissed her cheek. 'Stay warm, topolina.'

Her eyelids were heavy. She'd been up later than she was used to last night, enjoying her time with him. Then all the walking today. It had taken its toll on her body.

He left the room and his footsteps clumped downstairs. Vague snatches of doors opening and closing permeated her consciousness. Then the covers raised and Marcus slid a fur-covered hot water bottle in beside her. Its blissful warmth heated the blood on her hands and chest as she drew it close. He moved about somewhere nearby, probably getting dry clothes, then shuffled in behind her. He was on top of the covers, but he gently spooned her and she gave in to sleep.

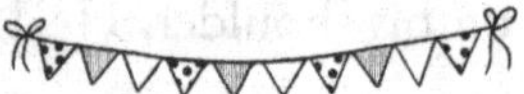

Snow covered the house, sparkling white and glittery like an advent calendar Willow once had. The glowing windows opened every day to reveal a vintage Christmas scene. But this time she was opening the door... From the inside. Marcus walked out behind her, following her into the sublime landscape. The dark blue sky twinkled with hundreds of stars and though it was dark enough to be night, it was still bright enough to see thanks to the gleaming white snow.

'I'll get the carriage,' he said.

Willow smoothed out her long dress as Marcus passed. He was in full Roman armour, gold breast plate shining in the winter sun and his red brush-topped helmet under his arm.

Willow's eyes flickered open, and she tried to hold on to the picture in her mind. She and Marcus had a house together – an old stone, Christmas-card-like house. Only he was dressed like a Roman general and she'd been wearing something more like a Victorian crinoline. Then he'd left. Oh no, he was leaving. Just to get the carriage... No, not the carriage. That was a mad dream. Where was she? Where was Marcus?

She was shaky but not cold. Her muscles and bones were in such a jumble, she couldn't quite feel where they were. The covers were moulded around her and her foot was spasmed. She tried to relax and stretch it, but it was a losing battle. Slowly, she inched her head around. Marcus wasn't behind her anymore. How long had she been asleep?

Straightening herself out took a while. She'd gone foetal and her body wanted to stay that way. This was what she'd feared would happen last night with Marcus. In a moment of passion, she'd get stuck and kill the mood completely, but it wasn't like that. He had ways of keeping her relaxed and the only tension and convulsions were the good kind.

She pushed herself into a sitting position. Light streamed in the window, and the snow-covered trees were dazzling. Had the snow stopped? The sky looked bright. At least that meant she hadn't overslept.

The clothes she'd borrowed from the spare cupboard were in the bedroom she'd been using. She had to get them. She swung her leg out of the bed and tested it. Her crutch was god knew where. Same with her phone. Her room was only a few doors down and across the landing. She could make it if she took it slowly. The decorative blanket on top of the duvet would keep her warm en route.

As she crossed the room slower than a moth moving through toffee, the door opened.

'You're awake.' Marcus beamed at her. He looked none the worse for his walk earlier. Had he showered and changed? Why was he in his coat? Not the soaked one he had on this morning, but the smart one he did his reports in. Her heart missed beat after beat. Was he leaving?

'Are you...?' She didn't have the words or the strength to continue.

'Hey.' He took her face in his hands. 'Don't worry. Everything's fine. Look, sit back down a minute. I want to ask you something.'

'What?' Her mind scrambled a bunch of ideas as he guided her back to the bed and sat knee to knee with her. She pulled the blanket tight.

'Willow.' He gazed at her for a moment as if drinking her all in. 'The easiest way to say this is just to spit it out, though you might think I'm crazy. The bottom line is, I'd like to keep seeing you.'

'Seeing me...' Smile! She should smile but wow. He'd said exactly what she'd been worrying about saying earlier. That had to mean they were on the same page. It could work. All of it... But ... 'I'd like to, yes, but I don't know how it would work.'

'Neither do I.' He laughed and leaned forward, pressing his forehead onto hers. 'I just don't want to give up on us. There is an us, I'm sure of it.'

'But I don't want to move back to Glasgow, Marcus.'

'I know, and I'm cooking up a plan. I have some ideas I think might work. Before I do anything though, I need to talk to my family and get some things sorted. You'll have to meet them too. I also need to do some damage limitation, otherwise Ginny will skin me alive. I should have predicted this snow. Anyway, my future might not lie in forecasting, but my plans include broadcasting, so I can't afford to alienate Ginny. She's very influential and I wouldn't like my name to be dragged through the mud'.

'She knows you're snowed in though, so you don't have to go straight away.'

'We *were* snowed in, but the plough went through ten minutes ago.'

'Did it? Have you told her? Are you going?' Did her voice sound panicky? Her limbs were trembling. *I don't want him to go.*

'No, I haven't told her yet and I know there could be other closures elsewhere. But if I can give her a story that diverts her attention from the snow, then I might be able to save my backside.'

'What kind of story? You mean the one about the school-house?'

'No. That's all fine. She replied to my email last night saying she'd given me the go ahead to make a special documentary. I only saw it a moment ago. I just hope she doesn't renege on that after this morning's fiasco. Next week we're going to put it all together and hopefully we can air it before Christmas. It'll probably mean I get to come back with a camera team too.'

'Wow. That's amazing.'

'I know and wait until you hear the best bit. I thought of an awesome way to get even more publicity for this place and that's the story I need to sell to Ginny.'

'What is it?' Willow was on the edge of the bed, gripping the blanket.

'Who do we know with thousands of social media followers who lives near here? If I can unmask Rocky Rainman now and persuade him to get his followers behind this place, then what a story that would be.'

Willow's heart was thumping again, too fast this time. She hoped it didn't show on her face like a guilty light. 'And... how...?'

Her brain kicked back to the walk earlier. She'd confessed, hadn't she? It seemed like a hazy memory, even though it could only have been a few hours ago. He hadn't understood her, had he?

'Now the road's clear I'm going to nip into Glenbriar and find this man. I honestly think this could be a winner. I've told

Ginny I've got a lead, so let's hope it turns out to be real and not just some mad local winding me up.' He flashed her his most beautiful smile and crossed his fingers in the air.

'What? But you can't.'

'Truly, Willow, it's ok. I'll take it slowly and it'll take ten minutes tops in the car. By the time you're dressed and downstairs, I'll be back and possibly with a story that could save this place.'

'Please, don't go.'

'Come with me then. I'll wait. I need to do this. It's for everyone. The schoolhouse can stay open. You'll keep your job and if I move up here, Toby might want to stay. If he knows I'm not too far away, it'll be easier. Come on. Then once I've dealt with the rainman, we can think about happier things. Like you and me.'

Willow tugged on her hair, twisting a strand into a knot, and stared into his eyes. How could this be possible? How was it that Marcus Bowman was saying these things to her? It was like all her dreams had come true. She wanted to fall into his arms and say yes, they could make it work somehow.

'Ok?' he said, and it was a question. He knew something was up. Very few people could read her, like really read her, and he was one of them. He saw when she was hurting and acted on it. Now he could see something was wrong, only it wasn't her body that was playing up.

Like she was being controlled by a remote, her head moved from side to side. 'No, not really.'

'Why not? Don't you want... Well, I mean...' He rubbed the back of his neck. 'Have I read this all wrong? Do you not want to see me?'

'I do. Really.' Christ. She wanted it more than anything, but she couldn't have him unless she told him the truth. Curse her heart. It was banging so loudly she could hardly think. 'But... Well, about Rocky Rainman.' The beating reached fever point. She looked away. *Hell. Don't cry.*

'Let me deal with him. It's nothing you need to worry about.'

'Yes, it is. That's the point. It's everything I'm worried about.'

'Why?'

'Because it's me.'

'What is?'

'I'm Rocky Rainman.'

CHAPTER TWENTY-SEVEN

Marcus

Marcus sat stock-still on the end of the bed, staring at Willow. Were his ears malfunctioning? Something, somewhere had gone wrong for sure. Willow couldn't be Rocky Rainman. Could she?

How long had he sat there, gaping at the woman he cared about so much? He'd rubbed the back of his neck raw. What was going on? Was she saying that to stop him from going out in the snow again?

'You?' It was the only word he could get out.

'I'm sorry, Marcus.'

'Sorry? I don't get it.' He got to his feet, paced to the window, and shook his head. A car was in the car park where he'd cleared the snow. Who'd parked there and why? No sooner had the thought landed than it took off again. 'How can you be Rocky Rainman? It doesn't make sense. Why...?' Why hadn't she told him before if it was true?

'I always wanted to be a weather forecaster but... Well, I don't like the idea of being on camera.'

'Seriously?' She could be a weather forecaster if she wanted. All she needed was a bit more self-belief and confidence, but instead of trying, she'd invented a persona to hide behind.

What to make of her now? Of course she didn't want to shout about what she was doing, and being anonymous would have suited her. *But why not tell me?* So typical of the women in his life to lie. 'Why keep up the front when you knew I was looking for him…? I went out in that snow today to find him. Why not speak up?'

'Because of this.'

'Of what?'

'Exactly what's happening now. I knew you'd be mad. I knew you'd hate me. I didn't set it up to annoy you or hurt you but I know Rocky's followers have said things about you.' She looked away. 'I tried to make them stop when I realised the damage it had done. I hoped I could get you and Rocky to come to a truce before I told you. I didn't want you to hate me.'

'Oh, Christ.' He clutched his face in his hands. 'I don't hate *you*. I hate being lied to. And I can't believe you're the one who started all this… the online bullying and…' What could he say? How could she have done this?

'HELLO!' A voice rang loud and clear from outside the room. 'Willow? Are you here?'

'Shit. It's Hayley,' Willow said. 'What's she doing here?' She glanced at Marcus. 'She's going to wonder what I'm doing in here with you, dressed like this.'

Willow was still in her underwear, wrapped in a blanket, and he supposed it looked problematic. 'Go and make up some story,' he said. 'You're good at that.'

The glare she threw him burned him. She shuffled up off the bed and left.

What the hell should he do now?

The voices in the corridor got louder, as if they were approaching his door. He froze, waiting for a knock, but they passed and got quieter. They were going downstairs. What did that say? Willow just passed by without a word. She wouldn't want her cousin to know what they'd been up to. Marcus could be her next big secret.

'Damn it, I won't be.' He threw open the cupboard and pulled out his suit hangers. The roads were clear. He could make his way back to Glasgow and leave this shitstorm behind. He'd done what he set out to do and had enough footage to make the documentary without Rocky Rainman. But the shine had been taken off the story. Ironic really. Willow was in the perfect position to save the schoolhouse herself. A few words from Rocky and people would be donating money left, right and centre to 'Scotland's favourite weatherman' and his chosen cause. *Pa*. This whole thing was a disaster. Marcus had to reassess everything. All the silly plans he'd made were in tatters and now he needed new plans – ones that didn't include romance. How could Willow have done this? Christ, he never learned, did he? A bitter taste rose in his throat.

Sweaters and socks flew into his case. Pell-mell wasn't his style, but he couldn't be bothered to sort it properly. Who was going to know or care? If he'd finally gone to the dogs, it had been long enough coming.

The corridors and rooms of this old place were so familiar now, almost like a home from home. So much had happened there in the past few days. But one thing was very different. In the office, a different woman sat on the desk, swinging her long thin legs, her phone clamped in her perfectly manicured nails. Her long chestnut hair tumbled around her shoulders with effortless elegance. Marcus guessed this was Willow's cousin, Hayley. They'd never been introduced. Would she even know about him? Maybe she wasn't aware anyone else was here at all. Would she get a shock if he spoke to her? Maybe he should just walk out without saying anything, but it would be easier to say it to this woman than to Willow herself.

He cleared his throat as he opened the door and she looked up with a wide smile.

'Oh, hello.' She put her phone down and got to her feet. 'Is everything ok?'

'Can you tell Willow I've left, please?'

'Sure.' She sucked on her lip for a second. 'Or you could stay and tell her yourself. She'll be down in a minute. She's just having a bath. It's good for her legs, you know?'

He nodded.

'I know you're Marcus Bowman.' She giggled into her hand. 'Sorry, stupid thing to say. You obviously know you're Marcus Bowman too.'

'I do.'

'I love *Destination Forecast*, even though Willow told me not to watch it.'

'Why?' he frowned.

She held up her hands. 'She told me she used to work with you and you'd fallen out. I heard it was a mistake, but I know she was sneakily watching every episode and drooli... I mean, enjoying seeing you again.' Her eyes raked his body and Marcus came out in goosebumps, imagining Willow watching his show to ogle him. If he wasn't so pissed off, he would have laughed.

'Oh, well, if she wants to see me again, she can always switch on the TV.'

'Aw, don't be like that.' Hayley cocked her head to one side. 'Just give her time to calm down.'

'She can have all the time she needs; I won't be bothering her again.'

'But why? Can't you give her a chance?'

'Why should I? I don't know if you're fully aware of the circumstances but I haven't actually done anything wrong. So please don't take some high ground over me.'

'I wasn't.' Her face fell. 'I was just asking you to be understanding.'

He shrugged. 'I'll do what I see fit. And if you all think I'm the bad guy, there's no point in me doing anything else.'

'I never said I thought you were a bad guy.'

'Well, let's be real. It's not like there's a future for me with Rocky Rainman, is there?'

She looked away and shook her head. 'If you say so, but I don't see why not.'

'After the online campaign he... she's led against me.'

'She didn't do that on purpose.'

'Are you sure? Because she didn't exactly try to stop it either. Now, please, just tell her I've gone.' He lifted his case and suit carriers and left by the front door. The sky was blue and sunshine reflected off the snow. It was dazzlingly beautiful and normally he'd want to get his camera and go snap happy but he couldn't bear it another second. He bundled everything into his boot, slammed it shut and drove off without looking back. It was the end of a wasted trip and the start of a shattered heart.

CHAPTER TWENTY-EIGHT

Willow

Frost in the air... Cold everywhere.

The bath water was cold. Willow couldn't move. Or she didn't want to. How could she face Marcus? She'd known this day would come but it didn't make it any easier.

In fact, it wasn't even as bad as she expected. Marcus hadn't got mad or shouted. Hurricane Marcus had often blown up a storm back in the office, but he'd taken this calmly. The agony in his eyes pierced her heart like an icy blade. Tears welled again and she pushed them back. How could she have hurt him like that? She should have told him from the start, but she didn't have the guts. This was her punishment. She deserved this pain and so much more.

A knock sounded on the door, followed by Hayley's voice. 'Willow, are you ok, my beauty?'

'Yeah. I'm just coming down.'

'Ok. I'll put the fire on so it's nice and warm. I just hope the wood burner works the same way as my mum's.'

Getting out of the bath was never easy but today it was worse than ever. Willow's limbs were shaky and she just wanted to curl up and cry. *Must not give in*. Where was Marcus now? Would he be downstairs too?

By the time she got to the common room, Hayley had worked out the fire and got a blaze going.

'Ah, there you are. I made some hot chocolate. Come.' Hayley indicated a chair and Willow sat. Hayley took the seat opposite, cradling a mug in her long elegant fingers. 'I brought some clothes round for you. They're in the office. When you're allowed back into the bungalow, I can come round and give you a hand sorting stuff out if you like.'

'Thanks.' Willow leaned on her hand, letting tears fall. 'Though everything will be ruined. The roof's caved under the snow.'

'Aw, Willow, my beauty.' Hayley jumped up and sat on the arm of the chair, stroking Willow's hair. 'It's ok. Or it will be.'

'Will it?'

'It's only clothes and stuff. It can be replaced.'

'I know. But what about Marcus?'

'Oh, Willow.'

'I've always fancied him. But I'm such a stupid child. I don't know what I'm supposed to do. Once, I sent him a Valentine card. It's cringy now I look back. When I left, I tried to forget about him. And now… I just can't believe he ever… liked me too.'

Hayley rubbed her back and Willow rested her head on Hayley's leg.

'Willow, my wee beauty. I hate seeing you like this. He's just really upset because he thinks you invented Rocky Rainman to get at him.'

'I didn't. But when all the comparisons started, I guess I liked thinking I was better than him. Why didn't I think how much I might be hurting him?'

'I don't know. Probably because it was easier to believe he hated you than like him from afar with no chance of ever having him for real.'

'But he didn't hate me. I just would never have believed…'

'I know. That's the problem. You never believe in yourself. I could tell from the way he was talking how hurt he was. If he didn't care about you, it wouldn't have cut so deep.'

'Wait… You spoke to him? Maybe I should go talk to him too. I could try to explain.'

'But he's gone.'

Willow pulled back and wiped her eyes. 'Gone?'

'He left about half an hour ago. He came in and asked if I'd let you know. That's when I spoke to him.'

'Oh no. I'm too late.'

Hayley placed her hand on Willow's shoulder. 'It's never too late. You can call him anytime. But maybe leave it a bit. He needs time to process things too.'

Willow let out a long sigh. 'Process the fact that I'm a liar.'

'He might think that just now, but once he's calmed down, he'll see your side of things too. You didn't set out to piss him off.'

'I know. I told him. But I played along with it when I was angry with him and when I was hurting. This has all been a disaster. I should shut down that bloody account and give all this up.'

'Please don't. You're good at forecasting. There's no reason why you and Marcus Bowman can't co-exist.'

'Do you think he'll drop this? He hates Rocky Rainman with a passion. He was dying to expose him. He's probably on the phone to Ginny right now, discussing how best to bring me down and make me look bad.'

'If he does, you'll know he isn't worth thinking about. If he cares about you as much as he made you believe, then he won't say anything.'

'Oh god.' Willow rested her head in her hands. 'This is awful.'

'I know.' Hayley resumed stroking her hair, almost like she was giving one of her clients a head massage.

Compulsively, Willow snatched her phone and scrolled social media for any inkling Marcus had gone public. He'd still be driving but with the power of the media behind him, anything could happen anytime. As pictures and words flew by, she spied nothing to suggest anything had changed.

'Has he said anything?' Hayley asked.

'Not that I can see.'

On her page feeds, people had posted photos of the snow with claps and cheers for the Rainman.

Another cracking prediction

Always trust the Rainman

Spot on Rocky!

Ten out of Ten for the big man once again.

Much as she loved the praise, she knew how fake it was. They thought she was a 'big man', but nothing could be further from the truth. She was a tiny woman, terrified of what people would make of the real her. When she hid behind the big man persona, it was easy to make predictions and get involved in the banter. If she made mistakes, it didn't matter. No one knew it was her anyway. Rocky took the flack and she moved on; no harm done.

'Why don't you come clean?' Hayley said.

'I already did. That's what caused all this.'

'I mean, with everyone. Tell the world you're Rocky Rainman.'

'So I can beat Marcus to it.'

'No. So you can own it.'

'I can't go on camera.'

'Of course you can. You've convinced yourself you already know what people will think and say but it's not true. Stop assuming you know how people will react. At least try. Stop hiding in the shadows. Let your light shine. Believe.' She grinned. 'You can do this. If you can bed a celebrity like Marcus Bowman you can do anything. That's no small achievement for a girl who hasn't had a boyfriend in at least two years.'

Heat bloomed in Willow's cheeks and she loosened her neckline. The fire was so warm.

'Do it,' Hayley said. 'Take a leap now and let everyone meet Rocky Rainman.'

'Just like that? Mum and Dad don't even know.'

'Easily remedied. Call them and tell them. Then go public. Step out of the shadows and show your face. We want to see the talent behind the forecast. If you lose followers, who cares? You might get thousands more. People are so nosey they'll want to know what's going on.'

Willow sighed and stared at the flickering flames in the stove. She'd not done it for followers, not in the beginning. She did it because it was what she wanted to do, but she was scared to do it the 'right' way. Now, she'd achieved what she set out to do but while the secrecy gave her the strength to do it in the first place, it was hurting people and that was never her intent.

Going public would be taking a leap that could change everything. And once it was done, there was no going back.

Chapter Twenty-Nine

Marcus

Ginny's lips were drawn into a pout as she eyed Marcus like she was scrutinising a student and figuring out which punishment would best suit their crime. He adjusted his tie and looked away, feeling like he was being virtually undressed. A shudder passed down his spine as he recalled his university lecturer, Janice, who'd shown him just how far he could go. He'd handed himself to her to get what he needed. She got off on the thrill, and he had too. He was a teenager; she was a beautiful woman and had fulfilled a lot of fantasies for him, just as he did for her. He squirmed, looking back at those memories. Was that what was happening here? Did Ginny want some action in return for a reprieve?

She considered him. *Don't you dare ask me for anything inappropriate.* He wouldn't give in this time. Janice's influence had got him his big break, and she'd got to take part in extracurricular activities she didn't get with her husband. He'd repeated the process with an executive producer when he started in broadcasting, but he'd learned his lesson. If Ginny tried it on, he would report her. He'd had enough.

'So, that little sojourn to the Highlands was basically a waste of time and money,' she said, her pout returning as soon as she stopped talking.

'Actually no. We got a great story about the schoolhouse that we can take on to be a documentary.'

'Yes. So we can get a few more desperate housewives tuning in to see how hot Marcus Bowman looked out in the snow.'

'That's objectionable.' He narrowed his eyes. Sometimes he wished he was four feet tall with a face covered in warts. 'And verging on sexual harassment.'

'Oh please,' she snapped. 'Pull the other one. Bottom line is, you spent a week fannying about interviewing people.'

'Which is what you sent me to do.'

'And now you want to make it bigger, so we're going to have to send a camera crew back. Sounds like a man desperate to boost his ratings. Why should I throw more money at it, when you've given me nothing of interest? What happened to your big scoop on Rocky Rainman? Where did that fizzle out to?'

Where indeed. And the biggest rub of all was Marcus couldn't tell Ginny. If only Willow hadn't lied to him. Nonetheless, he wouldn't expose her. He loved her too much to hurt her like that. Willow had her reasons for not revealing her identity. While he might not know for sure what they were, or agree with what he guessed they were, he wasn't going to expose her.

'Nothing is happening with Rocky Rainman. All the leads were false.' He let out a sigh and leaned back. 'Maybe we should drop it.'

'Hmm.' Ginny drummed her fingers. 'I'd be happy to let go of the damn thing except he draws so much attention from this station. I notice he's started being oddly friendly towards you while you were up there. What do you make of that?'

Marcus flicked lint from his sleeves, trying to come up with an answer that would appease her and keep Willow's secret safe. 'Christmas spirit?'

'What bullshit. Did you happen to meet Willow Roxburgh at the schoolhouse?' Ginny eyed him. 'It was some friend of hers who contacted us about the place originally.'

'Um, yes. I saw her there.' He gritted his teeth at his stupidity.

'Ah, poor little Willow. I liked her. She was a good worker but I don't think this was really the place for her. She scared herself off in the end.' Ginny shook her head.

'How do you mean?'

'She applied for the forecaster job, then flipped out. I got her application and her resignation almost together. She retracted the application, saying she didn't have the qualifications or qualities.'

'I didn't know that.' If he had, it might have helped put two and two together. That, coupled with the funny little poem on the Valentine card, would have roused his suspicions. Why hadn't he thought about her sooner? It was so obvious in retrospect.

'She was right, she didn't have the qualifications. I couldn't have taken her on for that reason.'

'Are you kidding? Sadie Greene has no qualifications either. Neither do half the people you employ,' he snapped.

'Sadie has the connections, which, as you know, is worth a lot more.'

'Ha. You admit it at last. Sometimes, it's degrading working here.'

'You would know.'

'Yes. I would and I do. I'm not sure forecasting is my calling anymore.'

He gazed out the window towards the Clyde and the oh so familiar view. He'd worked here so long.

'Did you consider that it might be her?' Ginny rubbed her heavily ringed finger around her chin.

'Might be her what?'

'It might be Willow behind Rocky Rainman. If she's a wannabe, then who knows?'

'I don't think so.' *Shit. Need to change the subject.* But Ginny was a bulldog. She didn't get where she was today by letting go. Once she got the scent, she was off.

'It could be, you know. Look at her name: "rocks-burgh" sounds like Rocky, add that to her history. It makes sense. Now, if I recall...' She opened up her computer screen. 'Her uncle works here. He's a camera operator, I believe. Let me see.' She clicked her screen and peered over her glasses at it. Her mission face was on and that was not good news. Ginny Lord was ten times sharper than Marcus Bowman when it came to investigative stuff.

He knew full well who Willow's uncle was, having used that as a good reason for him to keep away from her while she worked there. Even if Jonathan was one of the nicest, most easy-going guys in the building, Marcus had decided any relation of Willow was bound to object to her having anything to do with an alleged playboy like him.

'Here we are. Jonathan Hutcheson. Go check him out. Ask a few questions.'

'Are you serious?'

'Yes, Marcus. Leave no stone unturned. You started this, you're going to finish it.'

'Oh, Jesus Christ.'

'Call aid from whoever you like, but get me something to go on and soon.'

'But if Willow is Rocky Rainman, why did they not use her to drum up publicity for the schoolhouse? Why ask us? That makes no sense.' He already knew the answer – or suspected. The owners didn't know Willow's alias either and she didn't have the confidence or the belief that people would do this for her.

'Not a clue. But get yourself in to see Jonathan and find out what you can.'

This was ridiculous. He'd got himself into exactly the place he didn't want to be. If he refused or did nothing, Ginny wouldn't just hang him out to dry. She'd slap a ten-times more capable journalist in his place and they'd uncover Willow's secret in a second. He still needed to keep Ginny sweet if he wanted to do the documentary.

Laurenia was the only person he could tell any of this to. She'd been at her mother-in-law's house over the weekend with the kids and Toby. With the early Monday start, Marcus had barely seen her, but he needed to talk to her now.

He nipped out the front of the building into the wintery air and stood by the railings. Once he'd met Laurenia here when she brought Toby for an appointment at the children's hospital. Little did he know someone had been watching and reported back to Willow. She'd thought him a married man with kids. He should be a married man with kids. How was he thirty-seven with so little to show for himself? He'd missed out on so much. Why couldn't he love someone? Someone who wanted him for more than his body and his money.

The call connected.

'Hey, darling,' Laurenia said. She may be seven years younger than him but she always seemed like the older sister. More sensible; the voice of reason. Everything he should be but failed miserably at. The control he had over his life was gained by straightening his tie and lining up pens but it didn't change the big deals. He was still floundering while trying to find the right way.

'Hey.'

'Sorry, I didn't have the chance to talk much to you last night. What's up?'

'I want you guys to move to wherever you want. Find the dream house and take it. Don't stress about Toby. I'll look after him.'

'Oh, Marcus.' Laurenia let out a sigh. 'That's a lovely idea but how can you? Not with your job.'

He turned to look at the studio building he'd worked in for so long. A giant Christmas tree twinkled inside the glass-fronted reception, giving a false image of warmth and happiness. If some people still got pleasure working there, then good for them, because he didn't. 'I'm giving it up.'

'What? You can't.'

'I want to focus more on *Destination Forecast* and maybe other shows like that. It might mean Toby living with you for a little while but it won't be as constant as it is now. Ideally, I'll persuade him to move into an assisted-living facility but it can be gradual.'

'What has brought this on?'

'I don't even know where to start. Have you got time to talk? Like proper talk?'

'Sure, darling. Tell me anything. Sounds like you've been doing a lot of thinking.'

'I have, but I've messed up with someone I care about.'

'You mean a woman? I didn't know you were seeing anyone. When did this happen?'

He stared at the bright blue sky. 'It was all a bit sudden. But the crazy thing is, I love her more than anyone else I've ever been with.'

'Wow, Marcus. Are you sure you're feeling ok?' Her voice sounded half amused, half shocked. 'This sounds big. Who is this person? You've only been away a few days and you never mentioned anyone before.'

'I knew her a while ago. We worked together. Then last week at the schoolhouse, she was there and... Well, I fell for her all over again.'

'Again? I'm so out of this loop. Tell me more.'

He checked his watch. 'Ok, here goes.' His next stint on air wasn't for a couple of hours, so he had time to give her the full story. Hopefully he wouldn't forget anything and could keep it brief and not bore her.

Laurenia let him talk until he'd got it all out.

'Darling, she sounds wonderful. And she lives near Glenbriar, which is where I really want to live. It all sounds too perfect. Go back to her right now.'

'How can I? She is wonderful but she lied.'

'And you know why. Deep down you know. She was afraid of how you'd react and she was right. Of course she didn't want to make it public who she was. She's probably spent her life being scrutinised by doctors and physios. Look at Toby and everything he has to put up with. I don't blame her wanting to hide away.'

'Yeah, yeah, I know.' And he did. It just hurt like a punch in the gut.

'I bet she's hurting just as much as you. It sounds like she really cared about you too.'

'But how can I make it up to her?'

'You don't have to. If you want her, just go and tell her.'

If I really want Willow. His chest ached for Willow. She was all he wanted.

'Thank you. You've put it in perspective as only you can.'

'Ok, darling, see you later... And I'd love to meet this woman one day soon.'

'You will.'

He needed to get the forecast sorted before his next stint on air. He made a quick check of social media. Rocky had gone quiet. Guilt twinged inside. Had he knocked the stuffing out of Willow? This was her baby, her success story, and he'd pissed all over it. He didn't have the right to take her down. He shouldn't have done it with anyone. His head was stuck so far up his own arse he couldn't see it.

Later in the afternoon, when he'd done his forecast, a man beelined for him. *Oh no.* Jonathan Hutcheson. Either Ginny had sent him, or Willow had, and he was on his way to break Marcus's nose in the name of honour.

'Marcus?' he said cheerfully – a good sign.

'Hi.'

'I had an email from your producer saying you wanted to talk to me.'

Bloody meddling Ginny. She wasn't going to let this rest but at least Marcus could keep his nose intact.

'Yes. I did. Come and sit, if you don't mind.'

He made his way back through the newsroom to his desk and offered the spare seat to Jonathan.

'You're Willow's uncle, aren't you?'

'Yes, I am. I haven't seen her for a while.'

'I met her in the schoolhouse near Glenbriar.'

'That's good. How's she getting on?'

'She seemed very well.'

'My sister will be pleased to hear that. Poor Lorna, that's Willow's mum. She constantly worries about her. It's a tough position for her. She wants to give her the right amount of care but at the same time, she knows Willow needs to be independent.'

'She's definitely that, and she's capable of handling herself.'

'Aye, we all said that to Lorna. But she's always had trouble letting go. But what's this about?'

'Just a bit of background. I'm doing a feature on the schoolhouse where Willow works... I'm just looking for some background on her.'

'I'm not sure I can tell you much. I haven't seen her since she moved. Lorna and Martin went to see her in the summer but they're not confident drivers, especially in bad weather. They want to go for Christmas but I'm not sure they'll risk it if the weather stays bad. Willow's got her aunt Lisa, that's my other sister, so she isn't on her own. And Willow's very close to Lisa's daughter Hayley, but Lorna and Martin feel guilty about her being so far away. I think they'd like to move closer to her but they don't want it to look like they're interfering.'

Marcus tapped his finger on the table. This was a nice little chat but he couldn't ask Jonathan anything that might lead to Rocky Rainman. He didn't want to make anyone suspicious.

'Thanks,' he said. 'I wonder if you could give me contact details for your sister, Lorna. I'd like to chat to her too.'

Jonathan pulled out his phone. 'I'm sure she wouldn't mind.'

'That's great.' Marcus entered the number into his phone. Jonathan headed off and Marcus stared at the screen. An idea gradually formed in his mind.

A plan for a surprise Christmas which he liked, but it could go horribly wrong.

CHAPTER THIRTY

Willow

Willow folded one of her favourite tops and packed it in her bag. The builders had come earlier in the day and temporarily secured the roof of the staff quarters. It was safe for her to go in and rescue all her stuff, but it wasn't habitable with water dripping in. Some of her clothes that had been in the wardrobe and on the side where the roof was still intact were salvageable. But the kitchen area was completely wrecked.

Marion and Barry were finally back and everything had returned to normal. Except it wasn't. The schoolhouse had no residents and no guests. Willow had apologised for everything from the tree falling to the health and safety inspection but Marion had just smiled sadly and said, 'You did a wonderful job. I'm only sorry that after Christmas this job won't exist. Not unless Marcus Bowman's documentary works a Christmas miracle.'

Hayley held out some damp food packets and screwed up her nose. 'This is an excuse for a shopping trip if ever I saw one.'

'Except I don't have any money.' Willow let out a sigh. 'Or a place to live.'

'You can stay with me until you find somewhere.'

Hayley was so kind but she lived in a tiny flat and no way could they both live in it for long. Willow's head was spinning, swirling with cloudy thoughts about Rocky Rainman. 'If I'd just had the guts to be myself and not worry about what people may or may not think of me, none of this would have happened.'

'True, but if you hadn't invented Rocky Rainman,' Hayley said, 'Marcus wouldn't have come here in the first place, and the two of you would never have reconnected.'

'Maybe that would have been better.'

'I don't think so.' Hayley packed the clothes Willow had saved and shoved them into a bag. 'Even if nothing more comes of it, you still had that time. And that's been good for you.'

She didn't know the half of it. Willow came alive with Marcus, but even that was a hollow victory. She knew her own strength now, but she didn't think she'd ever want a relationship with anyone else. Maybe she needed to go back to what she thought before and use what they had as experience. But the idea made her sick. She'd already been imagining a house and a garden with a couple of dogs. Now she was back to being alone – jobless and homeless – before they'd even had a proper date. *Just proves my inexperience.*

'We're nearly done,' Hayley said. 'Good to get this sorted before Christmas.'

'Do you think if...' Willow stopped and took a deep breath.

'Think what?'

'If I asked people. I mean if Rocky Rainman asked people to get behind the schoolhouse that maybe we could save it?'

'Oh my god that's a genius idea. You could put it all over social media.'

'Do you think people would care?'

Hayley pressed her lips together and moved her head from side to side. 'Hmm. Do you know what I think would have more impact?'

'What?'

'If you confess to being Rocky Rainman, then explain who you really are and your connection to the schoolhouse. It makes it a more human story, not just some random faceless person.'

It all came down to confessing to who she was.

'And you could make that even better by working with Marcus.'

'Seriously?' Willow threw her a look. 'How can I do that? He wouldn't want me forecasting with him.'

'Not forecasting. If you appeared in his documentary, thousands more people would tune in to see Marcus going head-to-head with the Rainman.'

Willow groaned. 'I'm not sure I can do that.'

'Well, I think you should.' Hayley folded one last top and squashed it into the bag. 'You just need to go for it. Think how amazed your mum and dad would be.'

'Yes, they'd love it but I hate the thought of being on camera.'

'Maybe there's another way. Let me think.'

It was odd moving stuff into the main schoolhouse, especially when she wasn't sure how long she'd be there.

'It's much nicer having you here,' Marion said as she helped them up the stairs with the bags. 'I was always worried about you being stuck out there in that old bungalow. If we stay open, we'll be having both of them knocked down. It makes me ill when I think about what might have happened if you'd been in there when that tree came down.'

'Well, it fell over the kitchen, so it would have had to have been when I was cooking and we all know that's not exactly a priority of mine.'

Marion and Hayley both chuckled and shook their heads at each other.

Willow chose the room next to the stairs, highly aware of the room Marcus had been in last week just down the corridor. The door sat ajar, like he was inside and about to come out.

After Marion went back downstairs, Hayley marched along and closed the door shut. 'Listen, Willow, if you're going to moon about him this much, you need to talk to him.'

'I hate feeling like this.'

Hayley put her arm around her. 'I know.'

'But I betrayed his trust.'

'Then do something about it. How about you make a big announcement post?'

'Hang on. I've just had another idea. I need to make a phone call.'

She sank onto her bed and called a number she hadn't used for a long time and never thought she'd use again. The line connected directly to Ginny Lord's office.

'Hello. Who's this?'

'Willow Roxburgh. I don't know if you remember me.'

'Yes, I do. And how very strange. I was just talking about you the other day.'

Was she? With Marcus? Was he telling her the story perhaps? Maybe it was already out there and what she was planning wasn't going to make any difference.

'Why?' Willow asked.

'Marcus said he'd met you when he was doing the story on the schoolhouse. Wasn't it you who suggested the owners contacted us in the first place?'

'No. I knew nothing about it until after.'

'I see.'

'Did Marcus tell you anything particular about me?' Her heart pounded in her ears. Ginny Lord wasn't someone Willow was used to holding her own with. When she worked there, Ginny had trampled all over her – as she did with everyone.

'Nothing, no. He was curiously tight-lipped. Why do you ask?'

'Did he talk to you about Rocky Rainman?'

'He did. And as far as he made out, there was no sight nor sound of him.'

'Oh.'

'Yes. And that makes me very suspicious. I know you were once interested in a weather job. Your surname could be manipulated to sound like Rocky and you were present at the place identified in Rocky Rainman's pictures. It all seems to point at one conclusion but Marcus disagrees.'

The annoyance in her tone was clear but Willow's tummy flip-flopped. Marcus didn't tell her. He kept the secret and that had to mean something.

'I've got some info on Rocky Rainman.' Willow cleared her throat. 'And I'm willing to give it to you with a condition.'

'Indeed. Go ahead.'

'I'll tell you all about Rocky Rainman if... Well, if you give me a slot to talk about it live tomorrow.'

'I'm sure I could arrange that. But I need the info first to know if it's worth anything.'

'I'm Rocky Rainman.'

She snorted a little laugh. 'I knew it. God knows what Marcus was playing at and how the hell he couldn't see it.'

'He knows. He just didn't want to tell you.' At least she hoped that was his reason.

'Seriously? He's such an idiot sometimes. But it doesn't matter what he wants anymore.'

'Why?'

'He resigned this morning.'

'He what?' No. He couldn't have. 'What about the documentary on the schoolhouse?'

'Oh, he's still doing that. In fact, I think he needs another interview with you about it. You might hear from him soon.'

Willow's pulse rocketed again.

'Now, live on air tomorrow sounds wonderful. Let's have you on the *Afternoon Digest*. I'll have my assistant call you back with details later. This could be exactly what I need.'

Willow laid the phone on the bed beside her, closed her eyes and drew in a long, slow breath. Why did she get the feeling Marcus had a different agenda to her? And he'd resigned but the documentary was going ahead. Why did he want to interview her again? Or was it Rocky he wanted to interview? Would her little stunt backfire? She grabbed her phone and googled him, looking for news reports, social media rumours, or anything, but there was nothing new, just the usual pictures of his smiling face standing in front of his weather screen or sexy screenshots of him in exotic *Destination Forecast* locations.

After tomorrow, she'd have no more secrets. It was liberating and terrifying in equal measure, and she could only hope it wouldn't come back to bite her.

CHAPTER THIRTY-ONE

Marcus

Marcus glanced in the rear-view mirror and saw two faces shining back at him. Not his nieces, Toby, Laurenia or any of his other siblings. Two people he'd never met until the day before.

Random acts of kindness were not his thing. Maybe they should be. He'd been far too self-centred for a long time. Helping his family was one thing, but he'd ignored people in general. When he was married, he made no attempt to get to know his wife's family. He'd never made friends easily, and it had always seemed simplest that way, but this felt good – and right.

'Are you ok?' he asked.

'Yes, thank you,' Lorna Roxburgh replied. He saw Willow in her eyes, her face shape and even in her mannerisms – the way she toyed with her hair as she looked out the window with a slightly nervous expression.

'This is a very comfortable car,' Martin Roxburgh added with an appreciative nod. They'd both insisted on sitting together in the back, so Marcus felt like a chauffeur as he pulled out of the drive.

'Great. On we go then.'

When Marcus had called Lorna yesterday, he was still working for Ginny – just. Both Willow and her uncle had told him her parents weren't confident driving and how much they wanted to see her for Christmas. And she needed it too. She missed them – he understood how much. Being independent didn't mean she couldn't miss her family. Marcus missed Toby and Laurenia every day. Missed his other siblings too, and his mama, god rest her soul. He'd missed so much in his family. Things he couldn't get back. A fresh start was in order with or without Willow, but he'd much rather it was with her.

Lorna had thought it was a hoax when Marcus Bowman turned up at her door, offering to give her a lift to see her daughter for Christmas. Willow knew he was coming to visit that week. He'd emailed her and said he needed some last-minute footage for the documentary and could they put their differences aside for that. She'd agreed. But he had a lot more planned than that. It might all backfire and his stomach churned at everything that could go wrong.

'Willow told us yesterday she was behind this Rocky Rainman character,' Lorna said. 'And you spent a week looking for him, not realising it was her.'

'Yeah.'

'Did she learn it all from you when she worked at e-Broadcast Scotland?'

He pulled out the end of their street onto the main road. 'No. She learned it all herself. I think she already knew as much as me when we worked together. She figured out how to cross reference the charts and pull her own conclusions from them without any input from me. She used to help me, in fact.'

'I don't even know what that means,' Martin said.

'The bulk of my job is... *was* interpreting data into a way the public would understand. When I left school, I didn't know what I wanted to do. I studied maths because I was good at it and it helps with equations when building the weather models, but TV was never on my radar.'

'But you enjoy it?' Martin asked.

'I've got used to it but the forecasting schedule is relentless. Things have changed in my life and I need to move on.'

'Will you do more *Destination Forecast*?' Lorna asked.

'I think so, and maybe more shows like that if I can get them.'

'Sounds interesting.'

'You know, Willow's a smart cookie. She's as good at the job as me. She just didn't have the confidence to go on camera.'

'I'm always so worried about her,' Lorna said. 'She was such a fragile child and she had to go through so much. I've tried to let her be independent but she's so far away. It worries me every second that something will happen to her.'

'I can understand that, but whatever you did, it worked. She's getting on fine. She's definitely not fragile anymore, but she misses having her family around.'

'If she wants us to move back, I'd be more than happy. It's a much nicer place to live than Glasgow and it would be good to be near my sister again.'

'I think she'd like that. It's never a bad thing to have a support network. I know that too well.' Laurenia had moved her life to support him with Toby and he couldn't have done it without her.

It was a long way to Glenbriar and Marcus wasn't great at small talk. For a while, he and the Roxburghs chatted until he asked if they'd like the radio on.

'That would be great,' Lorna said. 'I enjoy the *Afternoon Digest.*'

Marcus wasn't in a rush to listen to his former colleagues. But he put it on, deciding to switch off inside his head and concentrate on working out how this plan would work. The main road had finally got to a dualled section and he pulled out to overtake a lorry just as the *Afternoon Digest* opening music came on.

'Today we have an exclusive interview with Rocky Rainman, the rhyming weather forecaster and internet sensation. We'll reveal live on-air Rocky's true identity. Be prepared for a big surprise.'

Marcus glanced in the rear-view mirror. 'Did you know about this?'

'No,' Martin and Lorna said together.

'Willow called us yesterday,' Lorna said, 'but I didn't get the impression she was going to tell anyone else.'

'Maybe it's not her,' Martin said. 'Perhaps they've got someone who's pretending.'

Marcus's mind cast back to his trek in the snow. 'There's a joker in the village who either believes he's Rocky Rainman or wants to pretend to people that he is. I wonder if it's him.'

The next fifteen minutes were excruciatingly dull and drawn out as they waited for the Rocky Rainman feature. Could they not just get on with it? Finally, the presenter spoke the words they were dying to hear and Marcus punched up the volume, for no reason other than he needed to do something.

'And now, the exclusive we promised you at the start of the show. Before we meet Rocky Rainman in person, we have some related news for you. Yesterday, Marcus Bowman, the frontman of e-Broadcast Scotland's weather team, announced he was stepping down from the role.'

It was hardly an announcement. He just handed in his resignation and walked out.

'Marcus has a famous love-hate relationship with Rocky Rainman, often making quips on air about Rocky's impetuous predictions while Rocky and his followers enjoy a bit of witty banter about Marcus and his no-nonsense forecasts. Well, I'm delighted to welcome Rocky on air with me. And don't be surprised when Rocky speaks, because you're about to find out Rocky isn't a rain man at all. Rocky is a young woman whose real name is Willow Roxburgh.

And I'm delighted to welcome Willow Rocky Rainman Roxburgh to the show. Hello, Willow.'

Marcus glanced in the mirror again and met the stunned eyes of Willow's parents. Any thoughts the studio had got the wrong person were doused in cold water. Why was she giving up her safety blanket and coming clean live on air?

'Hi,' Willow said.

'So, Willow. Tell us how this all began and why you invented the persona of Rocky Rainman.'

'I've always loved the weather. Even the wet days are interesting. A while back, I worked for e-Broadcast Scotland in the newsroom and I watched the forecasters at work. It became a hobby of mine and I started doing research of my own. I learned how to read charts, observe and cross reference different sources and interpret them. The forecasters had different ways of doing it. Some of them knew everything about it and interpreted the data themselves, others used researchers and just did the talking. I helped behind the scenes and I even thought about applying for a job as a forecaster.'

She seemed to say it all without taking a breath and Marcus gave the console a little smile. Poor Willow. She was nervous but apart from going a little fast, she sounded great.

'What stopped you?'

'I actually sent my application, then I chickened out. I was born with cerebral palsy, which means I don't always stand straight. In fact, I very rarely do. And I wear splints and walk mostly with crutches. On longer distances, I need a wheelchair. I didn't think

I suited life on the screen, so I changed my mind. It seemed like if I was employed there, I'd just be filling a quota and not doing the job on merit. That's when I decided to do it myself. I didn't expect to go viral the way I did.'

'Do you think that has anything to do with your famous way of starting your posts with a poem?'

'Maybe. I like making up silly rhymes but some days it's tricky to think them up.'

'I bet. Tell us, why didn't you use your real name?'

'Forecasting is an imprecise science. I knew there would be times I'd get things wrong and it scared me. I have a bad habit of assuming people won't like what I have to say. Making up Rocky Rainman was like hiding behind a front and detaching myself from the criticism.'

'Sounds like a wise move. I can relate. No one likes being wrong. What prompted you to come clean now?'

'Last week, Marcus Bowman was in my hometown of Glenbriar. He was doing a report on the place where I work which is under threat of closure. While he was there, he discovered through social media that Rocky Rainman may be based there. People had seen some of my posts and rightly identified the location. I had the opportunity to come clean to him then and save him a lot of trouble. But I didn't. I kept my secret but it wasn't right. I actually put Marcus in a dangerous situation and I hate to think I could have prevented it by telling the truth.'

'That sounds scary. What happened?'

'He went out in one of the blizzards looking for someone claiming to be Rocky when I knew all along it couldn't be him... Well, it was me, so, you know...'

'Do you think this incident has contributed to Marcus's decision to leave e-Broadcast Scotland?'

'I don't know anything about that. I just hope he's ok. I always... admired Marcus. He's one of the great forecasters who really knows his stuff.'

'So, this love-hate relationship between Rocky and Marcus. What started that? Did you and he have a fall out when you worked together?'

'I never meant for there to be any hate directed at Marcus. Some of my followers were rude about him but there are so many of them, there's no way I could look through all the comments and block them. I only ever meant to make the forecasts for myself and people who were interested. I admit I made some comments from time to time that I shouldn't have and were totally unfair and unkind. This won't be happening anymore and I'd like to ask everyone who follows me to show Marcus the respect he deserves from now on.'

'Totally. Let's have some love for Marcus Bowman this Christmas. But as we now know, he's dropped out of forecasting for now. We don't know what his plans are, so this could be an end to the Rocky-Bowman feud. But it definitely isn't the end of Rocky Rainman or Willow Roxburgh. In fact, we have a message from the newscast producer, Ginny Lord. She said she'd officially like to offer you the position of forecaster in place of Marcus. The skills *you've demonstrated while forecasting as Rocky Rainman have done more than enough to convince her you're exactly the person for the job.'*

Marcus's jaw just about hit the floor. Martin and Lorna looked equally as shocked. Had he left so Willow could walk into his shoes? He agreed she was more than qualified, but what was the point of him going all this way to throw himself at her feet if she was going to leave and go back to Glasgow? These interviews were all scripted and rehearsed. Surely, she knew they were going to ask her that. Maybe she *did* know. After all, she had no idea what his plans were.

She was taking a long time to respond.

'That's an interesting offer. Thank you. I'll speak to Ginny about it in person.'

'Sounds very promising,' the presenter said. 'Thank you for coming on air today, Willow. And I look forward to talking to you again soon. Perhaps even calling you my colleague.'

'You're welcome, but before I go, I have a request to make of the listeners on behalf of Rocky Rainman.'

'Certainly, let's hear it.'

'Earlier, you may remember I said the place I work at is under threat of closure. This place is a retreat and a live-in residence for young adults with additional needs. However, it needs funds. It also needs publicity, so people know it exists and what great facilities it has to offer. I'd like to ask every follower of Rocky Rainman who has enjoyed the forecasts to either donate to the cause or share the

word about The Old Schoolhouse. I've put all the links on social media. It's such a great facility it would be devastating to lose it.'

'A great cause, folks. I'm sure you'll all be very generous and full of Christmas spirit, especially as the Rainman has given us the benefit of his, or her, forecasts for free for a long time.'

'Marcus Bowman is also doing a documentary about it and it's airing on Christmas Eve,' Willow added.

'Wonderful. It's great to hear that these two great weather rivals have called a truce this Christmas to support a wonderful cause.'

The presenter finished up and moved on to the next article, and Marcus turned off the radio. He, Lorna, and Martin sat in stunned silence. He'd flipped to autopilot and was only just remembering to drive. His brain had zipped off down a hundred different paths, looking for answers.

'Should I call her?' Lorna said.

'No,' Martin replied. 'She might not have decided. That was a tricky spot to put her in. Let's give her the chance to make her own choice. We'll see her later and we can support her in whatever route she chooses.'

Marcus's mind was in turmoil. As they got closer to Glenbriar, his resolve almost failed, but he wanted to go through with his plan.

Lorna and Martin didn't know about it, and he'd asked them not to tell Willow who brought them, but to sneak an envelope into the schoolhouse for her to find. Lorna looked suspiciously at it but asked no questions as she tucked it into her bag. Marcus dropped them off outside the schoolhouse and turned back. It was tempting to go inside and speak to Willow, but he wanted her to have time with her family and he had another job to do. He smiled when he spotted Laurenia's car in the car park. She must be here already. He'd see Willow soon enough, and they'd find out 'weather' or not she wanted to be his Christmas Valentine. And he had a whole lot more to offer her. Or was she going back to Glasgow to take over his former job?

CHAPTER THIRTY-TWO

Willow

Hey, folks! It's Willow here, and just to let you know. There's still a chance for some of us to get some Christmas snow! Unusual things are happening, tricks hidden up my sleeve... Let's all hope for miracles for this year's Christmas Eve.

Willow sat, almost shaking, and Hayley held her hand. Thank goodness for her favourite cousin. She'd taken an afternoon off work so she could be on hand after the on-air interview.

'I'm so glad that's over.' It had gone well until they offered Willow Marcus's job. She still couldn't believe it. It was what she'd dreamed of forever, being a TV weathergirl. The opportunity was right there, waiting to be seized. But she hadn't given her final answer. Was it wrong to benefit from Marcus's leaving? But more to the point, was it really what she wanted? She didn't want to go back to Glasgow. She loved it up here, the peace, the scenery, the community and Hayley.

'It went really well,' Hayley said. 'You sounded great, not too nervous at all.'

'Why did they offer me that job?'

'It's exciting! Though it was naughty springing it on you like that. Take your time to think it through.'

'I will.' She really should go and see Marion, but some people were downstairs looking at the accommodation and she didn't want to interrupt. What could she do to keep her mind focused and her itchy fingers away from the computer? She was dying to look at the weather and do some forecasting, but she wasn't sure she could bear to look at her social pages. The comments would be off the scale and she couldn't face them.

'Let's go into the common room and I'll get you a drink.' Hayley said.

'But what if the people are still looking around?'

'I'm sure Marion won't mind. We make the place look more inhabited.'

The entrance hall was empty and Hayley pushed open the common room door. Marion was chatting inside to a woman with a sheet of dark brown, poker straight hair. She was tall and dressed elegantly in black with heeled boots. A little girl sat on her hip and another girl was on the floor by the fire. She was wearing flashing reindeer-antler deely boppers and laughing with a young man. Willow had seen this woman and the young man before. She was Marcus's glamorous sister and the young man was Toby.

'Ah, Willow.' Marion waved them in. 'And Hayley, hello, girls. Come in and meet our guests.'

Heat spread across Willow's cheeks. Now she knew this woman was Marcus's sister, she saw the resemblance straight away. She was elegance personified. Even beside Hayley, who was always beautiful and well-turned out, this woman was stunning.

'This is Laurenia Conway. She's Marcus Bowman's sister, you know.' Marion beamed and Laurenia smiled gently.

'Hi.' Willow kept slightly behind Hayley, feeling ridiculously small again.

'Lovely to meet you,' Hayley said. 'Your hair is glorious.'

'Thanks,' Laurenia said, giving her head a little swish. The Christmas tree lights highlighted the glossy sheen on her tresses.

'Hayley's a hairdresser, so she always notices people's hair. Goodness knows what she makes of my grey frizz.' Marion moved towards the young man.

'Your hair's lovely too,' Hayley said.

'Thank you, dear. And this is Toby Bowman, Marcus's brother. He visited earlier in the year, you might recall.'

'I do,' Willow said.

'We're going to give it another go.' Laurenia hitched up the girl on her hip. 'I'm moving up here soon. My husband works on the rigs and the next time he's off, we're house hunting.'

'Oh. Nice.'

'Gosh, I hope you find somewhere,' Hayley said. 'Properties are so hard to find up here.'

'Yes, we won't be able to be too picky.' Laurenia smiled again and her likeness to Marcus increased. Willow was reminded of his twinkling irises and the very slight creases under his eyes. 'Marcus talked a lot about you, Willow. You're a real favourite of his.'

'Am I?' Willow swallowed, hoping she wasn't as red as the little girl on the rug's dress.

Hayley sent her a private wink.

'That's lovely,' Marion said. 'Especially now we know Willow's secret. And we all know how much Marcus disliked Rocky Rainman. Just as well he hasn't let that influence him.'

'Marcus is very hard to please.' Laurenia kept her eyes trained on Willow. 'But he's also very loyal and very devoted.'

Willow's cheeks were burning. She caught Laurenia's meaning and she understood Marcus's personality enough to get it completely. When he loved, he loved hard. She'd sampled it just last week, but did that mean he still—

Voices from the corridor interrupted the conversation. The door opened and Barry stuck his head around. 'We have some visitors for you, Willow.'

'Me?' Her heart thumped. Was Marcus here with the camera crew already? How awkward would this be?

Barry stepped inside and two people followed. Willow held her breath, then she gaped. 'Mum! Dad! What are you doing here?' She moved as quickly as she could across the room to greet them.

'Willow.' Mum pulled her into a hug and Dad squeezed them both together.

'Why are you here?' Willow said, her voice muffled by the hug.

'For Christmas,' Mum said.

'I hope there's room at the inn,' Dad added.

'Oh.' Willow pulled back. 'Well, I'll have to ask Marion.'

'Of course there is.' Marion beamed and clapped her hands together. 'I'll start making one up.'

'Can I talk to you about something?' Laurenia said. 'I have a question.'

'Yes. Of course,' Marion said. 'Come to the office with me.'

'Ok, I'll just tell Toby and Emily where I'm going. Freya can come with me. She's tired.'

Hayley approached Willow's mum and hugged her. 'Hi, Aunty Lorna.'

'Lovely to see you, Hayley.'

'Did you drive?'

'We came in a car,' Dad said.

'Wow. You've got braver.' Willow raised her eyebrows.

They exchanged a glance, then gave her another hug.

'Would you like help with your bags?' Barry asked. 'I still have one arm in good working order.'

'Not at all,' Dad said. 'We'll manage. I hope you don't mind us staying here.'

'The more the merrier,' Barry said. 'It's been too quiet around here recently.'

Willow couldn't stop smiling as they disappeared up the stairs with their bags. She could still hear them talking just out of sight, like they had stopped. What were they doing? She was just about to check when Hayley said, 'Your mum told me to give you this.' She handed her a white envelope.

'What is it?' Willow took it. It had her name on the front in very flamboyant handwriting.

'Open it,' Hayley said, frowning. 'It's probably a Christmas card.'

Willow's fingers trembled as she prised the back up. Something told her this wasn't just any old Christmas card. She pulled out a card. On the front was a big red umbrella covered in snowflakes and fringed with fur; two people's feet stuck out the bottom.

She opened it and read.

Come rain or shine, will you be mine?

There's snow-one quite like you.

When the sun comes out, I will shout... I love you, Willow, my topolina.

On this snowy day, I'd like to say... Will you ride off into the sunset with me?

'Who's it from?' Hayley said, peering over her shoulder.

There was only one person who called her topolina. 'Marcus.'

'Why did your mum have a card from him?'

'I don't know.' She stared at the words. 'What do you think he means?'

'What do you think? He loves you; he wants to ride off into the sunset with you.'

'Do you think he forgives me?'

'He wouldn't have sent that if he didn't.'

'And you didn't write it?' She couldn't stop herself saying it.

Hayley laughed. 'No. Of course I didn't. No way could I have made that up. What's a topolina?'

'A name he calls me. I googled it. It means little mouse.'

'Ok. Not very flattering.'

'Maybe not.' But in Italian, it was a term of endearment and also, he had a point. She'd always been timid on the inside. Until him. Good or bad, he'd always spurred her to take action. If he wanted her, she was damn well going to do this. No more hiding and messing about. The Glasgow job she could live without. Marcus... Well, she could live without him, but she didn't want to.

'What's going on out here?' Marion appeared out of the office. 'What's that noise outside?' She pulled open the front door. 'Oh my goodness. What's this?'

'What?' Willow followed her to the door and her mouth fell open. In the carpark was Ross McPherson sitting at the front of the carriage they'd seen back in his stable. Two white horses were hooked up to it and… oh god. Marcus was on his way to the door. He was there.

'Is that Marcus's carriage?' Willow's mum said from behind. Willow hadn't seen her there.

'You know Marcus?'

'Um… Well…'

'What does that mean?'

Mum didn't respond.

'He's here for you,' Hayley whispered.

Willow turned around, aware of people behind her. Everyone had gathered at the door to watch. Laurenia beamed as her brother approached, all six foot five of him in his smartest coat, looking like the sexiest man that ever lived. Willow was sure she'd faint if she didn't grab something. Hayley took hold of her arm and smiled.

'Hey,' Marcus said, scanning around.

'Hello,' Mum said. 'I didn't know you had a carriage. If I did, I'd have asked to come in that, not the car.'

'You came with him?' Willow glanced at her.

'Marcus!' Toby ran down the hall and barged his way through the crowd.

'Toby, no. Watch where you're going. Sorry, everyone.' Laurenia pulled an apologetic face.

Toby launched himself into Marcus.

'Hey, Toby.' Marcus lifted him like he weighed nothing. 'You like this place now?'

Toby nodded.

'Good. Well, I'm going to come see your room later, but you need to go back to Laurenia just now and wait for a bit. I've got one more job to do.' Marcus kissed his cheek, put him down and nudged him back inside. Laurenia took his hand and held him back from the door. The girl with the deely boppers screamed and flung herself at Marcus next.

He laughed and picked her up. 'Hey, Emily. Loving the headgear.' He wiggled her antlers. 'Can you help look after Toby? I'll be back later and we can chat properly, ok?'

'Yeah. Are you going in that?' She pointed to the carriage.

'I am. And when I come back, you can have a turn.'

She squealed again, jumped down, and ran to her mum and Toby. 'Did you hear that? I can ride in that carriage when Uncle Marcus comes back.'

Marcus smiled down at Willow. 'Would you like to ride with me?'

'Into the sunset?' She twisted her hair around her finger.

'Ross will drive us wherever you want.'

'Well...'

'Go,' Hayley said.

'You absolutely must,' Mum said.

'What is going on?' Marion asked.

'Come on, Cinders. Let's go to the ball.' Marcus took Willow's hand.

'I'll get your coat,' Hayley said.

Willow couldn't pull her eyes from Marcus. Should she go to him in front of everyone? The moment she decided to do it, he moved too, and they crashed into each other. He laughed and pulled her to his chest.

Hayley threw a jacket around Willow's shoulders. 'Bye-bye, my beautiful lovebirds,' she said. 'Be good.' She leaned in close to Willow's ear and whispered. 'Or not.'

'I need some photos of this,' Mum said.

She followed them out, but Willow only had eyes for Marcus.

'Ready, topolina?'

'For what?'

'Can I lift you into the carriage now?'

'Oh... Yes.'

He swooped her up, and she heard Mum fretting.

'It's ok,' he said. 'I won't drop her.'

'Hi.' Ross grinned and waved.

Willow settled into the seat. Marcus jumped in beside her and pulled a blanket over their legs. A princess on the back of a chariot with her emperor beside her couldn't have felt better than this. Ross tapped the horses and they walked on.

'What's this all about?' she asked.

'My Christmas gift to you,' Marcus said. 'No matter what lies ahead, I need to tell you... I love you, Willow.'

She crumpled into his arms. 'Oh Marcus, I'm so sorry. I wish I'd confessed about Rocky straight away. I shouldn't have been so silly about it.'

He shook his head. 'I get it. Sure, I was angry, but hey, I'm no one to judge. I've made some questionable moves in my life. Don't beat yourself up. Rocky Rainman was something that was all yours and listening to me insulting him all the time can't have been easy.'

'It wasn't. And I was so scared if I told you that you'd give us a terrible report and this place would have to shut.'

'I can't deny I might have wanted to, but I don't think I would have.'

'Me neither. But that's my big problem. I always assume I know what people will think. It's kept me hiding away for long enough but no more.'

He ran his finger down her cheek and smiled.

'I'm glad you came back, Marcus, because... Well, I love you too.' She held eye contact, willing herself to say everything without letting emotion get the better of her. 'I don't want the Glasgow job. I just want you.'

His embrace was strong and warm. She adored being there. The fields were still white and the mountains beyond rose in impressive peaks.

'I want you too. That's why I ditched the job.'

'Will you still do the documentary?'

'One hundred per cent.'

'And can I do it with you?'

'You want to go on camera?'

She nodded. 'Yes. No more hiding. Let's do it together.'

'Perfect. The camera crew is coming tomorrow. Let's give them Marcus Bowman and Rocky Rainman going head-to-head and all out to save the schoolhouse.'

Willow beamed and clung to his arm.

'And you know what?' he said.

'No?'

'This could be the beginning of something beautiful. We could do *Destination Forecast* together or maybe a new show, something all our own.'

She chuckled and shook her head. 'Do you think we could?'

'Absolutely. You're as famous as me these days, maybe even more so. I heard you on the radio and you were awesome. Together we'd pull in the ratings. Especially if we're a real-life couple. Who doesn't love that kind of intrigue? That is assuming we are a real-life couple.'

'Yes, Marcus, I definitely want us to be that.'

He rested his hand on her cheek. She leaned up and placed a soft kiss on his lips. He returned it with interest. Closing her eyes, she soaked it up, welcoming this reunion.

When they broke apart, he smiled and she gazed into his eyes.

'Laurenia is moving back here,' he said. 'So are your parents. They want to be nearer to you. Toby's come around to the idea of the schoolhouse and I'm going to look for a house up here too. Maybe you'd like to help me.'

'Maybe I would.' She gave him a coy look. 'I might also like to live in it.'

'I wouldn't want to be in it without you. Neither of us can forecast the future, but I know whatever happens, I want to be with you.' He leaned in and kissed her again.

'For once,' she whispered onto his lips, 'Rocky Rainman agrees with you.'

CHAPTER THIRTY-THREE

Willow

Let's 'rocky' the night
away...

Willow stood in the snow next to Marcus, bundled up in her pink coat, a bobble hat, and scarf wrapped right up to her chin. Behind them was the schoolhouse and in front was her uncle Jonathan with his camera all rigged up. The light turned from red to green and Willow smiled, hoping her voice would work. Nerves were eating at her but having Marcus beside her calmed them, so they were nothing like as bad as they would have been otherwise.

'Well, well, well,' Marcus said, his breath visible in the cold air. 'It looks like I'm standing here with none other than my former nemesis, Rocky Rainman.' His eyes sparkled as he looked at Willow.

Willow rolled her eyes but grinned, clutching her crutch. 'Yes, everybody knows now I'm Rocky Rainman, the nation's favourite weather forecaster.'

'Ouch.' Marcus feigned putting an arrow in his chest. 'Caught the bowman right where it hurts.'

'Sorry, not sorry. But we're not here to talk about the weather today. We're here to talk about something more important.'

'That's right. And that cause is The Old Schoolhouse, a vital resource for young adults in our community and beyond. Willow and I are here at the schoolhouse and have some fascinating human stories from former residents, local people, and staff to share with you. We want to raise awareness about the importance of this place.'

Willow nodded. 'And we need your help. This facility is a lifeline for so many young adults who have additional support needs. It provides them with opportunities to socialise, learn new skills, and grow their independence.' She paused for a breath. Had she got it right? Marcus's hand gently touched her back. 'Without it, they wouldn't have the same chance to thrive.'

Had she blurted the words too fast? After hours reading them, she wanted to get them perfect. It would take time to be as blasé as Marcus, who winged it through his broadcasts.

'Plus,' Marcus said, 'I don't know about you, but I've had my fair share of rain, wind, and snow this year. I think we could all use a little sunshine in our lives, and that's exactly what the schoolhouse provides.'

Willow nodded, 'Absolutely right. And we're not just asking for your money. We need you to spread the word. Remember all the free forecasts you've had from Rocky Rainman this year? Consider this your chance to give just a little in return.'

'Even in the depths of winter, the schoolhouse provides a warm and welcoming space for these young adults.'

'And it's a lot more fun to have snowball fights and build snowmen with friends than it is to do it alone.' Willow scooped a ball of snow from the fence and waggled her eyebrows at Marcus.

He held up his hands like a shield. 'You heard it from the number one snowballer in Glenbriar. Now, first up, let's hear from Marion and Barry Corbett about their reasons for opening The Old Schoolhouse in the first place.'

The camera light went red and Marcus turned to Willow, letting out a puff. 'Wow. We did it in one. You're a natural.'

Willow tugged at her scarf. 'Was that ok? I felt like I was babbling.'

'It was great,' Jonathan said. 'And I'm so thrilled I was able to come and film it. It's good to be back with my family at Christmas.'

'Let's get the next section done,' Marcus said. 'Then we can go in and get warm.'

When it was finished, Jonathan packed away his equipment and they all went inside. Marion had set up Christmas nibbles and hot chocolate in the common room.

Willow took a seat beside Laurenia, who smiled at her.

'We've seen a house we like,' she said. 'It's close to the centre of the village. A lovely big Victorian property with a great garden too. We've put in an offer and the estate agent was confident it would be accepted, though it might be in the new year. This isn't a great time of year for buying houses.'

'That's so good you've found something,' Willow said. Her parents also had their eyes on a couple of houses nearby. Properties in the village were hard to come by and often expensive. Willow and Marcus hadn't seen anything that fitted with what they were looking for and neither could really say exactly what that was.

Hayley arrived with bags full of Christmas presents for everyone, including Laurenia and her children, though she hardly knew them. 'I just love buying things for everyone. I can't stop myself.' She slumped into a seat beside Willow. 'How did the filming go?'

'It was fun. Marcus and Jonathan are just sending the footage to the studio. They'll put it all together and it'll air on Christmas eve.'

'Fingers crossed it helps keep this place open.'

'Good news on that front,' Marion said. 'We've already had people inquiring since Willow posted the links on Rocky's social media page.'

'That's awesome.' Hayley beamed. 'Oh, and you know my cousin Aidan,' she said to Willow.

'Yes. Your other favourite cousin?'

'Haha, yes, him. You know he's away in Canada doing a coast-to-coast walk raising money for motor neuron disease?'

'Yes.'

'I was messaging him and he said even people over there have heard of Rocky Rainman.'

'No way.' Willow stared at her. Just how big had this got? Nerves played in her tummy but it wasn't a bad feeling. Quite exciting really, especially when she had Marcus beside her. She wasn't alone in this game anymore.

'Yup. And it's a miracle he even replied to my message. He's gone totally AWOL.'

'Is that the gossip you were going to tell me about him?'

'Kind of.' Hayley lowered her voice. 'You know before he left, he was dating my friend Elise?'

'Um, yes.' Willow often found it hard to keep up with all Hayley's friends; she had so many.

'Well, Elise got fed up waiting for him and she's started dating Finlay.'

Willow's eyes popped. 'Finlay? As in—'

'My brother. Yes, your cousin. And also Aidan's cousin. It's actually good Aidan's still away. I mean, he's been a total prat not giving Elise any indication of when he'll be back but god knows what he'll make of it when he finds out she's gone off with Finlay. I hate conflict and I don't see him being impressed.'

'No. He won't be. And is he coming home for Christmas?'

'I don't think so, but he's really rubbish at communicating, so who knows?'

'Probably best he doesn't by the sounds of things.'

Marion handed out the hot chocolates and Jonathan strolled in, ruffling up his slightly damp hair. 'Started snowing again.' He beamed at Willow. 'Marcus is taking a call but he asked me to get you. He's just in the office.'

'Oh. Ok.' Willow got to her feet and made her way to the office. Marcus was sitting at her desk and chatting on his mobile. He glanced up at her as she entered.

'Thanks again and merry Christmas to you.' He ended the call and stood. His expression was unreadable but a prickle of unease crept over Willow's shoulder. Something was going on.

'Was that bad news?'

He took both her hands and smiled. 'No. It was someone offering to sell us a house.'

'What do you mean?'

'It's in the perfect location but it needs some doing up.'

'Then spit it out.'

His lips quirked up, filling his face with his beautiful smile. 'I was talking to Ross McPherson. He heard we were looking for a house and he wonders if we'd like to buy his old barn. You know, the one with the all-year-round air-conditioning.'

'Otherwise known as a giant hole in the roof.'

'Exactly. But as Ross says, If there's a building there already, it's easier to get planning permission. And he's willing to sell us some land too. Think of the potential.'

Willow let her mind wander. 'But I can't afford that.'

'Willow.' Marcus pulled her into his lap and kissed her cheek. 'I'm buying our house. Stop worrying about that. But I'm not buying anything unless you love it.'

'I love it. It's in the perfect place, so close to the horses.'

'We could even get our own.'

'Oh my god. Really?'

'Absolutely... Though we should probably get a roof first.'

'And we can do a fancy barn conversion?'

'Whatever you fancy.'

'Well... You know I only really fancy you.'

He lifted her off the ground and spun her around. She squealed and clung onto his neck.

'We're going for the ride of our lives,' he said. 'And I'm finally going to stick my neck out and make a daring forecast.'

'Which is?'

'That you and I are going to have the perfect Christmas and a wonderful life.'

Willow clung to his neck and kissed him. 'Rainman concurs and so does Willow Roxburgh.'

'Then it must be accurate.'

'One hundred per cent.' Willow beamed at him. As long as they were together, she'd be on cloud nine, and perfectly content for Marcus Bowman to stroll off into the sunset with Rocky Rainman.

The End

MORE BOOKS BY MARGARET AMATT

Scottish Island Escapes

1. A Winter Haven

2. A Spring Retreat

3. A Summer Sanctuary

4. An Autumn Hideaway

5. A Christmas Bluff

6. A Flight of Fancy

7. A Hidden Gem

8. A Striking Result

9. A Perfect Discovery

10. A Festive Surprise

The Glenbriar Series

1. Stolen Kisses at the Loch View Hotel

2. Just Friends at Thistle Lodge

3. Pitching up at Heather Glen

4. Two's Company at the Forest Light Show

5. Highland Fling on the Whisky Trail

6. Snowdown at the Old Schoolhouse

7. Starting Over at the Crafty Bee Barn

8. A Surprise Proposal in the Rose Garden

9. Cutting it Neat for the Wedding

10. A Classy Affair in the Country

11. Mix Up under the Mistletoe

12. A Fresh Start on the Bridle Path

13. Last First Kiss at the Village Church

14. Fight or Flirt on the Scenic Route

15. Love Match on the Road Home

Love on the Edge – Barra Series

Acknowledgments

Thanks goes to my adorable husband for supporting my dreams and putting up with my writing talk 24/7. Also to my son, whose interest in my writing always makes me smile. It's precious to know I've passed the bug to him – he's currently writing his own fantasy novel and instruction books on how to build Lego!

Throughout the writing process, I have gleaned help from many sources and met some fabulous people. I'd like to give a special mention to Stéphanie Ronckier, my beta reader extraordinaire. Stéphanie's continued support with my writing is invaluable and I love the fact that I need someone French to correct my grammar! Stéphanie, you rock. To my lovely friend, Lyn Williamson, thank you for your continued support and encouragement with all my projects. And to my fellow authors, Evie Alexander and Lyndsey Gallagher – you girls are the best! I love it that you always have my back and are there to help when I need you.

Also, a thanks to the editors at Leannan Press for their work on this novel.

Of course a huge thank you goes to the readers who continue to support me in so many ways. I appreciate each and every one of you and hope that I can keep bringing you more books to enjoy! Big love.

Margaret XX

About the Author

Margaret Amatt

Margaret has told and written stories for as long as she can remember. During her formative years, she spent time on long walks inventing characters and stories to pass the time.

Writing books is Margaret's passion and when she's not doing that, she's often found eating chocolate, walking and taking photographs in the hills around Highland Perthshire. Those long walks still frequently bring inspiration!

It's Margaret's pleasure to bring you the ***Scottish Island Escapes*** series, ***The Glenbriar Series*** and the ***Love on the Edge – Barra*** series. Each series features interconnected stories for those who enjoy inhabiting Margaret's world but each and every book can be read as a standalone if you'd rather dip in and out.

You can find more information about Margaret on her website or by signing up for her newsletter

www.margaretamatt.com